DEATH IN T

Two armored electrov...
first pour five men in bulky riot suits. Gerswin
shrugged and hefted the heavy laser.

Hisssss. The Lieutenant fell with a laser burn
through his skull.

Thrumm! Thrumm! Thrumm! Thrumm! Gerswin
missed the fourth guard who, with quicker reflexes
than his compatriots, had dropped behind the
electrocar. The man in the shadow clothes eased
back to the emergency escape and slowly slid up it.
Once on the roof, he crossed to the front of the
building. The guard had not bothered to look up, a
sign of either poor training or no real opposition.

Hisss. The exposed guard crumpled, unaware he
was dead.

Still, no one had emerged from the second van.
While Gerswin would have preferred to finish off
the entire troop, he could hear the distant whine of
more Guard vehicles. He dropped to the street and
ran, in the effortless lope of a devilkid ahead of the
she coyotes, racing the landspouts and terrors of
Old Earth.

IN ENDLESS TWILIGHT

Tor books by L. E. Modesitt, Jr.

The Magic of Recluce

THE ECOLITAN MATTER

The Ecologic Envoy
The Ecolitan Operation
The Ecologic Secession

THE FOREVER HERO

Dawn for a Distant Earth
The Silent Warrior
In Endless Twilight

L. E. MODESITT, JR.

A TOM DOHERTY ASSOCIATES BOOK
NEW YORK

For Nancy
and her love of the not-quite-usual

IN ENDLESS TWILIGHT

Copyright © 1988 by L.E. Modesitt, Jr.

A Tor Book
Published by Tom Doherty Associates, Inc.
49 West 24th Street
New York, N.Y. 10010

Tor® is a registered trademark of Tom Doherty Associates, Inc.

Cover art by Maelo Cintron

ISBN: 0-812-52000-9

First edition: March 1988

Printed in the United States of America

0 9 8 7 6 5 4 3 2

THE ONCE-UPON-A-TIME SCOUTSHIP JUMPSHIFTED, AND FOR A moment that was both instantaneous and endless, black light flooded the two small compartments, the one containing the pilot and the crew space that contained no one. That instant of shift seemed to last longer than normal, as it always did when the actual shift was near the limit.

"Interrogative status," asked the pilot, a man with tight-curled blond hair and hawk-yellow eyes that swept the range of displays on the screens before him.

"No EDI traces. No mass indications within point one light. Destination estimated at four plus." The impersonally feminine tone of the artificial intelligence would have chilled most listeners, but the pilot preferred the lack of warmth in the voice of the *Caroljoy*.

In his rebuilding of the discarded and theoretically obsolete scout, the former Imperial Commodore could have programmed warmth into the voice when he had added the AI, just as he could have opted for more comfort in the spartan quarters, rather than for the raw power and extensive defensive screens the beefed-up ex-Federation scout now enjoyed. The pilot had avoided warmth in both the ship and the AI.

He leaned back in the control couch, trying to relax, as if he wanted to push away a particularly bad memory. He did, and as he often also did he whistled three or four notes in the odd double-toned style that was his alone.

The AI did not acknowledge the music, since the notes represented neither observation nor inquiry.

What was past was past. The two tacheads he had used on El Lido, along with the thirty thousand casualties, would certainly draw Imperial interest, but he doubted that they would call Impie attention back on him. Not yet. After all, one of the two targets had been CE, Limited, in which he, as Shaik Corso, had held the controlling interest.

Now, Hamline Rodire had control, and the former Commodore hoped that Rodire would use the influence that CE, Limited, represented for the benefit of all of El Lido.

He shook his head. He had run through the arguments all too often to change his mind, or the past. What was past was past. Time to concentrate on the future, on running down the rest of the research leads that he and the Foundation had neglected for too long. Time to refocus himself on the long range and eventual mission, on getting the technology he needed for the reclamation job on Old Earth, a job that was too big for the underfunded and ignored Recorps to complete.

"EDI traces at forty emkay."

"Interrogative signature pattern."

"Signature pattern tentatively identified as standard system patroller, class II."

"Course line?"

"Preliminary course line indicates target headed in-system. Probability exceeds point eight that patroller destination is planet three."

Former Commodore MacGregor Corson Gerswin nodded. That made sense, particularly since planet three was Byzania.

"Interrogative other patrollers."

"Remote EDI traces from exit corridor two. Probability exceeds point five that second system patroller is stationed within one hundred emkay of jump point."

"Interrogative other system targets."

"That is negative this time."

Gerswin's fingers played across the representational screen, checking the relative positions and travel times.

He pulled at his chin.

After the debacle on El Lido, he had plunged into trying to tie up a number of loose ends. That had been fine, but he hadn't bothered to update Lyr on those activities. Not what had happened on El Lido, but on his OER Foundation-related efforts, the ones she monitored and on which she had to keep records for the Empire's tax collectors and various departmental snoops.

First, though, he really wanted to take a rest, one of several hours while the *Caroljoy* cruised in-system.

He reached for the control couch harness release, then straightened.

Might as well do the update and send it. The energy required would be less the farther out-system he was when he dispatched the torp. And the less energy required for the message torp, the more left with the ship.

Who could ever tell what he might require?

From what he recalled, Byzania, while not unfriendly, was a rather tightly controlled society. But, first, the update to Lyr. Then he could worry about sleep and Byzania.

Once she got the update, she could be the one to take on the worries about the latest implications of what he was doing, not that she wasn't already.

He cleared his throat and tapped the data screen controls.

II

Buzz!

At the sound, Lyr dropped in front of the console.

The screen showed the face of the man with the curly blond hair and hawk-yellow eyes.

"You never change," she observed safely, since Gerswin was really not on the screen, his image only the beginning of a prerecorded torp fax for her.

She first tapped the controls to store the entire message and the mass of data that always accompanied his transmissions, then tapped the acknowledgment stud to start the message.

"Lyr. Finished the Grom'tchacher lead. Your first impressions were right. Leased the lab, took the cash, and left. Nice prospectus, though. Theory's interesting, if not down our line. Might be worth a commission job for one of your friends to investigate."

Gerswin looked down, then back into the screen. In the shadows behind him, Lyr could make out the accel/ decel shell/couch that dominated the control room, and the manual auxiliary control banks that Gerswin had insisted on retaining even after centralizing the direct controls in the simplified bank before him and, secondarily, in the AI center.

In scanning the background, she missed the next words, not that she could not have replayed them anytime.

". . . off to Byzania next. Hylerion—the precoded, accelerated tree grower—heard some interesting reports. Never collected the last installment of the grant. Suspicious enough to make me think the idea worked.

"Be back in Ydris to check their system after that. Send a report there."

He grinned at the screen.

"Since you're the cred worrier, some good news. In tracing down Grom'tchacher, ran across some business. Managed to broker a lab lease and some other property along with ours. Finder's fee arrangement. Took it personally, but felt some belonged to the Foundation. Means no draw on my operating account for a while. Remainder of the OERF share is coming through the general receipts. Code blue."

Lyr frowned. That she'd have to check. Credits were often the last thing the Commander worried about, the very last thing.

". . . off to Byzania. See you soon."

He always closed that way, she reflected, tapping the studs to store the message in the permanent file, but it had been more than five years since he had been anywhere near New Augusta.

She pursed her lips, knowing she should be somewhere other than before the console at 2030 on a spring evening. At less than seventy, she certainly wasn't novaed; her weight was the same as it had been years earlier; and her muscle tone, thanks to her exercise regime, was probably better. She looked far younger than she was.

"That could be the trouble . . ."

She cut off her monologue before it began and called up the general receipts account and the Commander's code blue entry.

"Unsolicited donation. Fyrst V. D'berg, Aerlion. One million credits. Codes follow. . . . "

Lyr ran her tongue over her chapped lips. Gerswin

and his unsolicited donations ran to as much as several million annually. Where he found them she wondered, but they always were supported.

And his ventures . . . she really wanted to ask him what else he had been doing besides tracking completed grants and projects and grantees who had failed to report or collect. Always the ventures, like the fabrication plant on Solor and whatever he was doing on Westmark with that plant protein substitute. Add to that the aliases. . . she worried at her lower lip with her upper teeth.

After forty years with the Foundation, she could see an accelerating trend, even more than in the first few years after the Commodore's retirement, a trend where things were building. To what, she didn't know, but once again she had the feeling that the Empire and the Commodore were going to clash.

She'd really have to talk to him about it—assuming he ever came back.

III

"SELERN? THE NEPHEW OF THE OLD EARL?"
The deep bass voice disconcerted Selern, coming as it did from the chipmunk cheeks and bright green eyes of a fool. But His Majesty Ryrce N'Gaio Bartoleme VIII was no fool, reflected Selern, not if his actions in removing the previous Eye indicated anything at all.

"That is correct, Your Majesty."

"Surprised, weren't you?"

"At becoming the Earl? Quite."

"That was not the reference I meant, Selern."

"Then I do not understand the question." Selern swallowed and hoped that the gesture had not been noticed.

"That I doubt." The current ruler of the Empire of Light pointed toward the single small chair on the other side of the inlaid and old-fashioned wooden desk. The occasional shimmer of dust motes that intermittently resembled a ghostly curtain revealed the defense screen that separated the two men. "Have a seat."

The newest Earl of Selern sat cautiously, keeping his eyes fixed on the Emperor. Ryrce wore neither circlet nor crown. Wispy strands of straw-tinted hair framed his all too-round face.

"Caution carried to excess, Selern. That warning about Calendra—the old Eye—could only have come from one or two sources. None of them would have had the nerve to deliver it, even anonymously. So I checked the peerage lists for the newly elevated and for recent heirs. Had to be you. Would you care to comment?"

Selern smiled. The smile was forced, but with a bit of humor. "You apparently have me on all rights, Your Majesty." He paused, then added, "I thought I was more discreet than I was."

"You were discreet enough—assuming your Emperor was trustworthy."

"Are you?" asked Selern, trying to keep the tremor out of his voice.

"No Emperor can afford to be trustworthy, Selern, except when he benefits by it." Ryrce laughed softly, a deep chuckling sound, before speaking again. "Then, he cannot afford not to be."

Selern waited.

"As of tomorrow, you assume the position of Eye. Both Eye regents have also been terminated."

Selern swallowed hard.

"What else could I do? Either they chose not to stand up to Calendra, or they agreed. I suppose they might also have failed to see his plans."

"Your action makes sense." Selern nodded slowly. "Unfortunately."

"You noted the question of certain nuclear weapons. What do you propose?"

"Finding them, if possible."

"If you cannot?"

":Trying to avoid situations where they might be used."

"And if that fails?"

"Waiting for the ax to fall when they are used again."

Ryrce laughed once more, this time a bass and booming guffaw.

"At least you understand for whom you work!"

Selern—the new Eye who had never desired the position—waited.

"There should be some records. Calendra implied that a single man controlled them. He saw that man would be my downfall as well."

Selern repressed a shudder. One man? One single individual with that kind of power?

"If the remainder of those missing tacheads and hellburners are used in the wrong way," commented Selern slowly, "that just might undermine all the centuries of peace."

"I doubt that any one individual could have that great an impact on the Empire," observed His Imperial Majesty. "But with nuclear weapons . . ."

The implication was clear. Selern's job was to keep the Empire whole and hearty, including the prevention of any one man from undermining its authority and image. Trust was the glue that held the Empire together, and the Empire was the structure of humanity, the one remaining web binding man in a common purpose.

Selern sighed.

Ryrce N'Gaio Bartoleme VIII nodded at the sound
from his new chief of Intelligence, nodded and stood to
signify that the private audience was at an end.

IV

GERSWIN RUBBED HIS FOREHEAD, MASSAGED HIS EYES, AND
looked away from the data screen on the right side of the
Caroljoy's control console.

"Two plus before Byzania orbit station." The AI
voice, the voice of the ship in real terms, was pleasant,
cool and clear, emotionless, unlike the warm and faintly
husky voice of the woman for whom he had named the
modified scout. The dichotomy did not bother him,
perhaps because he avoided thinking about it.

Gerswin rubbed his temples with the thumb and
forefinger of his right hand, closed his eyes, and leaned
back in the upslanted shell seat.

With each totally new system, it became a little
harder to assimilate the information he needed. But he
couldn't blunder around strange planets without at least
a fundamental idea of their government, customs, and
legal structure. Not doing what he was doing.

The standard structure he'd developed with the
Infonet professionals had helped, both financially and in
reducing the information to the absolute minimum he
needed. But it was still more than he wanted to learn,
time after time. And that was a danger itself, since it

pushed him toward continued dealings within systems
he already knew.

He frowned, and, eyes closed, tried to sort out
Byzania.

Government—quasi-military, despite the trappings
of more democratic institutions. Popularly elected sena-
tors formed an upper chamber which could approve or
disapprove any law or regulation, but which could not
propose either. Laws were enacted by the lower chamber, composed of delegates selected from each political
party's preference list in proportion to the total vote in
the general election. Head of government—prime minister, appointed from the military by the Chief of Staff.

Gerswin suspected that the preference lists
provided by the political parties were screened by the
military, which had its hand in everything.

Population—roughly thirty million, the majority
on the largest and first settled continent.

Economy—largely agricultural, with enough local
light industry to provide a small middle class. Two M/M
(mining/manufacturing) complexes on the largest moon
of the fourth planet in the system.

Culture—Urabo-Hismexic, with emphasis on male-
dominated honor.

Gerswin pursed his lips and opened his eyes.

By all rights, unless the ecology was hostile, and the
population and agricultural figures belied that, the system shouldn't need a military or even a quasi-military
government. Byzania produced nothing of high value
and low cubage, i.e., nothing worth the energy costs of
jumpship transport as an export, and wasn't strategically
located vis-à-vis the Dismorphs, the Analexians, the
Ursans, or the two other intelligent and technologically
oriented races found by the Empire.

"Search capabilities of Byzania orbit control?" he
asked the AI. He refused to personify the artificial
intelligence or to program in any human traits, or to
otherwise associate it with the ship or her namesake.

"Inquiry imprecise."

"Do they have the ability to pick out the *Caroljoy* from orbit if I took her down on the southern continent?"

"Probability approaches unity."

"Do they have the technology to crack the hull without fracturing the scenery if I set down at the shuttle port outside Illyam?"

"Probability is less than point one."

"What is their hard credit balance?"

"That is classified. Estimated as negative."

"The fact that it's classified tells me that. What about fax outlets? How many are independent?"

"Estimate point five of all media origination points, including fax outlets, are independent. No official censorship."

"It's a risk, but we'll go in. Evaluate the probability of acceptance—agent of Imperial family looking for a very private retreat."

"Probability of disapproval less than point two. Credibility less than point five."

"In other words, they'll let me do it, but won't buy the excuse. Well . . . let's hope so."

Gerswin wondered if he were being overdramatic. At the same time, when grantees didn't collect hard currency drafts, even at bayonet point, there was a reason, and the reason wasn't normally friendly. Still, he needed to get on the ground in one piece, and he wanted to find out if Hylerion had succeeded with those special trees.

Caution could be discarded later, if he had been overcautious. It was difficult to reclaim after the fact.

"Contact Byzania control. Arrange for landing rights and touchdown at Illyam shuttle port. Use code red three ID package."

"Contact is in progress," the console announced.

The control area went silent. Gerswin wouldn't have to say a word unless Byzania control and the AI came to some sort of impasse, which was unlikely. A private yacht meant hard currency, and Byzania needed whatever it could get.

In the interim, he went back to studying background information on the system, attempting to get a better slant on why such a largely agricultural planet had adopted such a strong military presence.

The climate on the two main continents was nearly ideal for synde bean production, and other easily produced foodstuffs. What land areas weren't under cultivation supported wide local forests, generally softwood akin to primitive earth-descended deciduous trees.

Some scientists had theorized that the lack of a large moon and/or light comet activity during Byzania's formative period plus the larger proportion of light elements were responsible for the low mountain ranges and slow crustal action, as well as for a general lack of easily reachable heavy ore deposits. For whatever reason, it was cheaper to mine the largely nickel-steel and other metallic deposits on the fourth planet's irregular asteroidal satellites than to sink deep mines on Byzania itself.

"Clearance obtained," announced the AI, breaking into Gerswin's study. "Anticipate arriving descent orbit in one plus point four. Our name is *Breakerton*."

"Acknowledged," growled Gerswin, returning his attention to the information before him. He couldn't afford to use the deep-learn technique, to have all the information he needed poured into his brain through direct input—not if he wanted to remain sane long enough to finish his self-appointed mission for Old Earth. Deep learn systematically used up brain cells, which wasn't a problem, given the millions available, if you expected to live a century or two only. Gerswin expected he would need all of his brain cells healthy for much longer. He might be disappointed—bitterly so—but it was a risk he chose not to take.

At least, when he scanned something, he could choose what he wanted to concentrate on and what he wanted to retain. While it gave him a short-term headache, he hoped it would lengthen his productive years.

"Better than a head full of useless data," he muttered as he turned to the cultural background.

"Input imprecise," noted the AI.

Gerswin ignored the comment. He had little more than a standard hour before he should be ready for touchdown.

V

GERSWIN CHECKED THE PUBLIC FAX LISTING FOR ILLYAM, KEYING in on all names beginning with "Hy."

"Hyler, H'ten Ker . . .

"Hylert, Georges Kyl . . .

"Hylon, Adrin Yvor . . ."

There was no listing for Jaime Hylerion. Either the missing biochemist lived elsewhere on Byzania, which was possible, but unlikely, since the Illyam listings held most of the planet's professionals, or he had emigrated, which was theoretically possible, but highly unlikely.

He sighed, and put the small screen console provided by the Hotel D'Armand on hold.

Glancing around the room, from the faded heavy gray, crimson-edged draperies that bordered the rectangular window overlooking the courtyard to the dull brown finish of the four-postered formal bed that looked uncomfortable rather than antique to the replica of some ancient writing desk that was too small to sit at, Gerswin felt cramped. More cramped than before the *Caroljoy*'s controls. More cramped than in the tightest flitter cockpit.

He stood up and moved away from the desk, stretching.

From the landing at the shuttle port onward, everyone had been *so* polite.

"Yes, Ser Corson."

"This way, Ser Corson."

"Will there be anything else, Ser Corson?"

His credentials as a purchasing agent for RERTA, Limited, as well as the Imperial passport, gold-bordered, and the maximum credit line on Halsie-Vyr, showed him as one MacGregor Corson, but the locals were scarcely interested in his name, but in the credit line he represented.

The Empire might, in time, find out about the name and wonder if MacGregor Corson and Commodore Gerswin were one and the same, but the Imperial bureaucracy could have cared little enough about him as Gerswin, and doubtless cared less about him as Corson, so long as no trouble was overtly attached to either name.

The former Commander wrinkled his nose, suppressed a sneeze. Despite the spotless appearance of the small suite, really a large room divided into two halves with a thin wall, it smelled musty.

"Assshooo!"

The violence of the too-long repressed sneeze sent a twinge through Gerswin's shoulders, made his eyes water momentarily. After rubbing his neck and shoulders with both hands to loosen the muscles, he stared at the list frozen on the console.

To search for all the names in the entire planetary listing which began with "Hy" would be enough of an alert to have every security agent in Illyam trailing him.

"You're assuming too much."

Gerswin realized that he had spoken aloud, and that there had been no echo whatsoever.

He frowned, ambling around the suite as if to familiarize himself with the furnishings, though he was more interested in the underlying construction.

The relative smallness of the window overlooking the courtyard had already struck him, but not the massiveness of the casement surrounding it, nor the thickness of the armaglass which did not open.

That the hotel had the latest in heavy-duty portals, rather than hinged doors, seemed out of character with the antique furnishings, unless Gerswin assumed certain things about the character of the government of Byzania. Those assumptions were solidifying as more than mere assumptions.

He returned to the console and seated himself.

"Time to get to work, Corson," he told himself and the sure-to-be listening agents as he reset the console and accessed land agents.

A dozen names appeared on the list. Gerswin picked the third and tapped out the combination.

"Cerdezo and Associates."

"MacGregor Corson. I'd like to make an appointment with Ser Cerdezo."

"Your interest, Ser Corson?"

"Must remain relatively confidential."

"Ser Corson . . . I know not how we can help you without adequate information," suggested the sandy-haired young man who had taken the call.

"I understand your problem. Perhaps my credentials would help to resolve the difficulty."

Gerswin placed his passport, credentials, and authorization for maximum credit in the scanning drawer, with a blot bar across all three. The thin strip was designed to prevent the scanning equipment from reading the magfield codes contained in each of the three flat squares.

"Ah . . . I see . . ." said the Cerdezo employee. "I will check Sher Cerdezo's schedule. She may have an availability this afternoon."

Gerswin waited, not volunteering more information, but retrieving his credentials from the scanning drawer.

"Would you be free at 1430?"

"Local time?"

"Yes, ser."

"That would be agreeable. I am at the Hotel D'Armand. What is the best way to reach your offices?"

After getting directions, Gerswin called two other firms and obtained appointments.

Now, if he could get access to another console, without using his identification . . . He shrugged. There were ways, even in Illyam. The important thing was not to be too impatient. While he had more time than most, he didn't have any more lives.

He spent the next hour or so retrieving background, tourist-type information from the console, and reading between the lines, before freshening up for his first appointment.

Leaving the hotel was another exercise in politeness.

"Good day, ser."

"Enjoy your stay, ser . . ."

Byzania was an interesting planet, reflected Gerswin as he strolled down the Grande Promenade toward his appointment with Raymond Simones. With the agricultural predominance and the military control, he had expected a climate warmer than the midday high of 18°C, as well as police on every corner.

Outside of the man in the standard brown tunic who had shadowed him from the hotel, and the one uniformed policeman in a small booth three blocks down from the hotel, he had seen no other obvious police representatives among the light scattering of people on the streets.

While there were some flitter-for-hire stands, the majority of citizens visible to Gerswin chose either to walk or to take the small electric trolleys that seemed to run down the center of all the major avenues.

The people in Illyam looked like people everywhere —no one extravagantly dressed, no one in rags. Some smiling, some frowning, but most with the preoccupied look of men and women with somewhere to go, something to do.

Tunic and trousers were the standard apparel for both men and women, but the men wore earrings, and the women did not. The women wore colored sashes, and the men wore dark belts.

One absence nagged Gerswin for most of his walk. Just before he entered the Place Treholme, he identified it. No street vendors of any sort. None! Nowhere had he traveled, except in systems like Nova Balkya, which was an out-and-out police state, and New Salem, with its religious fanaticism, had been without some street sales. Likewise, the streets and avenues were bare of comm stations or public comm consoles.

Gerswin nodded to himself. The pattern was becoming clearer, much clearer. Both absences fit in with the total lack of cash. Byzania was strictly a credit/debit economy. All transfers of credits went straight from your account to someone else's. All were doubtless monitored by the government. The principal formality at the entry shuttle port had been to open a Byzanian universal account for one MacGregor Corson.

Even the so-called free services of the society, such as console access to the public library facilities, required a universal account card. With such tight social control, Gerswin couldn't yet figure out why the military even needed such a high profile in government.

Raymond Simones, Land Agent Extraordinaire, had his offices on the third level of the four-level Place Treholme, which was more like an indoor garden surrounded by balconied offices than a place for transacting business.

"MacGregor Corson," he announced.

"Ser Simones is expecting you. He will be with you in a moment. Would you like a seat?"

Gerswin took the seat, only to stand abruptly with the bounding and enthusiastic approach of Simones.

"Ser Corson, I am honored. So honored."

He bowed quickly, twice, as he pronounced his honor.

"If you would care to join me in a liftea . . ."

"A small cup . . ."

The taller palms of the indoor courtyard leaned nearly into the conference room, although sonic shields kept both leaves and sounds out on the one side, while the closed and old-fashioned door presumably kept the staff excluded on the other.

"This liftea . . . straight from New Colora," offered Simones as he poured from a steaming carafe into two crystal demitasses.

"To your health and our mutually profitable business."

Simones lifted his demitasse.

"To your health," responded Gerswin, following suit, but taking only a small sip of the dark beverage.

"You are an agent of something called RERTA, Limited, you said. RERTA, Limited, has no real records. Obviously you are merely a front for someone or some group searching for a large tract of land, someone who does not want their identity known."

"Why would you say that?" asked Gerswin.

Simones shrugged his shoulders. "Is it not obvious? You have access to great credit; you are looking at a planet developed enough to have the necessary amenities, but one undeveloped enough to have large amounts of land available for purchase. Further, you arrive in a nonmilitary ship with screens of a class available only to the Court or the very wealthy, and you arrive alone. That means you are trusted, but expendable, that you have access to money, but that there is enormous power and wealth behind you. Alone, who would care? But you are not alone, merely an advance agent."

Gerswin laughed, not quite a bark, but not quite gently.

"I never claimed to be more than an agent."

"Ah, but what one claims is not always what is. In your case, however, the props are too expensive, too real, to be anything else but the truth. The real question is not just what you want, but why you or your patron wants it.

"Do you want farmland to provide an estate for the junior branch of a wealthy family? Or do you want a more isolated and scenic retreat for other purposes? Or perhaps a tract which offers both?"

Simones took another sip of the liftea and looked at the built-in console screen at his left elbow, as if to suggest that he was ready to begin in earnest if Gerswin were.

"My mission is rather delicate . . ."

"I can certainly understand that."

". . . and my latitude is broad within certain parameters. While RERTA is most interested in as pleasant a site as possible, and one which is somewhat off the beaten track, economics, especially these days, would indicate that it is prudent for any local site to be capable of being self-supporting, should the need arise."

Gerswin frowned as if to convey that he did not want to say much more, and waited for a reaction.

"That is a rather broad description, and without some general boundaries might be hard to narrow." Simones' bright blue eyes clouded, and he brushed a stray lock of blue-black hair off his tanned forehead.

"The optimal size," offered Gerswin, "would be ten thousand squares."

"Ten thousand square kilometers?"

"Depending on location, resources, transportation, and whether the property is virgin or improved."

"I see."

What Gerswin could see was that Simones wanted

to ask price ranges, but didn't know the client well
enough to broach the issue.

"While price is a consideration, it is not the sole
consideration. RERTA is always better served if the
price is as reasonable as possible for the value involved."

"Reasonable is a term open to a wide interpretation,
Ser Corson, and one about which there could be wide
disagreements."

"That is true. We need a better frame of reference.
While I could access the information myself, perhaps
you could give me the average price per kilosquare for
prime agricultural lands, for forest lands, and for wilder-
ness."

"Ah . . . averages. So deceiving, especially when the
transactions are large. Do you realize, Ser Corson, that
the average synde bean estate on Conuna runs about fifty
thousand squares?"

"I understand. Have any changed hands recently?"

"Last year, I believe, the Harundsa estate was sold
to General Fernadsa. The registered transfer was in the
neighborhood of 250 million credits."

"How many squares?"

"Sixty-three thousand."

"Assuming the registered price was the sole consideration, that means a minimum of four thousand credits
per square, or given the underlying considerations of
that transfer, more likely five thousand credits per
square."

"That was a bargain sale."

Gerswin got the point. He didn't know whether the
General Fernadsa who bought the property was the
Prime Minister or merely related, but the sale had not
been an entirely free-market transaction.

Simones was also testing Gerswin on Gerswin's
client. A Foundation might find Byzania not entirely to
its liking, while certain Imperial families could well end
up playing the local games better than the locals.

"RERTA might well be interested in obtaining property where future bargains could be had," Gerswin countered.

"One cannot predict bargains," answered Simones. "They happen, and they do not."

"True, and that is why one must be fully informed on the market and the players."

"Ah . . . yes. So many players, and some so well connected, particularly in the land business." Simones shrugged, then frowned. "I might offer you some advice, strictly an observation, you understand."

Gerswin nodded.

"You will doubtless interview other agents, and some will appeal to you, and some will not, but, should you deal with a noble lady, be most careful."

"I was not aware of an Imperial family here."

"Local noblesse, Ser Corson. Fallen nobility of a sort. The name is Cerdezo, and the lady can be most charming. Most charming. You might find her socially entertaining, and quite brilliant."

Gerswin nodded again. "I appreciate your . . . observation."

"Now . . . in regard to your search . . . let me check certain aspects of the situation, and I will get back to you." Simones rose to his feet.

Gerswin rose also, and half bowed. "A pleasure to meet you, and I hope to hear from you before too long."

"Doubtless you will, Ser Corson."

A tacit agreement had been struck. Simones had gotten some idea of what game Gerswin was playing and warned him that the locals played hard. Gerswin had accepted the information and indicated that he was still interested. Simones had concluded by saying that he would see what was really available, or might be, at what real price.

The one thing that bothered Gerswin was the out-of-character reference to Sher Cerdezo. Was Simones tied into security? Did he know that Gerswin had contacted Cerdezo Associates? Why was Gerswin being warned off? Because the lady was sharp and dangerous, or because security wanted to keep off-worlders away?

Gerswin did not frown as he kept his face pleasant and bowed again before turning to go.

Outside the Place Treholme, the slender man in the brown tunic was waiting as Gerswin hopped an electric trolley for his 1430 meeting with Sher Cerdezo.

VI

THE FLITTER CIRCLED THE HOLDING WEST OF THE THIN AND glittering green river that split the neatly and mechanically cultivated synde bean fields.

The few buildings, obviously used for storage and machine repair, stood at the top of a gentle rise, scarcely more than thirty meters higher than the gentle rolling hills covered with the rust brown of the synde beans about to be harvested.

Gerswin, in the right front seat of the four-seat flitter, could see from the indentations in the hilltop that other structures had been removed.

"This was the original estate house of the Gwavara's, but when the grandfather of the present Colonel married Vylere's daughter and consolidated the holdings of both families, the estate house was moved to Vylerven. That's about one hundred kays east," added Constanza Cerdezo, who sat directly behind Gerswin, providing a running commentary.

The silver-haired land agent reminded Gerswin more of a dowager aunt than the sharp-dealing professional the other two agents had warned him to steer clear of.

"Why is this available?"

"It is considered too remote, and the production levels have fallen considerably in the last four or five years. Neglected shamefully."

"Not much scenery here," groused Gerswin.

"That is true, but as I indicated earlier, were you to indicate a firm interest in this land, and your client's desire to maintain and improve it, the Ministry of Forests and Agriculture Development would look most favorably upon your application to purchase, say, twenty thousand squares of the adjoining Forest Reserve. With the stipulation that your client retain all but a small fraction in forest, of course. Still, two percent of twenty thousand squares is four hundred squares, and that would be adequate for any estate house, landing field, roads, and local produce gardens."

"And the normal fee for consideration?"

"I would suggest something in the range of five thousand credits, with a deposit of one million credits on the Forest Reserve application."

Gerswin didn't bother to ask if the deposit were refundable. Whatever she said, in practice, no deposit for special consideration would ever be returned.

"Could we swing over and see the Forest Reserve lands you're talking about? I've seen maps and holos, but there is no substitute for seeing the actual parcels."

"Forest Reserves are protected from overflights," the pilot stated baldly.

"How can I recommend RERTA buy something I have not seen?"

"You could rent a landcruiser," suggested the pilot.

"That would take days," complained Gerswin. "And I still would not have the sweep, the overview necessary."

"I sympathize, Ser Corson, but the regulations are regulations."

"Regulations are regulations, I know, but isn't there some exception, some variance, for special circumstances?"

"Ah, an exception permit," offered the pilot. Then his voice fell. "But you must apply in advance."

Gerswin shrugged and turned to Constanza Cerdezo. "Have you any suggestions?"

"Ser Corson, must you overfly the whole parcel, or merely see it from the air?"

"Perhaps if I could see at least part of it from the air, I could decide whether more flights were necessary, and then I could decide whether to apply for an exception permit."

Constanza addressed the pilot. "Michel, can you fly the demarche line?"

"Ah, yes, Sher Cerdezo. If I inadvertently stray . . . the fine is five hundred credits."

Gerswin picked up the hint. "Michel, I can understand your concerns about such delicate piloting. Should you inadvertently stray onto the wrong side of the line, I will be responsible for the monetary fine. If you are successful, as I know you will be, and you are not fined, the five hundred credits that would go to the government will be your bonus."

"Ser Corson and Sher Cerdezo, I will do my best."

The flitter banked left and swung toward the low hills thirty kays west of the old Gwavara holding.

As they neared the low hills, covered with a uniform dark green carpet of trees, with scattered clearings that appeared more as gray smudges, Gerswin thought he saw a faint line of smoke.

"Is that smoke?"

The pilot and Constanza both stiffened, almost imperceptibly, and the pilot swallowed.

"Ser Corson, why do you ask?"

"It seemed strange. Everywhere else the air is so clear. Even in the forests outside Illyam. First smoke I've seen."

"Perhaps it is smoke."

Michel brought the flitter around heading south-ward, along the gently curved line separating the rising and treed hills from the cultivated fields. Between the trees and the bean fields ran a dust-covered and narrow road. For fifty meters on each side of the road the ground was grassy, the grass a purple-tinged gold.

From his viewpoint, Gerswin studied the Forest Reserve. The low trees were gray-trunked, the foliage more purple–olive-green than the green of New Augusta or even of New Colora. He could see no towering monoliths, but a regularity in height, despite the obvi-ously irregular and natural growth spacing of the indi-vidual trees.

Several distant glimmers, either lasers or light re-flected from polished metal, twinkled in the distance, from what looked to be the second or third line of the hills that rose gradually as their distance from the cultivated area increased.

About the reflections Gerswin said nothing.

"The smoke . . . ?" he asked.

"Ah, yes, the smoke . . . it may be smoke."

Gerswin turned to Constanza. "Perhaps I under-stand. Even in the most ideal of societies, there are those who would not work for what they receive, who would rather live like savages . . ."

He could sense the relief in the pilot and the land agent, which indicated he was either off-track totally or had reassured them with his observation.

"Yes, Ser Corson," answered Constanza, "we do have a few of those. And occasionally their campfires go out of control."

"And the Ministry of Forests and Agriculture De-velopment is spread so thin that it would welcome someone who could protect and manage a small section of the Forest Reserve?"

As he asked the question, the flitter passed a small clearing, and Gerswin thought he saw the charred remnants of three identical houses side by side before the view was obscured by the flitter's stub wing and the intervening trees.

"There have been other lease/purchases granted on that basis."

Gerswin nodded, thinking more about the sight of three identical burned ruins in a small clearing.

"I take it that in normal circumstances, building in the Forest Reserves is not allowed? That is true on most worlds, I believe."

"That is true on Byzania as well. How else could a reserve remain a reserve if any savage could . . . build a . . . dwelling . . . anywhere he wanted?"

Gerswin noted the hesitancy in word choice and filed it mentally for future reference.

"Who actually protects the forests? The Ministry of Forests and Agriculture Development?"

"Protects?"

"Keeps people out, makes sure that savages don't destroy the trees, that sort of thing."

"All protection is the responsibility of the Chief of Staff. Any guard duty, whether at the shuttle port, or in the Forest Reserves, is the duty of the Armed Forces." That was from the pilot.

"So your Armed Forces are concerned with both the prevention of crime and the protection of natural resources?"

"Ser Corson, we have little crime here on Byzania. Surely you have already noticed that."

Gerswin had noticed that and said so before changing the subject.

"How far would twenty thousand squares go?"

Constanza had a map on the console screen in front of Gerswin, and with her instructions and the map, he could see how the combined holding would indeed be a most attractive property. Most attractive.

Attractive as it would be, he thought he also understood Sher Cerdezo's game.

RERTA would apply for the Forest Reserve purchase, and the government would turn it down. The deposit would be forfeit, unless RERTA could bring pressure to bear, in which case the deposit would become the processing fee or the equivalent. Whatever the eventual result, RERTA would be out an additional 1,005,000 credits, of which a large share would probably go to Sher Cerdezo.

A further refinement would be the requirement that RERTA purchase the estate land before it could apply for the Forest Reserve purchase. If the Forest Reserve purchase failed to go through, the Foundation, in RERTA's ostensible name, would have overpriced farming land, unless it resold at a loss, possibly through Sher Cerdezo.

He almost smiled.

The locals played rough, too tough to be ultimately successful, particularly if a few experienced Imperials moved in.

Gerswin could see another smoky patch in the forested distance, which he ignored, as well as a longer flash of light from the same general direction.

He could not ignore the three combat skitters, presumably carrying the troops for which they were designed, which zoomed through a low ridge between two hills and spiraled up into a holding pattern above the smoldering patch in the Reserve.

"Forest fire?" he asked blankly.

"I do not know," answered the pilot.

"Nor I," chimed in Constanza.

They both lied. Gerswin did not press the issue, but merely studied the skitters for a moment before turning his head to look at another area of the Forest Reserve.

"Most attractive land parcels, Sher Cerdezo. Most attractive."

"Do . . . do you think your client might be interested?"

"RERTA might indeed be interested. There are several other possibilities I have yet to investigate."

"I doubt that they measure up to this."

"They may not. If so, then I can honestly report that this is the most attractive." Gerswin looked at the pilot. "If there is nothing else you think I should see . . ."

"Of course. Michel, let us return Ser Corson to Illyam."

Gerswin leaned back as if to relax, then sat up and half turned in his seat.

"Sher Cerdezo . . . you are so familiar with so many of these estates. Almost as if you had . . ." Gerswin looked down and did not complete the statement.

". . . as if I had been raised on one?"

"My apologies if I have created some awkwardness."

"No." She laughed, and the laugh was the practiced easy kind that comes to those who make it their stock in trade. "My origins would be obvious to anyone raised on Byzania, even without the name Cerdezo. My uncle was once the Prime Minister—before he had an unfortunate accident while hunting turquils in the Western Reserve."

"Then you moved to Illyam, away from the memories?"

"They were good memories, but times change. I enjoy the city life, and the chance to meet off-worlders now and again. When one has a small household, one has no need for estates, and what I have is adequate, more than adequate, for my needs."

"I did not mean to pry."

"No, Ser Corson. You did not intrude. You understand a great deal more than most off-worlders, and for that understanding I am grateful."

Gerswin turned back to stare out the front of the armaglass canopy at the dim blotch on the brown horizon, the dim blotch that would become Illyam.

No matter how he turned the problem over in his mind, he couldn't see any quick solution. Not one that didn't point the finger at one MacGregor Corson long before he could track down what he needed.

That left the option of action, and of using others to force the issue before his cover was thoroughly shredded.

All he could do was wait until touchdown. Wait and hope that there wasn't a welcoming committee yet, not that he expected one until the locals had figured out how to get their hands on as much hard currency as possible.

As he expected, there was no greeting party when the flitter landed at the shuttle port, not if he excluded the small groundcar that waited for Sher Cerdezo at the edge of the tarmac where Michel had set the flitter down.

Gerswin observed the military style of the landing, which confirmed another of his suspicions.

As Michel shut down the thrusters, Gerswin stretched, began to unbuckle his belt harness.

"Uhnnnn . . ."

The pilot slumped forward over the stick, his beret sliding off his head and onto the control board.

"What . . . what happened?" asked Gerswin, swiveling away from the outside view and leaning over the pilot.

"Michel!" added Constanza Cerdezo.

Gerswin pocketed the pilot's credentials and universal credit card as he laid the man back and across the seat.

"He's breathing . . . heartbeat seems all right . . ." Gerswin looked at the land agent. "Is there . . . I mean . . . how do you call for an emergency health vehicle?"

"Perhaps we should take him to the dispensary in my groundcar," suggested the land agent. "By the time—"

"Good idea."

Gerswin fumbled around with the controls more than necessary before locating the door and steps release and activating them.

As the canopy slid back and the doorway opened and steps extended, the groundcar purred toward the flitter.

Gerswin edged the limp pilot to the doorway, climbed out, and gave the impression of staggering as he lifted the man into his arms and over his shoulder. With one hand on the single railing, he lurched down and toward the olive drab of the groundcar.

The driver wore the standard armed forces uniform
and had leapt out to stand by the open front door of the
car, his right hand on the butt of the holstered stunner.

"Sher Cerdezo, what happened?"

"Michel collapsed right after landing. He breathes,
but he is not conscious. Can we take him to the dispensary?"

"That would be no problem." The driver raised his
eyebrows as he surveyed Gerswin.

"We'll just bring Ser Corson with us, Waldron. He is
a client of mine, but Michel is the important thing."

As they talked, Gerswin eased the pilot's form into
the rear seat, and pulled himself in as well, shutting the
door behind him. Waldron seated Sher Cerdezo before
returning to the wheel to begin the trip toward the
dispensary.

"Medical, medical, this is Waldron. Pilot Michel
unconscious. Request emergency team upon arrival."

As the car whined toward the low building that was
the dispensary, Gerswin could see a glide stretcher and
two white-clad figures waiting under the emergency
entrance's portico.

No sooner had the groundcar come to a halt than
the armed services medical technicians were easing
Michel out and onto the stretcher.

The way they handled the unconscious pilot verified
another of Gerswin's suspicions.

As the medical team bundled Michel off, Waldron
turned in his seat so that he half faced Constanza, in the
front, and Gerswin, in the rear.

"What really happened to Michel?"

Gerswin could have taken offense and been in
character, but decided against it. Waldron was more
than a driver. More like Constanza's jailer.

"He just fell forward. One minute he was fine. The
next minute he was slumped on the controls."

"Before or after the doorway was opened?"

"Before, I think," answered Gerswin. "I wasn't looking at him at all."

"Why not?"

"Because I was considering what I would do with the land parcels that Sher Cerdezo had shown me."

"Did you see anything, Sher Cerdezo?"

"No. I was picking my case up from the floor. When I looked up, Ser Corson was looking at the groundcar. Then Michel groaned and fell forward." She glared at Waldron. "And if you are through treating us . . . like trainees . . . would you be so kind as to take us back?"

"Of course, Sher Cerdezo. Of course. And what about Ser Corson?"

"Unless you have any great objection, he comes with me. Michel's seizure stopped us from completing our business."

Waldron said nothing as he squared himself in his seat, seemingly oblivious to the lady's biting tongue. The whine of the electrics increased, and the car pulled away from the dispensary. The front glass darkened automatically as the car turned into the late afternoon sun.

Constanza sat straight, facing forward, silent. Gerswin followed her example, hoping he had read the lady correctly.

As the electric vehicle pulled up the long circular drive to a house—which, while appearing modest by the standards of the larger estate holders, would have been the envy of many an Imperial functionary—Gerswin had to wonder in what sort of splendor had Constanza Cerdezo grown up. She had referred to her quarters as small and modest.

At the portico waited two other men, both of whom wore livery that marked them as servants, but both with the manner of military personnel.

Before the car pulled away, Gerswin turned as if to help the white-haired lady from the front seat. One of the guards had already opened the door for her.

"Sher Cerdezo, I am not familiar with this section

of Illyam. Once we are completed, finished, is there some sort of transportation?"

"I am sure that Waldron would be more than happy to drive you back to your hotel."

"Most assuredly," said Waldron, smiling broadly.

At the smile, Gerswin hastily revised his plans again.

"My study would be best," said Constanza, "since I have my console and the larger maps there."

Gerswin followed her through the double doors and through the hardwood-floored foyer to another doorway on the right and a smaller hallway, with rough-finished white walls. At the end was the study, a long high-ceilinged room with rows and rows of built-in wooden bookcases, nearly all filled with old-style books, on the right, or the exterior wall. On the left was a nearly solid expanse of glass looking into the low gardens of the central courtyard.

"Might I borrow your console for a moment or two?" asked Gerswin.

"Certainly. I will get the maps out."

Gerswin used Michel's card to ask for the planetary directory and three names. General Juen Kerler and General Raoul Grieter had been mentioned in the faxnews, while Jaime Hylerion was the name he really wanted.

Hylerion was not listed. Period. The generals were, but only by name, with just a vidscreen drop number for messages.

As he sat at the console, Constanza walked over, placed her hand on his shoulder. Gerswin looked up, ready to remove her hand at the first sign of trouble. Her eyes widened at the Hylerion name.

Gerswin took a sheet of print paper from the console and printed an inquiry.

"Does the armed services keep samples of the house trees?"

He studied her face.

She looked at the question and shook her head. "Could we finish up now, Ser Corson?"

He crumpled the paper, but put it in his belt pouch.

"If you would pardon me, if I could make one other rather quick inquiry?"

"If it does not take too long. I do have other engagements, and I would like to finish."

Translated loosely, he didn't have much time.

Gerswin pulled a datacube from his belt pouch and dropped it into the scanner, tapping out the five lines of instructions he had memorized. He hoped the information worked as advertised.

Then he stood.

"I'm not sure what else we have to discuss, unless you have some recommendations on guarantees for obtaining a Forest Reserve purchase. Without that, it would be difficult to recommend buying only the estate lands. It is the combination which is so desirable."

"I am afraid I misunderstand you, Ser Corson."

Gerswin took her arm in his, and guided her back toward the front of the town villa.

"No misunderstanding, Sher Cerdezo. We may not be far enough along to finalize this. I have sent off the information, and I thank you for the use of your console, for further relay. Now, if you would care to see me off. Or do you have to meet someone in town?"

He squeezed her hand gently with the question.

"Perhaps I should. I had not thought . . . ah . . . it is no matter."

The car, and the smiling face of Waldron, were waiting at the portico for them.

"Are you going somewhere, Sher Cerdezo?"

"Yes. I had forgotten that Diene had asked me to stop by. So you can drop me there, and then take Ser Corson to his hotel."

"But . . . Sher Cerdezo . . ."

"I am sure you can arrange this, Waldron."

Gerswin helped the slender woman into the backseat, then walked around and sat down behind the driver.

"Hotel D'Armand," he offered in his most helpful voice. He could see the driver shrug slightly.

"En route Boulevard Fernadsa, then to the Hotel D'Armand," Waldron mumbled into the speaker.

Constanza shifted her weight as the car whined forward and down the drive.

Gerswin watched as Waldron wheeled out onto the nearly vacant boulevard, then stretched, his hands extended near the driver. He waited.

As the driver started to slump, Gerswin slid over the seat into the front, yanking the man from his spot behind the wheel with a single-armed vengeance that left the older woman openmouthed.

The car careened toward the left curb. Gerswin twisted it back on course, while removing Waldron's beret and jamming it low on his own forehead.

Already, Gerswin could see some of the results of his handiwork as lights began to flash on and off at random throughout Illyam.

After touching his datalink to the *Caroljoy* and punching in the emergency standby code, he twisted the electric's power up full and headed down the Boulevard Eglise toward the shuttle port.

Their arrival was anticlimactic, since the *Caroljoy* was grounded on the civilian side with a single military guard, still looking bored as Gerswin whined up.

"Halt!"

Thrummm!

The sentry never even had the time to look surprised.

Gerswin continued with the groundcar right to the point where the ship's shields, now pulsing blue, touched the tarmac. He jumped out, opening the rear door.

"Coming?"

"Now . . . ?"

"One and only chance."

She looked around the port, from the civilian receiving area where amber lights alternated with white, to the flat western horizon where the golden greened sun was about to touch the flat smudged line that represented the endless squares of synde beans, to the muddied gray of the tarmac, and across the gray to the armed services compound a kay away where sirens blared and intermittent lights seared the late afternoon sky.

At last, her glance strayed to the groundcar and the slumped figure within.

Constanza Cerdezo swallowed, and squared her shoulders.

"Yes. I'll go."

"We're not done yet, you know?"

"I'm scarcely surprised at that, Ser Corson, if that is indeed even your real name."

Gerswin was half listening as he jumped the screen out over them and began to guide the former land agent/prisoner toward the *Caroljoy.*

VII

GERSWIN TAPPED HIS FINGERS ON THE BOTTOM EDGE OF THE control keys as his eyes darted from the main screen to the representational screen to the data screen in a continuing scan pattern.

"Private yacht *Breakerton.* Private yacht *Breakerton.* This is Byzania Control. Byzania Control. Please acknowledge. Please acknowledge."

"Request instructions," the AI asked.

"Do not acknowledge. Maintain screens."

"Maintaining screens. Unidentified object departing orbit control. Probability exceeds point seven that object is orbital patrol with tachead missiles."

"Query!" growled Gerswin. "Interrogative probability of orbit control destruction through field constriction drive swerve."

"Inquiry imprecise."

"If we force the patrol to fire at an angle that will cause the missile to skip off the atmosphere, can we use the mag band constrictions to control the missile course for a return to orbit control, with subsequent detonation?"

"Probability of damage to *Caroljoy* exceeds point four. Probability of damage to orbit control exceeds point nine."

"No good. What kind of tachead does orbit control use?"

"EDI proximity is employed by more than point nine five of all orbit defense systems."

"Can you maneuver us so that, when you blank out EDI traces, the tachead will seek out orbit control?"

"Not within current gee restriction envelope."

"What is the minimum gee load requirement for a probability of orbit station destruction exceeding point nine with a probability of damage to the *Caroljoy* of less than point one?"

"Point eight probability of successful maneuver, defined as a point probability of destruction combined with a point one probability of damage to *Caroljoy*, can be obtained with an internal gee force loading peak of six point three for up to ten standard minutes."

"Interrogative time before maneuver commencement."

"Ten standard minutes, plus or minus two."

Gerswin stood up and walked across the narrow space and into the tiny crew cabin that was normally his. Constanza Cerdezo sat on the built-in bunk that doubled as an acceleration shell.

"Constanza?"

She turned, letting her feet hang over the side. "You have a problem?"

"I need an answer. What sort of physical condition are you in?"

"Why do you ask?"

"Because I need to know. Do you have any heart or lung problems? What's your chron age? Estimated bio age?"

"A lady . . ." She broke off. "You are serious. I know of no heart or lung problems. My age is fifty-seven years standard, and three years ago my biological age was set at fifty."

"Query," Gerswin asked the empty air. "Interrogative probability of severe biological damage, assuming standard profile, female, biological age fifty-three, slender frame."

"Probability of severe bruising exceeds point eight. Probability of internal bleeding less than point one. Probabilities based on maximum maneuver time of less than ten standard minutes at peak gee load of six point three."

Gerswin looked down at the white-haired and tanned woman, straight into her black eyes.

"The problem is simple. We have two choices. Cut and run. That's one. Without finishing my mission. Or use some fancy shipwork to knock out orbit control."

"You cannot come back and try again?"

"No. Excluding the costs, after what I did to the communications net, and to their air defenses on the way up, they will doubtless change things to prevent any recurrence. Next time, they just might destroy any untoward private ships who visit."

"There are risks?"

"Risk to you. About a five percent chance you'll be injured. Maybe more."

"And if you succeed?"

"I will get what I came for and, in the process, probably upset the current government."

"Would the Empire step in?"

"No. Against policy. Never have, and never will. Could quarantine the system until a local government regains total control."

The silence stretched out.

"Time until arrival of orbit patrol is five minutes plus or minus one." The AI's clear tones echoed in the small cabin.

The silence dropped over the two, with only the background hissing of the ventilation system.

Constanza Cerdezo looked at Gerswin, then lowered her shoulders. "Do what you must. I can do no less."

Gerswin lifted her off the bunk and set her standing on the deck. Next he ripped the sheet and quilt off the bunk and slammed them into a locker beneath. He touched the controls to reconfigure the bunk into an acceleration shell and, as quickly as he had made the changes, just as quickly lifted Constanza and placed her in the shell. Three quick movements, and the harnesses had her webbed firmly in place.

"Now. Once the acceleration hits, don't even move your head. Leave it straight between the support rests here. Don't lift it, and don't try to shift your weight once the gee forces start.

"At times you may have no weight, or things may seem normal. Don't believe it. Don't get out of here for anything. Is that clear?"

"Time for orbit patrol arrival at estimated firing point is three plus or minus one."

Gerswin dashed from the cabin to the control, scrambling into his own shell and adjusting the overrides for fingertip control.

"Use your six point three gee maneuver to get that tachead orbiting back at the control station."

"Command imprecise."

"Commence the maneuver you computed earlier, using a six point three gee envelope, to place the *Caroljoy* in a position where any tachead fired at the *Caroljoy* can be skip-deflected or otherwise placed in a position to allow it to home back on orbit control."

"Instructions understood. Due to delays and the position of the orbital patroller, maneuver with same probability of success requires an envelope of seven point one gees."

"Do it! Commence maneuver."

A giant fist slammed Gerswin deep into his accel/decel shell.

He tightened his stomach muscles to fight off the blackness, to keep his eyes open enough to see the readouts projected in red light into the sudden darkness of the ship.

"Orbit patrol readjusting position, holding on tachead release."

The pressure on Gerswin eased, back to five plus gees, he estimated. Because of the differentials in orbits, the strategy was to change positions rapidly enough while moving toward the patroller to force the patroller to fire quickly enough not to be able to compute the probabilities. Plus, the patroller did not know the configuration of Gerswin's ship would allow him to blow all EDI traces.

Gerswin hoped it was enough.

The gee force continued to ease as the *Caroljoy* boosted her speed at a decreasing rate.

"Closing on patroller. Tachead released. Commencing evasive maneuvers."

This time, the gee force blow to Gerswin did roll him into the blackness, though only momentarily.

"Patroller has released second tachead."

"Evade it, idiot," grunted the pilot.

"Stet. Evading."

Gerswin felt like he was being stretched across the couch. Supposedly, yachts, not even former scouts, were not capable of maneuvers like atmospheric craft, but Gerswin felt the *Caroljoy* was being handled more like a flitter than a deep-space ship.

For a moment, the *Caroljoy* went weightless, almost seeming to flip on her longitudinal axis.

The pilot's stomach ventured toward his throat before being jammed back below his hips by the next gee blast.

When the acceleration eased, Gerswin rasped out another command before he was pressed farther into his shell.

"Put Byzania tactical comm on audible."

"Stet. Frequency available."

Another gee burst slammed more breath from Gerswin than he thought he had left, and just as suddenly, all weight left him.

"Full screens, and complete EDI blockage," announced the AI.

The minutes dragged by.

"ByzOps. Hammer one. Returning. Target avoided both persuaders."

"Stet, Hammer one. Understand persuaders avoided."

"That's affirmative."

"Do you have visual on target?"

"That is negative."

"Interrogative EDI."

"Negative. Lost EDI after first release. No visual."

". . . don't like this . . ." Gerswin smiled wryly.

"Maneuvers completed," stated the AI.

"Interrogative closures? Position status?"

"One quarter orbit distance plus two relative Byzania orbit control."

"Aren't we close to an orbit relay?"

"Relay inoperative."

"I take it you rendered the relay inoperative."

"That is correct."

Gerswin shivered. That was one facet of releasing

control to the AI that he did not relish. It was also the reason why neither the I.S.S. nor any commercial ships linked their AIs to the controls directly. No one yet had figured out a workable system that embodied the day-to-day ethical and human considerations required. Every direct "ethical" system ever attempted froze or took too much time to make decisions. The only workable systems were those designed without ethical parameters.

"Return to advisory status."

"In advisory status."

"Give me at least five minutes warning of *any* approaching object, anything at all."

"Five minutes warning of all objects."

"Stet."

Gerswin scrambled out of his shell, wincing at the instant stiffness his muscles seemed to have acquired, and staggered into the small crew cabin.

A quick study indicated that Constanza was breathing, but her face and tan and white tunic were streaked with blood.

The white-haired woman's chest rose and fell regularly, but the beginnings of heavy bruises were showing on her uncovered forearms.

He fumbled for the medstar cuffs, finally plugging them in and attaching them.

"Interrogative medical status of subject."

"Subject unconscious. Probability less than point zero one of internal bleeding. Gross scan indicates no fractures."

From what he could tell, the blood had come from a nosebleed. He wiped her slack face as clean as he could, but left her in the harness to wake up naturally.

No sense in taking chances.

Back before the controls, he also strapped himself in.

The audio crackled.

"ByzOps. Unidentified object approaching orbit station."

"Hammer two, scramble. Launch and destroy."

"Two scrambling. Interrogative clear to launch."

"Cleared to launch. Cleared to launch."

"Affirm. We're cradle gone. Cradle gone and clearing."

"Vector on incoming, plus one five at two zero seven. Plus one five at two zero seven."

"Understand vector plus one five at two zero seven."

"Stet. Vector and intercept. Intercept and destroy."

"Intercept impossible. Intercept impossible."

"Can you impact?"

"You want me to ram it?"

"That's affirmative."

"ByzOps, this is Hammer two. Clarify your last. Clarify your last."

"Hammer two. If intercept not possible, use full thrust to impact and deflect incoming. Identified as persuader, class two."

"That's impossible, ByzOps. That's—"

EEEEEEEEEEEEE.

"Energy pulse indicates probable destruction of Byzania orbit control."

"Does that mean all incoming traffic will have to communicate planetside directly."

"That is correct."

"And the planetary commnet is effectively out of commission," mused Gerswin, "at least until they scrub the entire link.

"So it's time to drop in on our friends the savages and see if they do have those tree houses of Hylerion's."

The *Caroljoy* began to drop from orbit toward the patches of Forest Reserve Gerswin had tentatively marked from his orbit and map scans.

VIII

THE TALLER GENERAL LOOKED OVER HIS SHOULDER. THREE silver triangles glittered on his shoulder boards. Otherwise, his khaki uniform tunic was unadorned.

"Are you sure it's secure?"

"Nothing is secure now. With the communications links down, we're operating on emergency power, and we don't have the energy for sonic screens. I doubt anyone else on Byzania has the energy for peepers."

"Gwarara, summarize."

Colonel Gwarara squared his shoulders and faced the three generals.

"Generals, the situation is as follows. First, Ser Corson, whoever he is, dropped a trap program into the comm-link system. It was an expanding and replicating program. Furthermore, it ordered a printout of the program itself from every hard-copy printer on Byzania that linked into the net before we shut down the power grid."

"Shut down the power grid? The entire grid?" That was General Somozes, Chief for Atmospheric Defense, blond, stocky, clean-shaven, and square-chinned.

"Every minute that the system remained operational, another two hundred to one thousand vidterms were locked in. We estimate that it will take between twelve and thirty-six hours to scrub the entire system. That's if we can use all available personnel. We will have to return power in sections. If we miss one link, it could repeat the original lock."

"What did this devilish program do?" asked the
other General, the short, thin one named Taliseo who
headed the Marines.

"General, it was a simple program. All it did was
link together terminal after terminal, and leave the
connections open. That did several things." Gwarara
paused, took a deep breath before continuing. He
wanted to wipe his damp forehead. The bunker was
getting warmer with each passing minute.

"First, no comm system actually stays on line all the
time with all terminals. The actual link times are pulsed,
compressed if you will. Corson removed the pulse feature and made all the contacts continuous. Enormous
increase in the power requirements."

"Is that what caused the blinking lights and the
power fluctuations?"

"Before we shut the grid down? Yes."

"What else?" asked the tallest General, Guiteres,
the Chief of Staff.

"Second, as I mentioned earlier, this was a replicating program. Each connection transferred the program
to the new terminal and left it displayed there, as well as
printing it wherever possible."

"You mean, there are hundreds of copies of this . . .
this monstrosity printed all over Byzania?"

"More like thousands, but the distribution would be
very uneven. When we shut the grid down, the penetra-
tion of Conuno was close to ninety percent. Probably
only about seventy percent for Conduo, and less than
twenty-five percent for Contrio. Most of the terminals
don't have power-fail memories. By killing the power,
we automatically destroyed close to ninety percent of the
vidterm duplicates."

"What about hard copy?" asked the Chief of Staff.

Colonel Gwarara frowned. "A rough estimate
would be close to fifty percent of all hard-copy facilities
with power-fail memories."

"But every dwelling in Illyam has a hard-copy

capability. That's more than two million."

"It would be less than that, General," corrected the Colonel. "The access was only to vidterms with on-line printers, not backup units."

"The point is the same," sighed General Guiteres. "There are more than enough copies available that anyone who wanted to repeat the program could."

"No, ser. We can shield against this program being used again by anyone."

Guiteres stared at the Colonel. "You can shield against this particular program. Can you shield against another that has a different introduction? Or a different mechanism? Can you hide the basic concept?"

Gwarara looked at the hard and gray plastic of the bunker floor. "No, General."

"Gentlemen," Guiteres said softly, "the revolution is over. And we have lost."

"What?"

"Are you insane?"

The Chief of Staff waited until the shock silenced the other two generals. The Colonel had said nothing.

"I do not propose admitting this publicly. Nor have we lost the immediate control of the situation. But the society we have today is doomed, no matter what we do. We have been able to maintain control because we held all communications, because the distribution of food, information, and transportation was monitored and regulated through the communications network.

"Ser Corson, whoever he really is, has handed those who oppose us both the format and concept of shutting down those communications channels. How many blockages can we take before the entire fabric unwinds? Three . . . five . . . a dozen?

"He has also destroyed orbit control, somehow. We do not have the resources to replace it, nor can we purchase a replacement if Byzania is quarantined, which seems likely. Further, without the satellite control links, our access to the relay monitors is limited to line of sight.

That will give the savages more time to act and to avoid our patrols. To keep the communications relays operating will require maintenance from the shuttle port, which is expensive and energy intensive."

"So . . . ?" asked Taliseo. "So it costs us more. So it requires a stepped-up patrol effort to keep the savages in line. So what?"

"Don't you see?" responded Guiteres. "To maintain control under our present system will require more troops, more force. More overt use of force will create more resentment and unrest, which will generate other blockages, requiring greater force."

He stopped and looked around the bunker, wiping his own forehead with the back of his left hand.

"Assuming you are correct, and I have some considerable doubts, what do you suggest?" asked Taliseo.

Somozes frowned as he watched the two senior generals debate.

"In general terms," answered the Chief of Staff, "the answer is clear. We have to build a more decentralized system and society, using the existing political framework and economic structure, and we have to begin before the savages and the other opportunists understand the real situation."

"I disagree," interjected Somozes. "Why should we give anything away? We've given them prosperity, eliminated most crimes, and a pretty honest government."

"How many dissidents have vanished? How many radical friends of students have taken 'trips' and never returned? Do you think that a prosperous people ever considers the hardships that otherwise might have been?"

"That doesn't matter. We still hold the power."

"How many personnel in the Armed Forces?"

"Three hundred thousand."

"How many people on Byzania?"

"Thirty million."

"How many spacecraft?"

"One cruiser, one light cruiser, ten corvettes, ten scouts, and five freighters. Plus the orbit patrollers."

"And how many savages in the outer forests? How many student dissidents we know nothing about?"

Somozes shrugged, as if to indicate that he didn't know and could have cared less.

"More than four thousand, on all three continents," answered Taliseo. "That's not counting the underground within the cities."

"Half our Armed Forces is required to keep the forest groups in check. Half! Do you not understand?" Guiteres glared at Somozes, who seemed to ignore the look. "With our credit account system, we could isolate individuals. Does Miguel order more food than a family of three needs? We knew. Who does he call? We knew. What electronic components are produced and shipped? To whom? For what? We knew, and we could cross-check. Now, it is only a matter of time before the dissidents discover that they can destroy that tracking and control system. Even a single blockage will allow uncounted tons of material to be diverted."

Guiteres raked the three others with brown eyes that radiated contempt.

"Because we controlled the education, we could keep track of those who had the training on comm systems. We perpetuated the myth that great education was necessary to understand and engineer and program them. In one stroke, Ser Corson has begun the destruction of that myth. How soon will we see the students trying to duplicate his efforts?

"I do not know, but I doubt it will be long. And what will you do to them? If you can find them?"

"I doubt it is that grim," answered Taliseo. "Why do you think that?"

"For one thing, the Imperial offices have already been evacuated, and their ship lifted as we met, possibly leaving to recommend quarantine."

Taliseo frowned as the implications sank in.

Somozes frowned also, muttering under his breath, asking a different question entirely. "But what did we do to Corson? What did we do to him?"

Gwarara looked from one general to the next, then to the floor, as he wiped his streaming forehead with the back of his sleeve.

Guiteres shook his head slowly as he surveyed the three other officers and the emergency communications board behind Gwarara, an expanse of unlit screens and lights, totally lifeless.

IX

THREE QUICK TAPS ON THE CONTROLS, AND THE FIGURES reeled onto the data screen.

Gerswin had enough power for two more lift-offs and touchdowns—that plus boost out to jump point.

Two clearings had proved fruitless, merely burned-over ashpits long since deserted by the elusive rebels or the pursuing Armed Forces.

The one toward which the *Caroljoy*, operating as private yacht *Breakerton*, now settled was the most isolated he had been able to find, which seemed to meet the theoretical parameters outlined years ago by Hylerion.

"Any luck?"

Despite her recent ordeal, Constanza's voice came from the cabin with remarkable lilt and cheer.

"Know shortly."

The open space in the clearing was barely enough

for the short touchdown run of the scout. Once down, Gerswin swiveled the craft slowly in order to leave her in position for a quick departure. He also left the screens in place, despite the additional energy requirements.

"Anyone around?"

"Detectors show no heat radiation above background within two hundred meters."

Gerswin almost snorted. All the rebels had to do was lie in a ditch to avoid heat detection in the warmth of Byzania.

"Let's have a sweep from all the exterior scanners."

Unburned, the clearing was covered with a ground-hugging blue-and-gold-tinted grass Gerswin had never seen before. The trees were low, lower than the pilot had expected, and wide-trunked, the branches of the tallest reaching less than fifteen meters into the washed-out green-gold of the sky.

The fine dust raised by the scout's landing had already settled, giving the closer grass and trees a gray overtone.

"Freeze on the last image."

The image he had caught showed a regularity, a hint of an oblong structure, in the right lower corner.

"Expand the right lower corner."

Gerswin studied the blurred image.

"Constanza? Would you come here?"

"I am." The closeness of her voice, right behind his shoulder, jarred him. He started, unsettled that she had managed to move so close without his noticing, then frowned briefly at the thought that his skills might be deteriorating.

"I did not mean to surprise you."

"What does that look like to you?"

"A dwelling."

"The scale is wrong. Less than half size. Unless . . ."

"Unless what, Ser Corson?"

He turned his head to look at her, his eyes moving past the dark blotches on her arms.

"Unless someone is building half-sized houses, or half-sized people," he temporized, unwilling to voice his own hopes.

"There are rumors . . ."

"Of what?" he snapped.

She drew back from the intensity in his voice and hawk-yellow eyes.

"You seemed to know already . . . of houses that grow like trees . . . of the Marines burning them wherever they find them to keep the rebels . . . the savages . . . on the run."

"We'll have to see." He stood up and stepped away from the control panels.

"Keep full screens in place," he ordered the AI.

"Full screens in place," replied the AI impersonally.

"Do you want to come?"

"Certainly. If you think it is safe."

"Nothing's safe. Not totally. Stay inside the screens. They'll stop any energy weapon, or explosives, or projectile guns."

He touched the panel by the lock. The inner door opened.

"It's tight," he observed as she crowded in with him.

As the outer door opened, Gerswin's first impression was of desert as the flood of hot and dry outside air washed over them.

He bounded down the extended ramp and held out an arm to help the former Prime Minister's niece.

No sound marred the stillness. No breeze moved a single stalk of the blue and gold ground cover. Only the muffled crunch of the vegetation under Gerswin's black boots could be heard as he walked toward the rear of the scout to see if he could get a better look at what he hoped was Jaime Hylerion's house tree growing behind two older trees.

Gerswin stopped a meter inside the twinkling and faint blue pulsation that marked the screen line and peered through the first line of trees.

He frowned, bit at his lower lip.

The second line of trees obscured his view, but a regularity existed behind the trees. Whether it was man-made or a house tree was another question.

Whhrrrr.

"Corson!"

He ducked and turned, but not quickly enough, he realized as he felt the sharpness bite into his right arm. He glanced down at the stubby arrow imbedded there, shaking his head at his slowness, and his stupidity at not having kept himself in fighting order.

Without hesitating, he moved, grabbing the light-boned woman in his left hand and forcing himself up the ramp and into the lock.

"An arrow, for Hades' sake . . ." he muttered.

He blinked once, twice, as he stumbled into the control area, releasing Constanza as he felt his knees turning to jelly.

"So dark . . ."

The night struck him down with the suddenness of lightning from a landspout.

X

COOL, COOL . . . GERSWIN COULD FEEL THE DAMPNESS ACROSS his forehead, a contrast to the heat of his body.

He tried to open his eyes, but the dampness blocked his vision. His arms felt leaden, and his throat was raspy and dry.

"Uhhhh . . ." he croaked.

The faint pressure on his forehead eased as the cloths were removed from across his eyes.

A white-haired visage wavered in and out of focus.

"Corson? Can you hear me?"

Corson? Who was Corson? Corson was dead, dead at the hands of the Guild? Was it Allison, asking for her son? But Allison was long gone . . .

"Urrr . . ."

For some reason, he could not speak.

"If you hear me, blink your eyes."

Gerswin blinked.

"That's good. At least you understand. You shouldn't be alive, but Hyveres says if you have made it this far, you should recover completely . . . in time."

Corson, Hyveres—who were they?

Frozen—that was the way his face felt, with the hint of needles tingling under the skin.

He wanted to ask how long he had been immobilized, but could not. Instead, the darkness, with its hot needles and forgetfulness, crept back over him.

When he woke again, the cabin—and this time he could tell he was lying in the crew-room bunk—was dim. The hot points of needles burned and jabbed through most of his body, but the pain was worst in his legs.

"Urrr . . ."

The woman—was it Constanza, Caroljoy, Allison —must have heard him, because she appeared with damp cloths to help soothe the drumming staccato of the needle jabs behind his blistering forehead.

"Just relax. You should be better soon."

Relax? How could he, lying paralyzed with needles driving through him? What if the paralysis were permanent? How had anything gotten through the screens?

The questions spun in his head until the overhead blurred into red dimness, and then into hot blackness.

When the darkness lifted once more, the jabbing of the needles seemed less intense, nearly gone from his face. He tried to move his arms, but while they twitched, they did not lift from his sides.

". . . hello . . ." he rasped.

He could hear the light pad of footsteps, and a face appeared. He pulled the name from his recollections.

"Constanza?"

"Yes. I'm here, Corson. Can you swallow?"

"Can try."

"Please do. You're terribly dehydrated."

He could feel the coolness of the water against his lips, wetting the cotton dryness inside his mouth. Nearly gagging, he concentrated on swallowing, managing to force the water down.

"That's enough for now. In a bit, we'll try again."

The pounding in his temples eased, and the blurriness of his vision cleared, although his eyes seemed to wander at will.

"Could . . . more water?" he husked.

"A little."

She was right, he discovered, because the second sip felt like lead as it dropped like lead into his stomach.

Closing his eyes, he waited, letting himself drift back into the not-quite-so-hot darkness.

When he woke again, the throbbing in his head was gone, and only a tinge of the needlelike pain remained, and that in his lower legs and feet. The cabin was lighter, but he did not hear Constanza.

Should he try to lift an arm?

Gerswin realized he was afraid he might not be able to. At last, he concentrated on reaching his belt.

Shaking, almost as though it did not belong to him, his arm strained up and touched the square fabric edge of his waistband. Slowly he turned his head toward the arch between the crew cabin and the control area.

No Constanza, not unless she was standing nearly on top of the control screens.

Where was she? How long had he been totally out of commission? What had happened?

At that, he remembered his right arm and turned his head. A pressure bandage from the first-aid kit covered the spot where the arrow had entered.

An arrow! He would never have thought of that.

A scraping sound caught his attention, and he gently eased his head to where he could view the inner lock door as it was manually cranked open.

Constanza came in with a basket of food on her left arm and a loop of cord in her hand.

"Hello."

"You seem much better."

"I am, I think."

"Can you restore the power?"

"Power?"

He blinked, recognizing for the first time since his collapse that the only illumination was from the emergency lighting.

"How long has it been?"

"Three days."

"Is everything down except the screens?"

"I think so. I didn't want to experiment much. I don't understand the manual controls, and the ship did not recognize me."

"Not designed that way." He licked his dry lips and tried to ease himself into a sitting position.

"Let me help. You're still weak, and I'm not sure Hyveres believes me when I keep telling him you're still alive."

"Hyveres?" The name still meant nothing to him.

"He is the rebel leader in this forest cell."

She stood behind his left shoulder and folded the quilt into another pillow, then slipped it behind him. Gerswin could feel the tightness in his muscles protesting the movement.

"More water?"

He was too tired to object to her holding the beaker for him.

Three days? He shivered. By now, even the most

disrupted of governments should have been getting the power system back into service.

"Has the government resumed scouting flights?"

"Not here. Hyveres says there are reports of some limited resumptions on Conuno." She perched on the end of the bunk.

"Conuno?"

"First continent. We're on Contrio. That's why I asked about power. Hyveres was hoping we could leave. He doesn't want to use the few weapons they have collected in trying to destroy your ship. They don't want the government seeing it and attacking."

"Probably couldn't destroy us. Jolt it enough so the concussion might kill us."

"Can you take off?"

"Technically, yes. Once I can get to the controls. Not sure I could last through the sequence to jump. Besides . . . not done here. Don't have what I came for."

"And what was that?"

He saw no point in dissembling further.

"I wanted seeds, spores, whatever the propagating mechanism is, for the house tree. We funded the original research."

"House tree?"

"What we saw through the trees just before your friends the rebels stuck me with their little arrow. What was on that arrow? Did they tell you? How did you get the food with the ship shut down?"

Now that he was beginning to think, the unanswered questions were piling up.

Constanza laughed. "You will recover, Ser Corson." Her face smoothed out, and she went on. "Hyveres told me that no one could cross the screens without dying. Is that true?"

"Yes. Form of field inhibitor. Stops most energy, and since thought is energy . . ."

"I pointed out that unless I could get you to recover, which takes food and water, sooner or later the Armed

Forces would find your ship and do their best to destroy it."

Gerswin nodded for her to continue, but this time reached for the water beaker himself. He managed to take a solid sip with a trembling left hand.

"We reached an accommodation—"

"What about the house trees?" interrupted Gerswin.

"They have hopes, but none of them grow much bigger than what you saw."

"Know why," he answered. "And the arrow?"

"They have found a local nerve poison. How did the arrow get through the ship's screens?"

"Arrows . . . non-energy . . . low velocity . . . should have thought about it." Suddenly he was drained.

His abrupt weakness must have showed because Constanza stood up from the end of the bunk where she had been sitting.

"Lean back; just relax."

Could he afford to? What about the government?

"Until you are stronger, you cannot do any more."

He let the held breath out through his teeth, trying to relax and not wanting to. There was so much to do . . .

. . . but he dozed.

When he woke once again, he discovered two things. He was soaked, and the tingling in his legs was gone.

He eased himself upright and let his legs dangle over the edge of the bunk.

The gentle sound of breathing from the control room told him that Constanza was sleeping.

He stood slowly, and began to peel off the stinking trousers and tunic. Then he leaned against the bulkhead to rest. A moment later he straightened.

"Activate—status." He followed the command with the activation codes.

"Returning to active status," the AI acknowledged for the ship, and the normal lighting returned.

Gerswin dragged himself into the fresher, standing there while the spray cleaned him of grime, sweat, and urine. By the time the charged air had dried him, he was leaning against the inside of the stall.

After dragging himself back to the lockers, where he pulled out shorts and a black shipsuit, he struggled into the clean clothing.

All the time Constanza slept, which told him how tired she was.

Finally, he stuffed his filthy clothing into the cleaner, along with the quilt and the sheet, then collapsed onto the uncovered bunk to catch his breath. In time, he sat up and finished the last drops in the water beaker on the bunk ledge.

A few minutes later he shuffled toward the controls, where he half leaned, half sat on the bottom edge of the accel/decel shell seat where Constanza lay curled into a half circle, her tiny white-haired figure fragile against the black yield cloth.

"Interrogative power status."

The figures appeared on the data screen. He nodded. The loss wasn't as bad as it could have been. He still had enough for lift-off and through two jumps, with minimum reserves.

"Exterior views from the sensors."

The scenes in the screen had a reddish cast, indicating it was night and that infraheat was used for imaging. Outside of the footprints from the lock ramp, there was no sign of any activity. The rebels must have swept up their tracks every time they had brought food to Constanza.

The lady moaned in her sleep and turned, her foot striking his back.

He waited until she seemed settled again.

The acrid scent of air recycled too little burned his nose.

"Full interior recycle. Exterior air through filters."

All he could do now was wait. Even if he woke her,

trying to find the rebels in the hours before dawn would be useless, except to find another batch of arrows aimed in his direction.

"Wake me with the alarm if anyone approaches the ship or if she leaves the control couch."

With that, he shuffled back to the bunk and stretched out, not willing to make the effort to remake it.

Cling!

Gerswin started out of his sleep at the alarm, slowed his reactions as he sat up gingerly while Constanza peered through the arch at him.

"You restored the power."

"While you were sleeping."

Gerswin felt guilty. She still wore a now grimy tan and white tunic and tan trousers, while he was relatively clean in fresh clothing.

"Would you care to use the fresher?"

He stood and headed for the control couch, by way of the water tap, where he refilled the beaker. His legs felt steady.

"After you're through," he said, "we need to make some decisions."

"What about my clothes?"

Gerswin remembered he had never removed his own outfit and bedding from the cleaner.

"Put them in the cleaner—the brown and cream tab there. You'll have to take out my things. Put them on the bunk for now."

"Why don't you—" She broke off the sentence. "It is hard to remember how sick you are when you talk so clearly."

"Not that bad now."

"Hyveres says you are the first to survive the poison."

"Wonderful."

He turned away to devote his attention to the control readings and data displays.

"Can you pick up any commercial news?" he asked the AI.

"Negative. No satellite relay."

"What about audio?"

"Byzania has no separate commercial radio."

"Armed Forces tactical freqs?"

"Imprecise command."

"Pick up the strongest Armed Forces tactical signal."

The only sound Gerswin could hear at first was static, which was barely audible over the hiss of the fresher. As he concentrated he began to be able to distinguish some phrases.

". . . Red command . . . blue attackers . . ."

". . . corvette down . . . Illyam . . ."

". . . flamers . . . flamers . . ."

". . . grid still down . . . Jerboam . . ."

". . . forest cell tiger . . . fire at will . . ."

Gerswin shook his head slowly as he listened to the story play out with each fragmented transmission.

"It is that bad?"

He had been aware of Constanza's return and her listening with him, but not how much time had passed until she touched his shoulder as she asked the question.

Turning his head, he nearly whistled. The lady looked nearly as picture-perfect as before their first tour of the countryside.

"Amazing what a ship fresher and cleaner can do," he marveled.

"Thank you. What is occurring?"

Gerswin told her.

"But why?"

"My guess is that someone wouldn't believe someone else. Once the secret is out, they can't keep control the way it has been. Probably why the Armed Forces kept after the tree houses, because free shelter would have been a first step to escaping the generals."

"The house trees do not grow large enough."

"They would if they had more time and water. You can't grow them too close to other trees. Need a lot of solar energy. But any time someone grew them out in the open, I'd bet the Armed Forces fried them."

"I still don't understand why there's fighting between segments of the Armed Forces."

"Someone believes there will have to be change, and someone else disagrees. Power shortages are going to get worse, and there's no real backup system. The Empire will quarantine the system, as soon as they can get a fleet here. That's another reason why I need to get some seeds or spores and lift out."

Constanza sat down beside him.

"I don't know whether I should like you or not. You rescued me from a prison, and then you destroyed everything I grew up with."

Gerswin shrugged. "Not much I can say to that."

He waited.

She said nothing.

He cleared his throat. "Do you want to leave Byzania with me? I'm sure you would be welcome on . . . in a number of places."

"You are gracious . . . and very cautious. But, no. No, thank you. I think I would be welcome with Hyveres, more welcome than in the cities, and happier than on a strange world."

Gerswin touched the controls and the screens filled with the exterior view and the morning sunlight.

Constanza rose.

"I will tell him, and we will get you your seeds."

"You know, Constanza, the future on Byzania rests with Hyveres."

"I know. You have determined that. Like a god, you change worlds. Yet you will never have what a man like Hyveres will, for you will never rest. You will never be content, no matter how long you live."

Gerswin stood and took her hand. He bent slightly

and brushed the back of her hand with his lips. His legs remained steady, but he sat down as he released her fingers, afraid that his legs might yet betray him.

She put her hand on his shoulder, squeezed it, before stepping back.

"I think I am grateful to you. I can now look forward to the unexpected."

She reached forward to touch his shoulder again, gently, before moving toward the lock door.

"We will bring you the seeds you need. And you will go. You will fight your fate, and we will fight ours. What else is there to say?"

Gerswin lifted the screens and watched from inside the ship as the slender woman went out to touch hands with the rebel captain for the first time. A rebel captain nearly as slender as she, nearly as white-haired, and who sported a bristling white handlebar mustache.

Although she had looked not at all like Caroljoy, neither when his lost Duchess had been young or old, Constanza reminded him of Caroljoy, though he could not say why.

Then, again, perhaps he did not want to know why. The young woman who had been his single-time lover and Martin's mother had become a dream, and no man wants to examine his dreams too closely. Not when the dreams must constantly battle the realities of the present.

Besides, in her own way, Caroljoy had made it all possible.

Yet Constanza had some of the same iron strength.

He shook his head slowly as he watched the screen.

He watched. Watched and waited for the seeds of the house tree. Watched and listened to the beginnings of a society and an Empire crashing into anarchy.

XI

The pilot tapped the last control stud of the sequence and dropped his hand, which was beginning to tremble.

He wanted to shake his head, but, instead, laid back on the black yield cloth of the control couch while the modified scout shivered . . . and jumped.

At the instant of jump, as always, the blackness inundated the scout, blinding the pilot with the darkness no light could penetrate, then disappearing as the ship reappeared tens of systems from where it had jumped.

Gerswin reached out tiredly and touched the control stud that would recompute the *Caroljoy*'s position. He could have asked the AI to do it, but even as exhausted as he was he still hated to ask the AI to do what he felt the pilot should.

He could feel his hand shake, and he compromised.

"Position. Interrogative possible jump parameters."

His voice even shook, and he wanted to scream at the weakness. His eyes flickered down at his right arm, where the slight thickness under the long sleeved tunic indicated a pressure-tight medpad. The ship's medical system had assured him there was no infection. He was just tired—totally exhausted from fighting off the effects of the nerve poison.

Constanza had questioned whether he was up to leaving, especially to handling a long flight, but he had insisted, not wanting to wait until there might be an Imperial quarantine force in place or until some faction of the Byzanian Armed Forces happened onto his ship, particularly given the shortness of his power reserves.

Now there was nothing he could do but finish the trip.

"Position at two seven five relative, distance two point five, inclination point seven. Ship is in opposition," the AI announced in its professional and impersonally feminine voice.

"Interrogative short jump. Power parameters."

"Short jump possible. Depletion of reserves to point five. Interface probability is less than point zero zero nine. Power consumption will leave ship with three point five plus stans at norm, plus half reserves."

"Jump."

"Commencing jump."

This time he let the AI handle the jump, with the milliseconds of apparent jump time so short he scarcely noticed them.

"Time to Aswan?"

"Two plus at norm."

"Normal acceleration. Notify, full alarm, if *anything* approaches the ship or if any anomalies appear."

The odds were that he'd hear the alarm at least three times before they hit orbit distance, but he obviously wasn't up to watching himself.

Four alarms later, the *Caroljoy* was in orbit, ready for planetdrop over the planet he called Aswan.

None of the alarms had amounted to anything besides debris, not that Gerswin had expected them to, since the system was out of the way, to say the least.

Aswan was the fourth planet, and the one of two that orbited the G-2 sun in the "life zone." The third planet of the relatively young system might develop intelligent life someday, unless it already had, but without overt signs of such development. Gerswin doubted it, but since no one had intensively scouted the surface, who could say?

The fourth planet, Aswan itself, offered a different dilemma. Certainly some intelligent life had built the wall of white stone across the flat plain of the perhaps once-upon-a-time ocean. Bridge? Dam? Who could say?

With no moons other than tiny and captured aster-oids, and a thin atmosphere mainly of nitrogen, Aswan was not on anyone's list of places to visit. But someone or something had indeed built a bridgelike structure nearly two thousand kays long, straight as an arrow, running from northwest to southeast, or, if one pre-ferred, from southeast to northwest. The bridge was clearly visible from orbit against the maroon dirt/dust/crystal that covered most of the planet, the two-thirds that was not out-and-out rock.

While the dam, as Gerswin mentally identified it, rose out of the maroon crystalline to a height of nearly one kay, the high point was not at either end, nor in the center, but two-thirds of the way from the southeast toward the northwest end. As if to balance, in a strange way, one-third of the way from that southeast end, connected to the dam, rose a four-sided diamond-shaped tower—provided a set of unroofed walls rising more than three hundred meters skyward above the level of the dam itself could be called a tower.

The tower itself was roughly two kays on a side, while the dam was only four hundred meters wide.

The stones which composed both dam and tower seemed identical for their entire length. Identical and huge—each as large as the *Caroljoy* and each a glistening white shot through with streaks of black.

When he had first scouted Aswan, he had taken scans and samples for analysis. Granite, that had been what the geologists at Palmyra had said, but a variety they had never seen, with an internal structure that suggested tremendous building properties.

Gerswin had refrained from laughing.

The samples he had obtained by trimming the interior of the tower. He had found no stone unattached to the dam or tower. None.

The flush-fitted top layer of stones made touch-downs and take-offs easy, with nearly as much ground effect as on Old Earth.

The pilot shook himself out of his reverie and began the descent that would take him to the base he had built within the tower, the core of which was the atmospheric power tap system, which had cost enough, but which produced power in abundance, in more than abundance.

"Descent beyond limits," advised the AI.

Gerswin shook himself and made the corrections, forcing alertness until the *Caroljoy* was settled next to the power tap connection.

Slowly, slowly, he unstrapped, and pulled on the respirator pack and helmet, dragging himself to the lock.

Once the ship was connected to the power system, he could and would gratefully collapse.

The cable system was bulky, obsolete, but relatively foolproof, and did not require constant monitoring, unlike the direct laser transfer systems used by most ports, and particularly by deep-space installations.

"Still," he muttered, under his breath and behind his respirator, as he touched the transfer stud to begin the repowering operation, "what isn't obsolete? You? The ship? Your self-appointed mission?"

He licked his upper lip.

"Who cares about Old Earth? Do all the Recorps types really want the reclamation effort to end? Will anyone really remember the devilkids and the blood they spent on a forgotten planet?"

He snorted. The thought occurred to him that, if by some remote chance, his biologics actually worked, that he would be the one in the legends and the devilkids who had made it possible would be the forgotten ones.

As if that would ever happen!

He glanced at the white stone rising overhead into the maroon twilight, stone that seemed to retain the light long past twilight, though that retained light never registered on the ship's screens.

He sighed, shook his head again, and trudged back to the ramp up to the *Caroljoy*, up to swallow ship's concentrates and water, up to sleep, and to heal.

XII

LIKE THE PIECES OF A PUZZLE SNAPPING TOGETHER, THE FRAG-
mented ideas that had been swirling around in the
Commodore's head clicked into place as a clear picture.

He shook his head wearily.

So simple, so obvious. So obvious that he and
everyone else except, perhaps, the Eye Service had
overlooked it. No wonder the Intelligence Service had
not acted against him. No wonder the majority of the
biologic innovations developed by the Foundation had
gone nowhere except when he had pushed and developed them. And he had thought the ideas had been
accepted on their own merit!

It might work to his own benefit, and to the benefit
of the Foundation and Old Earth. It might—provided
he could lay the groundwork before the Empire understood what he was doing. Once they understood . . .

He paced around the circular table on the enclosed
balcony, stopping to look across the valley, over the
black of the lake toward the chalet under construction
on the high hill opposite his own retreat. That other
chalet would be needed soon, he expected, sooner than
he had anticipated.

He smiled in spite of himself, before resuming his
pacing, as he considered what to do next.

"Profit isn't enough. It never has been. Profit only
motivates those who lead."

That wasn't the whole problem. How could you
motivate people toward self-sufficiency when the tech-

nology was regarded as magic by most, when few understood the oncoming collapse when the power limit was reached? Not that there had to be a power limit, but the current technologic and government systems made it almost inevitable.

He halted and looked down at the small console he had not used, a console built into the simple wooden lines of the table, a console with a blank screen still waiting for input.

Smiling briefly, he tapped the stud to shut down the system.

"Since the political leaders follow the people, and the people follow the true believers, that means they need some new true believers to follow."

The Commodore in the gray silk-sheen tunic and trousers that looked so simple yet could be afforded by only the richest pursed his lips as he began to plot the revolution.

XIII

THE GANGLY MAN WITH THE ALTERNATE BRAIDS OF BLOND AND silver hair squirmed in the hard chair, shifting his weight as he reread the oblong card once more.

He studied the cryptic note attached to it yet again, trying to puzzle out what lay behind it.

> What would you do with the grant you requested? Be specific. Be at my office on the 20th of Octe to explain. Call for appointment.
>
> S

The card was stiff, formal, and nearly antique stationery, with a single name embossed in the upper left-hand corner. The name? Patron L. Sergio Enver.

The man with the blond and silver braids frowned. He'd assumed that Enver was related to the commercial Baron Enver who had founded Enver Enterprises. Certainly the local Enver office had been accommodating when he had faxed for confirmation.

"Yes, Ser Willgel. You are on the Patron's calendar. At 1000." That was all they had said, as if that had explained everything. Either that, or they did not know any more than he did, which made the matter more mysterious than ever, particularly since he had never expected a response from the routine inquiry he had made of a number of newer enterprises.

Because the Appropriate Technology Institute was five small rooms in the back of a rented warehouse, Willes Willgel had arrived early and sat waiting for the mysterious Patron Enver.

He checked the time. One standard minute until his appointment, not that promptness meant anything to the commercial barons. Willgel knew he could be waiting hours after his scheduled time, and he dared not complain. He was the one asking for funding.

The former professor sighed, aware as he exhaled of how thin he had gotten, of how baggy his tunic felt.

"Ser Willgel? Would you come this way?" A stocky woman stood by a closed portal.

Willgel leapt to his feet, then swallowed a curse at his own eagerness, and forced himself to walk slowly the four meters to the portal. He frowned, and tried to wipe it away, but failed. He worried more about the promptness of the Patron than if he had been summoned later.

"Unless the Patron asks you to remain, you have ten standard minutes. Do you understand?"

Willgel nodded. "I will do my best."

"Go ahead. He's waiting." The dark-haired greeter did not return the nervous smile that finally came to

Willgel's lips, but gestured toward the opening portal.

Willgel crossed through the gateway and into the office in three strides, head bobbing from side to side on a too-long neck as he tried to take in everything.

The office was large, but not imposing. The wall to his left was covered with a blue-black fabric on which was reproduced a night sky which Willgel had never seen before, from a system farther out in the galaxy, apparently, where the stars were more widely scattered. The ceiling was a faintly glowing gold, while the sheer gold curtains covered the full-wall windows to his left and directly before him. Standing straight in front of him was a smallish man, with tight-curled silver-gray hair and yellow eyes.

Beside him stood two modernistic armchairs, and behind the Patron was a combination desk and console, where all surfaces were covered with a tight-grained ebony wood.

"Sergio Enver," offered the Patron. "Have a seat, Ser Willgel."

His voice, while a light baritone, filled the office.

Willgel sat.

Enver did not. He stepped back until he was leaning against the wooden desk, a functional piece with no apparent projections besides the console itself.

"Your proposition did not explain what you meant by 'appropriate' technology. How would you define it?"

"That is probably the most difficult challenge the Institute faces, Patron—"

"Harder than fund-raising?" asked the Baron, lips quirking.

"Others raise funds easily. I, obviously, do not. But no one has really defined what technologies are appropriate to man, or to society, or whether differing societies should seek differing levels of technology, and what those levels should be."

"Put that way, what are the parameters of an appropriate technology?"

Willgel swallowed. "I'll try to be as succinct as possible. As you know, Patron, man's drive for more and better technology lies far back in history. Underneath that drive is the unspoken assumption that more technology is better and that improved technology will result in a better life for mankind. The problem with applying technology broadscale is that the benefits are uneven. Mass production of communications consoles may improve people's lives by allowing them more freedom in how and where they work and live. Use of technology in agriculture to concentrate control of production in the hands of a few at a cost which prevents competition allows economic control by a small elite. A standardized communications network allows a richer cultural life, but reinforces the possibility of social control by a few."

"Wait." The Patron held up his hand. "Generalizations address no real problems. You have also not defined what you mean as 'better.' Is 'more appropriate' better? Why do you think that certain types or applications of technology are better or more appropriate than others?"

Willgel licked his lips, then licked them again. Outside of the fact that Enver was generally linked into biologic technologies and was a major agricultural supplier, he really hadn't been able to determine what the Patron's economic interests were.

"I take it that your need for funding is warring with your ethics," observed the commercial magnate dryly. "If you don't wish to offend me, you might consider that intellectual dishonesty offends me more than attacks on my income or products."

Willgel swallowed again. "I see, Patron."

"Do you? I wonder. Go ahead, Professor, and try to get to the point."

Willgel coughed.

"As you suggested, I was leading to the question of appropriateness. 'Better' and 'appropriate' are tied together, because both are value judgments. Personally, I find that a technology or a use of a technology that increases individual freedom is better than one that restricts it. A technology that radically decreases liberty, even if it reduces costs of products, is not."

"Aren't those definitions arbitrary?" asked the Patron. "You are stating that decentralization and greater freedom are 'better' than centralization and a possibly higher standard of living. What about interstellar travel? What about the need for defense against outsiders? What about the great cramped artistic communities of the past? What about the still unsurpassed technology of crowded Old Earth?"

"Perhaps I am arbitrary," answered Willgel with a shrug that ignored the perspiration beading on his forehead. "The problem with larger and more concentrated societies, Patron, is that they require increasingly more complicated social codes or laws, or both, and more social restrictions, to maintain order and to avoid violence. Human beings are distressingly prone to violence and disorder. Further, increasingly concentrated societies create concentrated wastes. Higher technology can support more humans in a smaller area, which spawns a greater and more toxic waste problem, which requires, in turn, a higher level of technology to handle. And for what purpose?"

The scholar plunged on. "While you can argue that the creation of jumpships requires high technology, and that an interstellar society requires the communications they supply, it is harder to argue that low population societies like Barcelon really require the centralized control of agriculture and communications for either order or food. History has shown that a moderate number of privately owned agricultural enterprises is normally more successful than large and highly concentrated ones. History has also shown that centralized, but nongovernment communications systems are more successful—both in terms of maintaining freedom and lower costs—than are government monopolies or the

anarchy of small competitors. If you will, there is a level
and a type of technology ideally appropriate to each
human culture or sub-culture. Our mission is to define
what those types and levels might be, along with the
ramifications."

Willgel paused to catch his breath, then waited as he
watched Sergio Enver nod.

"What happens if your Institute declares that the
current use of technology on Barcelon amounts to totalitarian slavery and the Barcelon government protests to
the Empire? Or if you declare that the Imperial policy of
using synthetics is creating a totally inappropriate toxic
waste problem that is diverting unnecessary energy
resources for ongoing cleanup? What if the Empire
decides to ban your publications?"

Willgel smiled. "We are a long ways from either.
First, we must study the energy and personnel parameters for critical technologies, balance the input and
output against the wastes and other diseconomies, and
then pinpoint areas of diminishing returns, where the
use of more high technology may not produce commen-
surate benefits."

"Diminishing returns? A jumpship is certainly an
example of diminishing returns for a small system. But I
wouldn't advocate doing away with them."

"No. But you would not advocate building millions,
either, I suspect."

Abruptly Enver straightened and stood away from
the desk/console combination.

"There are a considerable number of fallacies in
your reasoning, Ser Willgel, as well as monumental
naivete in the implications of what you propose. I have
neither the time nor energy to disabuse you of the
fallacies, nor to better inform you on some hard realities."

Willgel could feel his face fall.

"But the core of your reasoning is sound. So is the

Institute, although I would suggest that you need some solid crusaders and true believers to spread the word. Pick up your draft authorization on the way out. And, Ser Willgel," added Enver as he walked around the console.

"Yes?"

"Make sure you not only do those studies, but that you publish them. Circulate them, and—I shouldn't have to tell a former professor—get as much of the academic community involved as possible. A good idea circulated and discussed in the schools is worth a million brilliant ones buried in the archives. Good day."

Willgel shook his head and turned. Such a brief discussion, if he could call it that. Enver had given him the impression that the Patron had already considered much of what was only speculation on Willgel's part. Willgel shivered.

The portal closed behind him as he stood in the dimmer green confines of the outer office once more.

"Ser Willgel?"

"Yes?"

"Your authorization."

Willgel walked to the console where the stocky woman sat. She handed him a single sheet.

He took it and read it. Then he read it a second time, and a third before he lowered it.

One hundred thousand creds! For one year. One year. Renewable at two hundred thousand for a second if published standards and educational efforts met the technical standards of the Patron.

Willgel didn't pretend to understand. For whatever obscure reasons he might have, Patron L. Sergio Enver had decided that there should be a strong Appropriate Technology Institute, one with technical excellence and a strong outreach program.

Willgel let himself smile as he held the authorization. Technical excellence and outreach—backed by sound reasoning. Enver had made it all too clear that he wouldn't stand for studies or reports that said nothing, or for fuzzy definitions.

The former professor wondered whether the Baron fully understood what such an Institute was capable of, given time and some financial support.

His stride lengthened as he marched down the corridor to the public tube train that would take him back to the warehouse and his budding Institute.

XIV

THE HEAVYSET PROFESSOR TRUDGED FROM THE ENTRY PORTAL into the small sitting room that opened onto the high balcony overlooking the University Lake.

"Who . . . who . . ." Her mouth grasped at the words as she saw the curly-haired man sitting in the recliner, sipping from one of her antique wine glasses.

"Professor Dorso, I believe."

"Uh . . . who . . . what are you doing in my home?"

"I apologize for the intrusion." His voice was light, but compelling, and his hawk-yellow eyes glimmered in the twilight dimness. "I've come to collect."

"Collect? What in Hades are you referring to?"

"Roughly twenty years ago, you accepted a modest grant from the OER Foundation. In return, you promised to develop a certain line of biologics based on your published works, and to hold that material until called for, up to fifty standard years, if necessary. I have come to collect."

The professor collapsed into the other chair with a plumping sound, the synthetic leather squeaking under her bulk.

"My god! My god!"

"Did you develop what you promised?" The man's tone was neutral.

"I . . . worked . . . just took the drafts . . . never questioned . . . but no one ever came . . . wondered if anyone ever cared."

He had stood so quickly she had missed the motion, so quickly she had to repress a shudder and failed. Taking a deep breath, then another, she could smell an acrid odor, a bitter smell, a scent of fear. Her fear.

"Did you even attempt the work?"

She began to laugh, and the high-pitched tone echoed from one side of the room to the other.

Crack!

The side of her face felt numb from the impact of his hand.

She stared up at the slender man. For some reason, her eyes tried to slide away from his body, and she had to concentrate on his face. Hawk-yellow eyes, short and curly blond hair, sharp nose, a chin neither pointed nor square, but somewhere in between—he could have been either an avenging angel or a demon prince. Or both at once.

"I did what I promised." Her voice was dull. "You don't know what it cost. You couldn't possibly understand. Don't you see? If I had failed . . . if I had died . . . but I didn't. I was right . . . and I couldn't tell anyone."

His face softened without losing its alertness. "You will be able to. Before too long. Wish I could have come sooner. All of us pay certain prices. All of us."

"How soon? When?" wheezed the professor as she struggled to sit upright.

He handed her a thin folder. "Study these specifications. I would like to have your spores packaged that way."

He held up his hand to forestall her objections before she could voice them.

"The fabrication group you are to use is listed on one of the sheets. I have already set up a line of credit for your use. Your authorization is included, and I will confirm that tomorrow.

"I want it done right. That's why you're in charge. That was also in your contract."

The woman sank back into her recliner, her eyes half-glassy.

The stranger turned and gazed out at the now-black waters of the University Lake, beyond the dim lights of the balcony, where the twilight submerged into the clouded start of night itself.

After a moment, he touched the panel. The armaglass door slid open, and a hint of a breeze wafted in, nearly scentless, except for the trace of water hyacinths underlying the cool air.

"Shocks . . . we all get them," he mused. "Things are not what they seem. Memories from the past appear as real people. People who were real disappear as if they never existed. Work overlooked becomes critical after it seems forgotten . . ."

Abruptly he turned and stepped back before her.

"Look at the last sheet."

"I can't see it."

He laughed, a harsh bark, and touched the light panel, watching as the illumination flooded the room, as she fumbled with the sheets from the folder.

"Oh . . . oh . . . that much! Why?"

"Look at the date."

"Five weeks from now? After twenty years?"

"That's for payment for your work, for your supervision in building the equipment. Turn it over."

The professor slowly turned over the uncounterfeitable credit voucher drawn on Halsie-Vyr. The amount represented ten years' salary. On the reverse was a short inscription.

She read it once, then again.

"I can? I really could?"

He smiled, faintly, understanding that the recognition would be worth more than the massive credit balance she would receive.

"The actual release form is also in the packet. If you complete the work on schedule, you will be able to publish your work immediately, including all the earlier research results, and the ATI Foundation will undertake its wide-scale distribution."

Her hands trembled as she methodically went through the sheaves of sheets, looking for the single release form, finally pulling it out, checking the authentications. Her dark brown eyes flickered from the certificate to the stranger and back to the certificate. Back and forth.

He turned again to the lake and beheld the darkness surrounded by the lights of the University Towers. Where the waters were clear of the hyacinths, reflections of the lights twinkled like the stars hidden above the clouds.

"Who are you?" Now her high voice was steady.

"I am who I am, Professor. No more and no less." He did not turn away from his view of the darkness and the reflected lights in the black waters beneath the balcony.

"You won't tell me."

"No. Except that I represent the Foundation. That's what counts. That and the fact that your work will be spread throughout the galaxy. It will be. My purposes are more immediate and selfish."

She pursed her lips, and her brow wrinkled, as if she were trying to remember something.

"Even so, it can't be that quick."

"I know. And we should have recognized the value of what you did earlier. At least we have now."

He turned back and faced her, looking down as if from an immeasurable height.

"The packet tells you where the packaged materials should be delivered." He frowned, as if debating with himself. "Would you be interested in other biologically related research? Completing some unfinished projects from notes, fragmentary materials?"

"That would depend."

"The conditions would be the same. Not that way," he interrupted himself. "All results could be released within a year of completion, whether or not it was picked up or used. Each project would be separately compensated, and well."

"Provided that I could start my own organization, with independent facilities, I would be very interested."

"How much?"

"I don't know."

"If you're interested, work up a proposal. Send it to the Foundation. Probably be accepted. Plenty of work."

"Who are you?" she asked again.

"I'd rather not say. Just a man with a job to do, and one running out of time." His lips quirked before he resumed. "Once the applicators are finished, this job is done. If you really are interested in doing more work, send that proposal. If you do, I may see you again."

"May?"

As she opened her mouth to ask the last question, the slender man had already turned and slipped toward the portal.

"Good night, Professor," he called as the portal closed behind him.

Slowly, slowly, the woman stood, placing the folder on the table by the recliner, and looking down at the maroon-bordered patterns of the threadbare, but irreplaceable, ancient carpet.

Leaving the folder on the table, she took four long steps to the open door onto her railed balcony. She stood there, the light wind pushing her short brown hair back away from her ears, watching the muddled lights reflected from the blackness of the lake.

After a time, she sighed and turned back to pick up the material laid upon the table. She left the door gaping wide, remembering the feel of the wind in her hair, remembering the stranger beholding the lake as if it were a treasure.

XV

"SER WADRUP?"

Hein Wadrup raised his slightly glazed eyes to the brown uniform of the guard, not bothering to offer a response.

"Ser Wadrup, your counsel has posted the necessary bond." The guard's magnetic keypass buzzed as he touched it to the lock. The door swung open.

Wadrup frowned.

"I don't have a counsel. Don't have the funds for one. What kind of joke is this? Another one of your 'build-his-hopes-up specials'?"

"No joke, Ser Wadrup. You make the jokes, it seems. Ser Villinnil himself posted the bond, and that one—he never works on good faith."

Wadrup struggled off the flat pallet, his legs still rubbery from the going-over he had received from the guards the day before.

The sharp-nosed guard, a man Wadrup had never seen before, turned and led the way down the block.

None of the other prisoners, one each to the uniform cells, two meters by three meters, even looked up.

From what the former graduate student could tell,

the guard was retracing the same route along which he had been dragged two weeks earlier.

By the time Wadrup had traversed the less than seventy-five meters to the orderly room, he was breathing heavily.

"That Wadrup?" asked the woman sentry stationed in the riot box outside the armored portal to the orderly room.

"That's him."

"Ser Wadrup, please enter the portal."

Wadrup paused. Either it was a subterfuge to get him to walk to his own execution, or he was being freed. He looked at the guard who had fetched him, standing ready with a stunner, and the sentry with a blastcone. Finally, he shrugged and stepped through.

The portal hissed shut behind him, and for the first time in two weeks, he was away from the cold black of the plasteel bars and flat floor pallets.

In the orderly room stood two men—a booking corporal of the Planetary Police accompanied by a heavyset local wearing a gold-banded travel cloak and a privacy mask.

"Ser Wadrup?" asked the anonymous civilian.

"The same."

"Could you trouble yourself to tell me the title of your unpublished article on the role of agriculture and government?"

Shaky as his legs felt, Wadrup almost grinned, but as quickly as the hope rose, he pushed it aside.

"I beg your pardon, but do you mean the last one submitted for publication, or the one rejected by the Aljarrad Press, to which I may owe my present residence?"

"Whichever one you sent to one Professor Stilchio."

Wadrup wanted to scratch his scraggly beard and squinted under the unaccustomed brightness of the lights.

"Oh, that one. That didn't have a title, because it was submitted for the 'Outspeak' column, but the subheading was 'Prosperity Without Force.' The other one was titled—"

"That will do." The civilian turned to the Police corporal. "I'll accept. Direct all further communications from the Court to my office. The bond is standard, nonrefundable if the charges are dropped."

"Your print, honored counselor?"

"Certainly. Here is my card, and the verification of the credited bond deposit."

Wadrup squinted again, fighting dizziness, trying to hold his vision in focus.

The civilian counselor turned.

"Ser Wadrup, if you can manage another fifty meters, my electrocar is waiting for us . . ."

"I'll manage."

Wadrup followed the heavier man through another portal and down another corridor, passing Planetary Police as they went. A third portal opened into the main lobby of the University Police Station, from where the police insured order for the complex that included five colleges and three universities. There were no others on Barcelon, and the reasons for such centralization had become clear to Hein Wadrup only after he had been picked up after trying to obtain forged working papers necessary to get a job to raise the funds necessary to leave Barcelon.

Outside the station stood a squarish, high-status electrocar, shining black. The rear door was being held open by a narrow-faced and well-muscled woman in a tight-fitting olive uniform.

Wadrup collapsed through the opening and onto the soft seat.

Almost immediately, the door shut, and the car began to move, smoothly, but with increasing speed.

Wadrup relaxed, too exhausted to hold on to consciousness.

"Wadrup!"

"Just carry him. Get him to the flitter."

The former student could feel himself being half

carried, half lifted out of the car and through the dampness he had come to associate with Barcelon.

Hands strapped him to some sort of seat, and beneath him, he could hear the whine of turbines.

Again he lost consciousness.

When he woke, he could feel the stillness around him, broken only by the faint hiss of a ventilation system.

"Passenger is awake."

"Thanks."

"Passenger?" he blurted, even as he tried to sit up in the narrow bunk into which he was strapped.

"Just lie there. Nothing wrong with you that rest, food, and a good physical conditioning course won't solve."

Wadrup turned toward the voice, but his eyes refused to focus on the blackness that seemed to speak.

"Don't worry about your vision. You can't see me. Partly for your protection, but mostly for mine."

"I am obviously in your debt, whoever you are, but would you care to offer any explanation?"

"Let us say that there are few enough people around with the capability to think, and it would be a pity if the iron-fisted government of Barcelon or any other water-empire system wasted that ability."

"You want something."

"Yes, but not anything with which you would disagree."

"Are you going to explain?"

"Shortly, but take a sip of this first."

"Drugs?"

"No. High sustenance broth. Want you thinking more clearly."

Wadrup watched as what seemed an arm of darkness touched the underside of the bunk, and the harness released. He sat up and took the cup of broth, half-amused that he could not see his benefactor, even while the man stood nearly beside him. From the light baritone timbre of the voice, he assumed that the speaker was male, but who could be sure? Who could be sure of anything these days?

He sipped the broth slowly.

"Be back in a moment. Please stay where you are."

The graduate student found he could drink less than half the liquid, so shrunken was his stomach. Holding the cup, he surveyed his quarters.

The bunk where he sat propped up was set into metal walls. Across the room to his left was another metal wall, punctuated with a closed and narrow doorway, four lockers, and two sets of four drawers built into the wall. The actual floor space measured less than three by four meters, perhaps as little as two and a half by three. The metallic ceiling was slightly more than two meters overhead.

In the middle of the bulkhead which ran from the foot of the bunk to the wall with the lockers was a squared archway into another compartment, but from the bunk all that Wadrup could see was another indistinct metallic wall, lost in the dimmer light of the adjoining room.

Wadrup puffed out his cheeks in puzzlement. He was missing something obvious. He squinted and lifted the broth to his lips, taking another sip and slow swallow.

"Feeling better?"

"What can I call you? Ser Blackness? I don't like not being able to see people."

"Well . . . you could use Blackness, or Hermer. That's not my name, but it means something to me without meaning anything to you."

"All right, Ser . . . Hermer. You posted a fifty-thousand-credit bond. You didn't do it for nothing. What do you want?"

"It was a hundred thousand, all told. Fifty for you. Forty for Villinnil, and ten to bribe the police. That's the beginning."

"Beginning?"

"Beginning. You need a new name, identity, prints,

and enough financial backing to continue your work."

"But what do you want?"

"For you to do what you've been doing. But with more understanding and a little more common sense. You've been acting like most student radicals, assuming you were half playacting, half gadfly."

Wadrup sighed.

"I'm lost. Really lost. Could you start at the beginning?"

"Suppose so. We've got another five hours."

"Until when?" The question was out of Wadrup's mouth before he understood what had been nagging him. The room where he was recovering looked like the crew room of an antique scout, the sort of thing that might have come from the early days of the Empire, or even from the Federation.

"Where are you taking me?" Wadrup demanded.

"For some rest and, after that, wherever we decide."

"Who's we?"

"You and I."

Wadrup sighed. "Questions aren't getting me anywhere. Why don't you start at the beginning?"

The unfocused black figure pulled up a ship chair and sat down across from Wadrup, who could see now that the man wore a black privacy mask over his face, and that the mask was the only feature that seemed to stay in focus.

"Too complicated. Let me start another way. With a series of questions. Let me ask them all. Don't try to answer.

"First, are there any truly powerful systems which do not produce an agricultural surplus? Second, could any system operate a centralized control of the economy and a large armed forces without control of the communications network and the food supply? Third, why is the Empire discouraging the biological and technical development of what might be called appropriate technology? Fourth, doesn't the use of centralized resources for local agriculture and communications actually reduce the energy and resources available for interstellar communications and travel? Fifth, hasn't history proven that State control is the least effective in maximizing resources for the overall benefit of the people?"

Wadrup took another sip of the broth before clearing his throat.

"I agree with you . . . I think, but aren't you assuming a great deal?"

"You will have a chance to make that evaluation firsthand. Assume for purposes of discussion that the Empire has resisted biological innovations. Assume that at least one system has attempted to destroy a tree genetically programmed to grow itself into an inexpensive house. Assume that someone has rediscovered the earth-forming techniques of Old Earth that created the biospheres of many Imperial systems, and that the Empire will shortly be hunting those techniques down."

"Ser Hermer, assuming that such farfetched things have or will happen is asking a great deal, even in view of my deep gratitude for your actions."

"Ser Wadrup. Think. You were imprisoned because you wrote a rather mild series of papers suggesting that war was not possible without the control of agriculture, that social control is linked to central control of the food supply, and that throughout history the people have been better fed when government refrained from meddling with agriculture and other forms of food production.

"Correct me if my reasoning is faulty, Ser Wadrup, but if you were wildly incorrect, why would anyone have bothered with you? Why would the government of Barcelon decide to spend hundreds of personnel hours chasing you long after you had stopped speaking publicly or writing? For no reason at all?"

"They jail people for no reason at all."

"How many students do you know who disappeared?"

"Plenty."

"How many? Name more than ten. You can't. Consistently, about ten students a year are jailed . . . or disappear. You were one of the ten. On a mere whim?"

"But no one paid any attention to my papers or speeches."

"That's right. And as soon as it looked like someone might, you were jailed."

Wadrup finished the broth and placed the cup on the ledge behind the bunk.

"So, Ser Hermer, what do you want?"

"I want you to found the 'Free Hein Wadrup Society.' "

"What?"

"You disappeared on Barcelon. Your body has never been found. There is no record of your leaving the system. The Barcelon government will deny it, but cannot prove you were not disposed of. The last record of your existence that was open to public verification was your time in jail. If the Barcelon government denies your death, it will seem as though they lie. If they say nothing, they can be charged with ignoring their own unpleasant actions."

"But it's suicide to go back to Barcelon, even with a new identity."

"Who said you were going back? You'll tour the systems that permit free speech, ostensibly agitating for the release of Hein Wadrup, telling why the Barcelon government has secretly imprisoned poor Hein Wadrup. Because they're totalitarian despots who control their planet through their control of the food supply. You will praise, faintly, more enlightened planets, while saying that it's still too bad that there isn't a better way to produce quality food for people."

"That's all you want?"

"Ser Wadrup, it seems a great deal to me. You give up your name, your family. You give up any fixed home for years to come. In return, I supply the necessary

unding and the factual information to supplement what
you already know."

"Hardly a great loss for me. My family is still
working in the pump works on New Glascow, and I
haven't been home in nearly ten years. I never had
enough money to concentrate on what I believe in."
Wadrup paused. "I'm not sure I like the charade of
freeing myself."

"If you have a better way of getting the message
across without ending up in prison again, I'm willing to
listen." The man in black stood. "I'll be back in a
moment."

Wadrup listened. He could hear another voice,
impersonally feminine, cool, clear, nearly icy. He shivered. Compared to that tone, the man in black seemed to
radiate heat.

"Interception course. Probability approaches point
seven."

"Lift one radian. See what they do."

"Lifting one."

Wadrup wondered who the pilot was, if she were the
narrow-faced cold woman who had acted as the guard
for the counsel who had secured his release.

"Ser Wadrup. Some evasive action is necessary."
The black-clad man returned, reached across Wadrup
and took the empty cup, placing it in one of the wall
receptacles. He returned to the graduate student.

"Please straighten yourself. Like this."

Wadrup found the harness around himself again.

"For your own safety, no matter what happens, do
not try to release the harness. Your success in doing so
could guarantee your own death."

The unknown man disappeared again.

Wadrup listened, not moving, but straining to make
out the conversation between the pilot and his captor/
rescuer.

"Interrogative time to jump."

"One point one."

"Margin for jump in five minutes."

"Less than point eight."

"Not worth it. Intercept probability?"

"Point nine without evasion."

"Intercept probability with evasion within standard stress envelope?"

"Point five."

"Probability within personal envelope?"

"Imprecise inquiry."

"Intercept probability with evasion maneuver within pilot's personal stress envelope."

"Less than point zero five."

Wadrup heard a clicking, realized that someone was strapping into a harness.

"Commence evasion."

An invisible piston crushed Wadrup into the bunk, squeezing, squeezing, until he felt the darkness rush over him.

Time passed. How much he did not know as he drifted between sleep, unconsciousness, pressures, and a half daze.

Then, once more, he could hear the inhumanly clear voice of the pilot before he was fully alert.

"Passenger is awake."

"Monitor. Interrogative time to jump."

"Three point five minutes."

"Screens?"

"Negative on screens. Patroller is at one point three."

"That's beyond range."

"Affirmative. Tentatively identified as class two."

"Probability of identification is climbing, isn't it?"

"Please clarify."

"Fewer patrollers, but more seem to be looking for us. Can you verify or offer statistics?"

"Statistically unverifiable. Variables too extensive. Gross number of patroller contacts up ten percent in last five standard years."

"Must be my imagination. Here we go."

The room turned simultaneously black and white around Wadrup, and he felt as though an electric shock had passed through his body. The moment of jump lasted no time at all, even while that instant of timelessness stretched and stretched.

Another shock, another white and black flash, and the crew room returned to its familiar metallic coloration.

"How far out are we?"

"Estimate three plus hours to orbit. Screens clear."

"Call me if anything shows, or if any abnormality reaches point zero five on the anomaly index."

"Stet. Will alert at point zero five on the anomaly index."

Wadrup turned his head toward the whispering sound of light-footed boots and watched as the shadowy black figure swept into the crew room.

"Sorry for the delay, Ser Wadrup."

Snick.

Wadrup stretched as he shrugged himself loose from the webbing of the restraint harness.

"Who are you?" Wadrup asked.

The other shook his masked head. Despite the fuzziness of the image the man in black presented, by looking from the corners of his eyes, the graduate student could get a better idea of the general motions of the man.

"All right. What are you?" Wadrup rephrased the question.

"You could call me a man with a mission. Won't tell you the mission except to say that the present attitude of the Empire, its systems, and those across the Arm threatens that mission. That's where you come in. You and a few others have been recruited to speak out, to give the people some ideas and some hope. If you will, to get the next generation's opinion leaders to think. To be receptive to change. That's what I hope."

"Nothing small, I see. Merely to change the thought patterns of millions in tens or hundreds of systems."

"No. Nothing small. But we have some time. Time and the fact that we are right."

This time Wadrup shook his head. He still knew next to nothing. Or did he?

Ignoring the black-clad figure across from him, Hein Wadrup added up what he knew.

The man was wealthy, wealthy enough to own and equip a high-speed scout as a personal yacht. He was not interested in personal luxury. He was able to find people like Hein Wadrup for his own purposes, which meant some sort of organization. He was opposed by at least some system governments, and he did not want Hein to see his face, which meant he was not totally unknown.

He couldn't be too old, because he wouldn't be able to accept high-acceleration evasive maneuvers, and his tolerances were higher than Hein's. He was also totally at home in the small ship, which meant a great deal of experience.

Wadrup frowned, shifted his weight, and dived at the man, hands reaching for the privacy mask.

Thud!

Wadrup sprawled on the deck. Before he could shake his head to clear it, he could feel the man's hands lifting him back onto the bunk, hands that conveyed the feeling of immense strength. Yet the man was obviously shorter and more slender than Wadrup.

"Ser Wadrup, even in your best condition, you would find your moves inadequate." He laughed, a single harsh bark. "Are you interested in my proposition? Or would you rather that I drop you off at the next port?"

"Next port?"

"New Avalon. I will supply the transportation free, but, of course, I could not bring your passport and universal ID, for reasons we both understand."

"That's blackmail!"

"No. On New Avalon you would be perfectly free to

stay. The Monarchy does not allow extradition. You would be safe, also, since they do not permit foreign agents."

"But I'd be stuck!"

"Ser Wadrup, I rescued you at great cost, with some risk, transported you to a place of safety, and am willing to let you go without any strings. I offered you a simple business proposition. You may accept or refuse. In any case, you are alive and free, and you would be neither by now had you stayed under the care of the authorities of Barcelon."

Wadrup bit his lip. He couldn't deny any of it.

"I'll have to think about it."

"I want a totally free decision. I will be here on New Avalon for several days. In the meantime, I will give you, say, one hundred credits. If you are interested in the proposition I made, contact me through the port. I will be registered under the name of DeCorso. If not, consider yourself a fortunate young man."

Wadrup frowned.

"In the meantime, I have some things to do. Please remain here. The narrow doorway across from you contains a small but adequate fresher, which you may use.

"The second locker contains those belongings of yours Ser Villinnil's staff were able to locate, including some clean clothes."

Wadrup looked up to see him passing through the archway and stopping to touch something. A flat metal wall extended from the archway, turning the crew room into a well-equipped cell.

"Strange . . . strange . . ."

The thought of getting clean again overruled more intellectual considerations, and he headed for the fresher. He'd have to give the stranger's proposition a fair evaluation, but not for a while, maybe not until he had the chance to see the situation on New Avalon.

XVI

"TELL ME AGAIN." BARON MEGALRIE'S VOICE DROPPED TO THE soft silkiness that was a telltale warning to those who knew him.

The Vice President of Marketing knew the tone also.

"Yes, Baron. We cannot meet the competition. Bestmeat—that is the firm—is selling to the restaurant distributors and the food centers for twenty percent less than we are."

"Our markup is more than twenty percent," observed the Baron in the same silky tone, looking pointedly at the real wood of the conference table, then brushing an imaginary speck from the left forearm of his long-sleeved crimson silk-sheen tunic.

"That was my first reaction, Baron." The red-haired man swallowed hard. "Statistics pointed out, however, that the twenty percent level was the maximum profit-maximizing level for Bestmeat. That is, low enough to take the roughly forty percent of the Westmark trade we don't have absolutely controlled, but high enough—"

"Spare me the basic economics, Reillee. To what obscure point are you leading?"

"Through happenstance, sheer happenstance, you understand, it came to my attention that Bestmeat was banking more than five million credits a standard month in their investment account alone."

"What firm?"

"Halsie-Vyr, Baron."

The Baron's voice dropped even lower. "And how much did this happenstance information cost you?"

"It was happenstance—"

"Reillee . . ."

"Five thousand."

The Baron stared levelly at Reillee.

"We have several problems, Reillee. You didn't pay enough for that information. That means everyone will know shortly that you were concerned. We will return to that problem later."

He glanced behind Reillee at the closed portal, then stared at the red-headed man.

"Can I draw the conclusion that since Bestmeat is not out directly to ruin us, which seems unlikely with their heavy profit margin, that they have some new meat source or process that means they actually can undercut our ranches and mutated beefaloes? Can I draw that conclusion?"

"Yes, Baron."

"Do you know what that source is?"

"I have reports, Baron."

"And you do not trust them?"

"No, Baron."

"Why not?"

"Because they all say that Bestmeat has developed a special kind of plant that produces protein better than the best meat steaks."

"Yes, that would be hard to believe."

Reillee tugged at his tunic, looked at the conference table, then at the Baron. He was unable to keep his eyes focused on the commercial entrepreneur's dark orbs and dropped his glance.

"And what success have you had in solving this problem?"

Reillee did not answer.

"Where are your successes?"

By now, the Baron's voice had dropped so low that

it had lost its silkiness, so low that it was a rasping knife cutting through the conference room.

"There . . . are . . . none."

"Can you explain why not?"

Reillee gave a shrug, as if to indicate the matter had passed well beyond his control.

"Because, Baron, it seemed clear that price cuts would not work. We still are banking a profit. We cut prices and run in the red, while Bestmeat cuts their prices and runs in the black."

"Reillee, your ingenuity seems limited."

"Yes, Baron, I know. I tried to block their suppliers by invoking the sole source clause with all of ours, but they don't deal with anyone who deals with us. I invoked the emergency power clause, and they jumpshipped their own generators in.

"I used the brotherhoods to deny local labor, and they brought in outsiders under the free work laws, and paid them higher wages. That left the brotherhoods most unhappy, and we had to match the Bestmeat wage levels. I pulled off the construction workers for their new employee housing, and they used some new technique to grow houses—"

"Grow houses?"

"I don't believe it either, but all four Infonet agencies came up with the same reports. And they did get the housing built, and to standards as well. It's virtually solid wood."

"Solid wood? Real wood?"

"That's right."

The Baron looked away from the trembling Reillee, then touched the wide band on his wrist.

The portal behind the Vice President of Marketing, Westmark System Division, opened. A thin and dark man with hooded and heavy eyelids, in a dark blue tunic and trousers, stepped inside the conference room.

"Ahmed, Mr. Reillee. Mr. Reillee has outlined a problem to me. He will outline it to you. If he has done everything he has said he has done, then he has done all that I could expect. Please check on it.

"If Mr. Reillee has done all these things, or even most of them, he deserves a ten percent bonus for calling this to our attention, and you need to take the necessary further steps. If not, Mr. Reillee needs a new occupation, and you will do what is necessary. In either case, I expect your ingenuity will be required. Please do take care of it."

Reillee looked down. Ahmed nodded, and the Baron stood.

"There is a problem on Haldane. After tomorrow, I will leave. Problems, problems. Such is the life of a Baron of the Empire. I will expect a report from each of you to be torped to headquarters within two standard weeks."

Reillee turned, realized that Ahmed was waiting to follow him, and departed. The Special Assistant followed as closely as a shadow, and as darkly.

The Baron frowned at the closed portal.

XVII

GERSWIN SCANNED THROUGH THE REPORT.

Should he follow his instincts and strike directly at the heart of the problem? Or should he let nature take its course?

Megalrie would certainly attempt a strong-arm operation—that was his style. And it would be one with maximum force. Finesse was not the Baron's trademark, nor was personal involvement. One of the Baron's special assistants would take care of it.

Gerswin tapped out the codes for access to the financial status and projections. Then he studied the figures.

If Bestmeat of Westmark were folded, left beached and belly-up, he could pull out roughly 100 million credits, but Megalrie would destroy the hytanks and the land under cultivation. On the other hand, if he could turn over the operation to someone, he could still come out with about fifty million credits and the chance for the operation to survive.

To fight Megalrie directly would take too many resources and, more important, too much time and visibility at a time when the Empire was becoming too interested in biologics. To remove the latest Special Assistant would only postpone the Baron's final actions.

Gerswin shrugged. The answers were obvious, not that he had much choice. He could not fight Megalrie, nor could he allow the Baron to win.

According to the report, Megalrie was about ready to leave for Haldane on his yacht, the *Terminia*.

He tapped out another code on the console screen.

"Ser Jasnow's office—oh, yes, Shaik Corso."

The screen blanked, and Jasnow's face appeared.

"Yes, Shaik?"

"Like to talk to you. In person. Now."

"Ah . . ." Jasnow's thin and pale cheeks became thinner and paler as he sucked them in.

"Now," repeated Gerswin.

"I will be there."

Jasnow blanked the screen before Gerswin did.

Gerswin laughed mirthlessly.

Within minutes, Jasnow was marching through the portal with an air of offended dignity that only an academic convinced of his own importance could have matched.

"Ser Corso—"

"Quiet."

Gerswin motioned to the chair across the console from him. "Sit down."

Jasnow sat.

"I would not have asked you if it were not important. Also aware that you have snoops in my office. Hope you are the only one with access to the cubes, for your sake.

"Now, Baron Megalrie is about to try another strong-arm operation on us, and this time it will be something impressive, like a power satellite misfocusing on one of our plants, or on this building."

Jasnow's white face paled even further.

"He wouldn't."

"He will. Therefore, in the interests of *your* survival, here is what you will do. You offer Chancellor Gorin control of Bestmeat, Westmark, to the government. It will be run as the same sort of public corporation as the linear rail system and the water system. With you as President. That will give him the popular support he has lost with the collared crew. His wife is a nutritionist. She will be offered the position, paid as well as you are, as consulting nutritionist for the State."

"As much as—"

"Right. If you want to keep your neck and your job."

"What if she weren't a nutritionist?"

"You'd offer her something equally exalted and highly paid." Gerswin paused. "Everyone will know it's a package deal, and everyone will know why you did it, and some will even be amazed that you had the common sense to do it. This way, though, you get to retain your considerable salary for a while, at least, and an operating corporation and fancy title."

"What if I don't?"

"Then you will be either dead or out of business and luck." Gerswin's flat tone conveyed absolute certainty.

"How will that stop Megalrie?"

"He's not about to take on a system government, especially if he's still making a profit. Besides, he'll figure that eventually the inefficiency in a government operation will drive prices up, and his profits will follow."

"You seem sure that Megalrie will see it that way."

"Megalrie will see it that way." Gerswin smiled, and he could tell it was not a friendly expression because Jasnow shrank back in his captain's chair. "He will."

Gerswin stood.

"Get through to Chancellor Gorin. I know you can. Be as candid as necessary. Gorin will buy the idea. Right now, he'll buy anything, and even if this doesn't give him the election next year, it will give him and his wife more than a year's high salary from her position."

"But—"

"But what? You've got less than a day to make the deal and make sure it goes public. Make sure that Megalrie's man Reillee gets the information as well. If you don't put this together, you'll have nothing."

"What about you?"

"Me? I'm selling out to you. That gives you absolute control. If you want to gamble, be my guest. It's your life."

Jasnow shivered. "You think so?"

"Have I been wrong before?"

"No."

"Then I'd suggest you follow through. In the meantime, I'll be completing the transactions to transfer my interest to you and setting up the form for you to follow in turning Bestmeat over to the government."

Jasnow pursed his lips, finally shrugging as he turned.

As soon as Jasnow left, Gerswin began to program the transactions necessary and to arrange the fund transfers to the shielded account in the local Halsie-Vyr office.

Shortly, he would use the private exit for his flitter and the trip back to the producing wastelands he had bought for next to nothing years earlier, back to the small strip and bunker where the *Caroljoy* waited while being repowered.

Too bad he wouldn't have a chance to check out all the plantings on all the scattered lands, the ones that neither Jasnow nor the staff knew about.

Once the secret was out, there would probably be a government effort to destroy all the meatplants not under government control. The thousands of plantings would probably thwart that, and if not on Westmark, then on the half-dozen other planets where Bestmeat operated.

XVIII

AS EYE, HE COULD ALMOST CONVINCE HIMSELF THAT HIS DUTY was clear. The gray-haired and rail-thin man flicked the console to standby and rubbed his forehead before leaning forward to rest his head in his hands.

The more he studied the fragmentary background, the surprisingly sketchy Service records, the more convinced he was that Calendra had been right—assuming the mysterious individual he had mentioned to the Emperor had indeed been Gerswin. There was more to MacGregor Corson Gerswin than met the eye, far more. And yet . . .

". . . who could disagree with his goals, at least in the abstract . . ." muttered the man charged with the ultimate control of Imperial security.

If it *had* been Gerswin who destroyed the Assassin's Guild, could he, especially as Eye, fault that destruction? Hardly. If it had been Gerswin who used the tacheads to

smash the tie between the oligarchs and the secret police
on El Lido, had not the results been in both the interests
of the Empire and the average El Lidan?

Without Gerswin's support and work for the OER
Foundation, would all the foodstuffs and medical advances from biologics have occurred so soon?

Eye sighed. Even worse, except for Gerswin's connection with the damned biologics foundation, there was
no proof. Endless probabilities poured from the Eye
Service stat-system, but no hard proof. Not that proof
was a limit to Eye.

As Earl of Selern, he was reluctant to employ the full
power of his Intelligence office without some shred of
hard evidence. Calendra had acted without proof and
without rationale too often, and look where that had led.

To complicate matters more, the majority of the
probabilities, except for the propaganda negatives associated with the use of nuclear warheads, indicated that
the actions attributed to Gerswin and his range of aliases
supported, or apparently did not harm, the Empire.
Virtually all were politically popular.

Eye frowned without moving his head. His instincts
told him a different story. Gerswin was not out to harm
the Empire, at least not in the short run, but the man
jumpshifted under different stars. If you could call him a
man. He also appeared to be one of the handful of
known biological immortals. How long Gerswin could
retain function or sanity was another question.

Selern took a slow and deep breath, touched the
screen, and scripted a compromise.

Should Gerswin himself, under his own identity,
dock in Imperial facilities or main systems territory, he
would be detained and restrained for a full investigation.

Eye smiled wryly. Gerswin might well escape, but
that would provide proof of sorts, and no one had ever
escaped the full might of the Empire, even with the
equivalent of a small warship.

Besides, he needed to report some action to the
Emperor.

XIX

GERSWIN STUDIED THE READOUTS ON THE DATA SCREEN. THE snooper he had left in orbit just beyond the *Terminia* had relayed the latest.

The EDI twitches indicated that the *Terminia* was being readied for orbit-out, probably as soon as a shuttle from Haldane arrived.

"Relay indicated approach to target." The AI's voice was as impersonally feminine as ever.

"Characteristics of object approaching target?"

"Object indicated as armed shuttle, class three. Characteristics and energy signature match within point nine probability."

"Stet. As soon as object departs target proximity, deploy full shields."

"Stet."

Gerswin took a sip from the open-topped glass of water, then swallowed the remainder of the water before standing up and heading into the fresher section to relieve himself.

The next few hours were going to be interesting, more than interesting, to say the least.

Gerswin had strapped into the accel/decel shell couch and was wondering if the *Terminia* would ever depart.

"*Terminia*, clearing orbit." The transmission was on the orbit control band.

"Happy jumps, *Terminia*."

"Shields up," announced the AI. "Target vector

tentatively set at zero seven zero Haldane relative, plus three point nine."

"Close to within one hundred kays, same heading."

"Closing to one hundred kays. Estimate reaching closure point in five standard minutes."

The two-gee surge in acceleration pressed Gerswin back into the shell.

He touched the console and reviewed the numbers again, pursing his lips. The maneuver should work.

At times such as these, he wondered if it wouldn't have been easier to have added offensive weapons to the *Caroljoy*. Probably no one would have discovered them, not the way he had operated, but the penalty risks were too high for the benefits.

Privately owned and armed jumpships were one thing the Empire was deadly serious about. So serious that entire Service squadrons had been deployed for years to track a single pirate. Since ship and jump costs were so high to begin with, and since the energy costs of avoiding the Service made any commercial piracy infeasible, and since the I.S.S. hadn't had that much to do since the mistake known as the Dismorph Conflict, there weren't any pirates. Not that lasted long.

Gerswin sighed as he waited.

While he had once "borrowed" the Duke of Triandna's yacht, with the help of the Duchess, that woman who he had known only as Caroljoy on a single warm night until long afterward, he had not considered himself a pirate. After all, he had only been carrying out the Emperor's promises. Even if the Emperor hadn't really wanted to supply those arcdozers for the reclamation on Old Earth. Even if the dozers had only been to buy time for the devilkids as they struggled to reestablish a foothold on Old Earth. Even if they were all dead or dying by now. Even if . . .

He shook his head violently. He needed to finish the business at hand. The sooner he could get it over with the better.

"Change heading to parallel target at distance of one thousand kays."

"Changing heading."

Gerswin waited until the readouts indicated the return to a parallel course.

His fingers began the rough computations that he could have left to the ship's AI.

"In one standard minute, commence maximum acceleration with internal gee force not to exceed five point five gees. Maintain for point five standard hour."

"Stet. Maximum acceleration possible with internal gee force not to exceed five point five gees. Will maintain for point five standard hour."

Gerswin waited for the force to press him back into the control shell, almost welcoming the physical pressure as a test with set and understandable limits.

"Commencing acceleration."

"Stet."

Test or no test, by the time the half hour ended, Gerswin felt sore all over.

"Stop acceleration. Maintain internal gee field at one standard gravity. Maneuver the ship back at full acceleration along target course line. Suggest forty-five-degree heading change for two minutes, followed by a reverse two-hundred-twenty-five-degree sweep turn."

"Recommend Kirnard turn."

"Proceed Kirnard turn," Gerswin affirmed. Damned AI! That was what he had wanted to begin with.

He wanted to come back in on the reciprocal course with as much velocity as possible. His generators would take at least twice the strain as those of the *Terminia*, perhaps more, since the other yacht was reputed to be filled with luxuries, and luxuries meant energy diversions.

"Interrogative closure time."

"Time to CPA estimated at point two five standard hour."

"EDI lock?"

"Negative on EDI lock. EDI trace available."

"Time to intercept?"

"Inquiry imprecise."

Gerswin frowned. Damned AI! He wondered if the AI had a sense of self-preservation.

"Interrogative. Are we confirmed on head-on-head reciprocal courses?"

"That is negative."

Gerswin sighed.

"Change course to maintain reciprocal courses. I want a head-on-head intercept."

"Probability of physical contact exceeds point zero zero five."

"I suspect so. Interrogative time to intercept."

"Point one five stans."

Gerswin waited, confirmed the AI verbal reports with the actual data on his own screen.

"Probability of physical contact exceeds point zero one."

"You may make any course changes necessary to maximize survival and minimize contact *after* screen contact."

"Stet. You are relinquishing control to AI?"

"That is negative. Negative. Allowing emergency override after screen contact to avoid physical impact."

"Stet. Override only after screen contact."

"Only after *defense* screen impact," Gerswin corrected.

"After defense screen impact," parroted the AI.

Gerswin could feel the sweat seeping out of his palms as he tightened his harness and leaned back in the shell couch.

He checked the fingertip controls, checked and waited.

"Time to contact?"

"Point zero five."

Gerswin wanted to wipe his forehead.

"Divert all power to defense screens. Minimal gee force."

"Diverting all power."

The control-room lights dropped to emergency levels, and the whisper of the recirculators dropped to nothing. Gerswin felt light in the shell as the internal gees dropped to roughly point one as the power from the gravfield generators was poured into the defense screens.

"Target commencing course change."

"Match it. Continue head-on-head intercept."

"Probability of physical impact approaching point one without course change."

"Understood. Maintain intercept course until full defense screen impact."

A drop of sweat lingered in Gerswin's left eyebrow, tickling, but refusing to drop. He wrinkled his brows, but did not move.

"Screen impact."

Whhhrrrrrr!

Gerswin was thrown sideways in his harness for an instant.

The lights flickered, then came back up to normal levels.

"Course alteration in progress."

"Turn it into another Kirnard turn."

"Stet. Converting to Kirnard turn."

"Status report."

"Number two main screen generator is down. All other systems functioning within normal parameters."

"Interrogative target status."

"Target has stopped acceleration. Negative screens. Negative EDI track."

"Interrogative turn status."

"Completing Kirnard turn."

"Fly by target. Drop torp probe for confirmation of target status."

"Stet. Full instrumentation check with torp probe. Note. Torp probe is last probe."

"Understand last probe. Reload on Aswan."

Gerswin finally wiped his soaking forehead.

The impact of the *Caroljoy*'s heavy screens should have blown every screen generator in the *Terminia*. Milliseconds later, the *Caroljoy*'s screens would have impacted the *Terminia* itself, with enough of a concussive impact to fragment everyone and everything within the hull.

That had been the theory. The torp probe would either confirm or deny the results. Too bad the *Caroljoy*'s only operating launch tubes were limited to message torps or their smaller equivalents. But he'd been through that debate with himself before. Probably better that he had no easy way to launch the remaining tacheads and hellburners. Then again, the thirteen remaining nuclear devices would probably outlast both Gerswin and the *Caroljoy*. After El Lido, and the expression on Rodire's face, he had no desire to launch mass death again, even in support of the greater life his biologic efforts represented.

As he was coming to appreciate, the best use of force was on a wide and diffuse scale. The Empire found it easy enough to recognize direct threats, but not those without an overt focus, such as the changes in society that his biologic innovations were beginning to bring.

No . . . the tacheads and hellburners represented the past, and best they remain in the past and unused in the future.

He pulled at his chin as he straightened in the control couch and returned his full attention to the display screens before him.

"Probe away."

"Stet."

Gerswin remained flat in the shell, just in case something went wrong.

He could see the end of the road ahead. Before too long, even the slow-moving Empire would begin to put the pieces together, to understand what he was attempting. Soon, all too soon, it would be time to fold his tent before they understood the implications or traced his real purposes back to Old Earth.

"Just what are your real purposes?" he asked himself in a low voice.

"Query not understood."

"That makes two of us."

He waited for the report from the torp readouts.

"Probe results. Negative screens. Negative EDI traces. Free atmosphere dispersing from target hull. Heat radiation unchecked and dropping."

Gerswin took a deep breath. End of Baron Megalrie. End of *Terminia*. Beginning of end for Gerswin's Imperial activities.

"Stet. Can you recover probe?"

"Negative."

"Set course to nearest early jump point. Full screens available. One gee."

"Understand fullest possible screens. One gee course to early jump point. Estimate arrival in one point one."

"Understood."

Gerswin unstrapped himself and swung out of the shell. While the system energy monitors would doubtless pick up the energy burst created by the screen collision, no one was going to find the dead hulk of the *Terminia*, not at the tangent created by the collision. Gerswin shook his head, not wanting to dwell on the yacht's crew, not wanting to think about the ever-mounting implications, not wanting to think about the decisions lying in wait ahead.

The peaceful years were over, assuming they had ever been. Assuming that such peace had not been a recently acquired personal illusion.

The disappearance of the Baron would be linked to Gerswin, as would all the other probabilities for which there was little or no proof.

He sighed.

Commodore MacGregor Corson Gerswin could never appear again in Imperial territory, at least not under his own name. And it wasn't likely to be long before all of his other identities would also be targeted, assuming that the Baron's efforts had not meant that he was already under indirect Imperial attack.

No, the peaceful years were over, for a long time to come, if not forever.

XX

DESPITE THE SILENCE IN THE KITCHEN, PROFESSOR STILCHIO looked from side to side, cleared his throat, finally touched the light plate and brought the illumination up to full.

He coughed.

In the corner next to the preservator was a shadow, an odd shadow. He tried to look at it, but his eyes did not want to focus.

A certain dizziness settled upon him, and he put his right hand out to the counter to steady himself.

"Professor." The address came from the shadow he saw and could not see.

The academic cleared his throat again, but said nothing.

"Professor, you might look at the folder on the counter."

Stilchio refused to look down, hoping the shadow might disappear. Slightly intoxicated on good old wine he might be, but shadows did not talk.

His right hand groped for more support and brushed something that slid on the smooth tiles.

In spite of his resolve, he looked down. By his right hand was an oblong folder.

"That folder contains an excellent short paper on the social implications of mass agriculture and its use in controlling populations and supporting centralized governments."

"So . . . what . . ." stuttered the professor, still trying to steady himself.

"It strikes us that it would be an excellent piece for the eccentricities section of the *Forum*."

"I'm not . . . not exactly . . . approached . . . this way."

"You have never published a single paper or article that suggested anything wrong with centralized agriculture or of government control of the food supply."

"Who would help the poor?"

"The government. If they are so interested in the poor, let them buy food for the poor. Better yet, let the governments stop blocking new biologic techniques that would let the poor feed themselves."

"But—"

"Professor, time is short for you."

Thunk!

Stilchio turned his head to gape at the heavy knife buried in the cabinet door by his head. His hand reached, then drew back as he saw the double-bladed edge, the mark, he feared, of the professional.

"You have been asked to do nothing which is not in keeping with your publicly professed ethics, nor which would in any way personally endanger you. The credentials of the writer are adequate, to say the least, and certified in blood. If this article is not published in the edition being released next week, the following edition will carry your obituary.

"You have a choice. Live up to your publicly quoted beliefs in free expression of ideas or die because you were a hypocrite at heart."

"The police . . ."

"Can do nothing, nor will they. Would you care to explain that while you were drinking, you were threatened for hypocrisy? Would anyone really ever believe you?

"Read the paper in the folder. You will discover no incendiary rhetoric, just facts, figures, and a few mild speculations. Tell anyone you were threatened over such a scholarly paper, particularly by this author, and they might lock you away or relieve you of your duties for senility or mental deterioration.

"Good night, Professor. We look forward to the next edition of the *Forum*."

Stilchio stood absolutely still as a black shadow walked up to him and withdrew the knife, effortlessly, from the wood of the cabinet. Then, just as soundlessly, the shadow was gone through the archway and toward the front portal.

Finally, the kitchen was silent, the loudest sound the beating of the graying professor's heart.

His hands explored the wedge cut in the wood. His eyes glanced at the folder, then back at the cut, then toward the closed portal.

He walked, slow step by slow step, toward the dispenser, where he filled a goblet with ice water, where he stood, sipping at the chill water whose temperature matched the chill in his heart.

With a sigh, he edged back toward the folder on the counter, from which he extracted the short article. Studying the title page for a long moment, he sighed again. Then he turned to the first page of text.

He had hoped that the proposed article would have proved poorly written, propagandistic, or threatening. He doubted it was. He recognized the author, who was, unfortunately, deceased. Deceased, it was rumored, at the hands of the Barcelon government.

Another sigh escaped him as he turned to the second page.

His eyes darted back to the wedge-shaped cut in the cabinet, as if to wish the mark would disappear. It did not.

He looked back at the brown tiles of the floor.

Too old, he was too old to refuse to publish such an article. It was well written. While he disagreed with the conclusions, to publish it would only bring praise from his critics and allow him to claim impartiality. Not to publish it . . . he shivered, recalling the pleasant tone of the professional who had visited so recently.

Too old—he was too old to be a martyr, not when it would serve no purpose, not when no one would understand why.

He shook his head as he shuffled toward the console in his study.

XXI

THE SUMMER PARK AT LONDRA, NEW AVALON, HAD ITS Speakers' Corner, as did all the public parks on New Avalon.

Constable Graham twirled his truncheon, smiling under the morning mist that was beginning to lift. Overhead, a few patches of blue appeared between the ragged gray clouds.

The constable slowed as he approached the paved area and the three public podiums. He studied the small crowd—less than fifty, and mostly university students on their midmorning class breaks.

Graham frowned as he saw that a number of the students were poring over identical leaflets. That was unusual, since most of the speakers were either expatriate politicians trying to recapture their glory days or political science students practicing for later campaigns. The reputation of the university was such that even a few of the younger sons of the first families of the Empire studied there. Few others could have afforded the jumpship passage costs.

Consequently, seldom was literature passed out. Even less often was it read.

The constable edged closer to the single speaker, seeing only a dark-haired young man, wearing the traditional and formal black university tunic.

"Power? I ask you—what is it? What is its basis? Power is the ability to control people's lives. Ah, yes, a truism. So simple. But look beyond the simplicity. Look beyond the mere words, beyond the obvious phrases. Ask what composes control.

"You need food. Whoever controls your food supply controls you. You need shelter. Whoever controls the providing of shelter controls you.

"Take that a step forward. Let us say a man gives you a handful of seeds. He says, 'One of these will grow into a house that will provide shelter, and the rest will become plants to provide all the good food you will ever need.'

"I ask you, is this in the interest of any government?

"No! A thousand times, no!

"Just take the food. If each man or woman could grow his own with little effort, what need would there be for millions of hectares of land for farms, for government agriculture pricing policies. And if each family grew their own food, how could the government ever produce enough of a surplus to maintain an army? Or a secret police force?"

Graham frowned again, letting his truncheon drop to his side.

"Rubbish," he muttered under his breath, looking up at the student on the podium, who seemed too old to be anything but a senior graduate fellow. The policeman studied the man. He did not recall seeing the speaker in the park before.

"You!" demanded the speaker, and Graham stopped, held momentarily by eyes that flashed yellow. "You! Constable! Do you believe a government's purpose is to serve its people? Or should the people serve it by feeding its soldiers?"

Graham retreated without speaking, grabbing a leaflet from the first bench he passed.

"Come, Constable! If the government has no massive farmlands and no great agricultural surplus with which to support a nonproductive bureaucracy and an unnecessary army, how could it remain oppressive?"

"What about feudalism?" snapped another student.

Graham ducked away, leaflet in hand, glad of the reprieve and to escape from the yellow-eyed speaker.

". . . feudalism was based on scarcity . . . on the fact that self-sufficiency was limited . . . outdated by modern communications and modern biologics . . . advances hidden away from you by the Empire . . ."

"Isn't that the same old conspiracy theory?"

"No conspiracy. People need organized society . . . need protection . . . but the lack of independence in obtaining the basics has left them at the mercy of government. It is no accident that repressive governments cannot exist on new frontiers, where individuals can support themselves or can readily leave. Repression exists where there are no alternatives . . ."

The constable continued away from the speaker, folding the leaflet and tucking it away to read later. It might actually be interesting. He resumed twirling his truncheon and checking the benches, absently noting the regulars and the newcomers, tipping his antique helmet

to the few mothers and their small children as he neared
the playground.

Idly, he wondered about the leaflet, about the quality feel of the paper. The whole business seemed strange.

He shrugged.

All the speakers had something strange about them,
but the commonwealth believed in free speech, always
had, and always would, no matter how strange the
students that flocked to the university. Even if they had
yellow eyes and strange ideas.

XXII

LYR CHECKED THE INVOICES AGAIN. SHE FROWNED, THEN
tapped in an inquiry and analysis program.

"What is he up to now?" she muttered as she waited
for the results. While she should have returned to
reviewing the budget flow, she decided against it, arbi-
trarily, and let her thoughts wander as the analyzer
sorted through the invoices and purchases made by the
Commander over the past year.

It could be her imagination. Then again, it might
not be imagination at all.

From what she could tell, lately his efforts had
moved from the research and new grants area far more
into field testing and production, in some cases even into
granting licenses.

All had generated substantial revenues and strange
amounts of new contributions to the Foundation; many
of which were from entities she suspected were no more

than aliases or ciphers for the Commander himself.

He seemed uneasy with the growing attention he received, and particularly when he learned that his own name had appeared in the listing of commercial magnates of the Empire (unrecognized section).

Lyr smiled wryly. She had no doubts that the total holdings of the Commodore she still thought of as a Commander were more than sufficient to place him well up among the barons of the Empire.

She had mentioned that, once.

"You had better hope that no one puts that together, then, for both your sake and mine."

"Why?" she had asked, but he had not answered the question, as he often did not when the inquiry revolved around his personal activities.

Cling.

She looked down at the screen as the results from the analyzer program began to print out.

As each statistic appeared, she nodded, smiling faintly as the figures confirmed her suspicions.

"Conclusion?" she tapped out.

"Probability of terraforming operation being developed with biologic technology exceeds point seven. No evidence of delivery vehicles included."

She frowned at the last. What would be needed for such a delivery system?

Her mouth dropped open as she recalled an obscure fact—one that Gerswin had mentioned more than once. The Empire had originally forbidden terraforming because it had been thought that the development of the techniques had been what had devastated Old Earth. While the prohibition had technically lapsed, the attitude had probably not.

She scripted another inquiry, hovering over the screen for the analyzer's response.

Cling.

Tapping the keyboard studs, she watched as the conclusion scripted out.

"Without Foundation data, probability of successful analysis of terraforming project is less than point two
within five standard years. Exact calculation of future
probabilities impossible, but trends analysis would indicate that successful analysis by outside sources possible
within ten standard years and approaches unity in less
than thirty years."

No wonder the man seemed driven, almost as if he
knew his projects would be discovered.

But what were they? What planet or planets did he
want to terraform? What planet would appeal to a
hawk-eyed immortal?

Lyr shivered, not certain she wanted to know the
answer to the question she posed. She did not frame
another inquiry for the analyzer.

Instead, her hands framed the sequence to delete the
entire file she had created.

XXIII

BLACK THE SHIP WAS, AND STREAMLINED IN THE ANCIENT
tradition that predated the Federation that had predated
the Empire that would precede the Commonality of
Worlds. Black the ship was, and with a nonjump speed
that indicated a scout. Black with the full-fade dark
finish that no eye could grasp in the dimness of space.

The pilot ignored the lunar relays and their inquir-
ies, flashed well clear of the geosynch station for the
High Plains port, and dropped the scout into a high-
temp entry that would have vaporized most ships that

attempted it, and one which required a deceleration beyond the physical limits of most ships and pilots. Such a deceleration was impossible for contemporary ships, with their automatically linked shields and gravfields.

The scout's full power was tied to the shields during entry. Using the gravfield would have diverted too much energy from the deceleration, particularly since the streamlined configuration of the scout was far from optimal for a gravfield inside an atmosphere.

The lunar detectors lost the scout in less than half a descent orbit, and the geosynch station picked it up later and lost it sooner.

"Scout, characteristics . . . high-speed entry . . ."

The entire data package was light-stuttered to the Entry Port operations at High Plains, filed in the lunar relay banks, and ignored in both locales.

The scout pilot, pressed into the accel/decel couch, looked to be perhaps thirty standard years, blond, curly-haired, and wore a dark olive uniform without insignia.

His fingers alone reacted to the data screen and the data inputs flashing before him.

A dull roar and rumble marked his passing through the clouds, that, and the puzzled look on the face of a duty operations technician.

"Captain's luck! Unauthorized entry, and they both lost it. Not even a hint of descent area. How are we supposed to find it?

"Old war scout, from the profile. Refugee, smuggler, or . . ." He paused because he could not think of a realistic alternative with which to complete the sentence.

Finally, he posted up the entry for the operations officer, who would have the final responsibility for action, not that Major Lostler could do much with neither locale nor down time. Then he punched the entry into the log, and completed his duties by relaying the bulletin to the other Recorps subposts.

He smiled briefly. Smuggler or refugee, what could the one or two people in a small ship do, particularly

with no energy sources left anywhere but in Recorps
territory?

By the time the scout had settled into the twisted
ecological nightmare that had once been called Northern
Europe, the tech had dismissed the reported unauthorized entry as insignificant.

XXIV

"INTERROGATIVE SHIELDS."

"Shields in the green."

"Interrogative outside energy levels."

"No outside energy levels."

The man at the control couch leaned back, sighed.
Outside of the momentary scan from the lunar detectors,
his return had apparently gone unnoticed. Either that, or
no one really cared.

"Current number of dispersal torps?"

"There are twenty full message-sized torps, one
hundred ten-percent torps, and ten thousand shells."

"Commence pattern Beta."

"Commencing pattern Beta."

The obsolete scoutship began the drop run over the
planet's most desolated continent, scheduled to receive
five of the full-spectrum torps and thirty of the ten
percenters. Because he was limited to the small message
torps by both the ship's limited capacity and the size of
the permitted launchers, the seeding would take time,
perhaps too much. But he was limited to what he had.
Even if but a few of his torps were successful, eventually

the spread would complete itself.

With luck, as much as twenty percent of the reclamation seeds and spores would survive.

Even if only one percent made it, over time, the ecology would recover. It would not be quite the same ecology as before the collapse, not with some of the additions and built-in stablizers, but what else could he have done? The dozers were still at it, and they had been far from enough. No pure mechanical technology would ever have been enough.

"Energy concentration at two seven five, five zero kays. Probability of long-range monitor approaches unity."

The pilot nodded at the mechanically feminine tone of the AI, but said nothing as his hands played over the screens before him.

"How long until the first turn?"

"Ten plus."

"That will bring us back toward the monitor?"

"That is affirmative."

"Probability of crew."

"No crew. Monitor is Epsilon three, stored burst, link transmitting type."

"Can you detect transmissions?"

"No transmissions detected."

Gerswin nodded. The monitor had not yet detected the *Caroljoy*, or an immediate transmission would have gone out.

He shrugged.

"Break Beta pattern. Commence Delta in two minutes."

Gerswin strapped himself in place for the high-speed drop series that was about to follow.

While a monitor could not harm the *Caroljoy*, the scout had no exterior weapons with which to silence the monitor, and as soon as the monitor discovered a scoutship where one did not belong, it would relay that information, and satellite control or some other authority might well decide to send something which did have the power to disable or damage the scout.

Why Recorps or the Impies were wasting energy on surveillance monitors was a mystery that could wait, one that he did not need to investigate at the moment.

"Monitor is ground scanning."

"Cancel Delta."

"Canceling Delta."

"Interrogative ground scanning. No other scans?"

"Monitor is ground scanning only. Scan pattern indicates that no other surveillance patterns are in use."

"Resume Beta pattern as planned. Notify me if monitor shifts from ground scan."

"Will notify if monitor scan patterns change."

Thump.

His ears picked up the sound of the first full message-sized torp launch. He waited to see if the Epsilon monitor reacted, but neither the AI nor his scan screens detected any change in the pattern of the Recorps monitor, nor any transmissions from it.

Thwip.

The softer sound of a ten percenter barely edged into his hearing. The AI was releasing the shells at a much faster rate, but they were so small he could not detect the individual releases.

Gerswin shifted his weight, waiting as the scout/yacht called *Caroljoy* continued to deliver the cargo he had promised so long before.

Thwip.

"Beta, section one, complete. Commencing pattern section two."

"Stet."

Gerswin split the far left screen and tapped a code. The homer signal, tight and far off-band, was clear. He should not have been surprised, but he was. The north coast refuge he had built so many years before was still there, still functioning, still apparently undiscovered.

Thwip.

"Get me a broad band sample."

He listened, trying to pick out intelligible phrases from the transmissions, most of them made a quarter of a planet away.

". . . Dragon two . . . tracs . . . home plate . . ."

". . . negative . . . is negative this time . . ."

"Outrider three . . . vector on . . . spout bearing . . ."

". . . have Amstar hold . . ."

". . . ScotiaOps . . . Dragon two . . . return . . . say again . . . return . . ."

For a time, static alone filled the speakers.

Thwip.

Thump!

"Completing Beta, section two. Commencing pattern section three."

"Stet."

Gerswin shook his head.

So anticlimatic. No guards, no armed flitters, no fanfares. Just blanketing wastelands with spores and seeds.

"What did you expect?"

"Query imprecise," answered the AI.

He ignored the artificial intelligence.

"Query imprecise."

"Withdrawn," he snapped.

Thwip. Another ten-percent torp launched.

The pilot massaged his forehead, rubbing his temples with the fingers and thumb of his right hand.

"What next, great reclaimer?"

"Pattern section four is the next section of the Beta pattern," chimed the cool and impersonal tones of the AI.

Gerswin wanted to shake his head, but just kept rubbing his temples. Usually, he tried to avoid asking himself questions when the AI was operational. He was slipping.

Slipping in more ways than one. Each year, it was

harder to separate the memories, harder to keep them all in order, to remember the differences between Caroljoy and Constanza, between Faith and Allison, between Lerwin and Lostwin, between beta- and delta-class flitters.

And it was harder to think things through, harder to separate the dreams from hard plans for the future.

He let his hand drop and looked up at the screen, the blackness showing the plot, the *Caroljoy*'s position and the distant blip that represented the ground-scanning monitor.

What next?

Shaking his head slowly, he let his eyes drop.

He had stepped up his physical training, in hopes that it would help his mental sharpness. The physical reflexes were still as good as ever, perhaps better, automatic and maintained with practice. But the mental abilities . . .

Soon he would have to face that question. That and the future. Would a single-focused project help? Give him time to sort things out while not juggling a thousand variables?

He couldn't think that through yet. Not yet. Not until the last shell, the last torps, until all had spread their cargo across the desolated spaces of Old Earth. But that would only be a few dozen hours away.

Thwip.

"Completing Beta, section three. Commencing pattern section four."

"Stet."

Thump!

XXV

THE PILOT SAT BACK IN THE CONTROL COUCH, STARING AT THE blank main screen.

"Now what?"

"Query imprecise."

"The query is not for you."

"Stet," responded the AI.

The refuges, north Europe coast and western continental mountain, were both waiting, apparently undiscovered. And he had done what he had promised them all, promised young Corwin, assuming the boy had survived and returned to Old Earth, and Kiedra and Lerwin and Caroljoy. He had carried out his trust, hadn't he?

Even now, the ecological torps were beginning their work, beginning the biological processes that would do what all the dozers he had stolen and begged and pleaded for so long ago could not.

Even now, people were reclaiming the planet of their birth, having children, slowly spreading from the reclaimed high plains and from the Scotia highlands. And soon, soon, they would have help from the biological agents he had seeded.

That aid would take longer on Noram because he had only been able to seed the outlying areas without too high a risk of detection. But he was done. Finished. Completed.

He had carried out his trust, hadn't he? Hadn't he?

"Haven't you?"

"Query imprecise."

"Withdrawn."

He tried to ignore the AI, still staring at the blank screen before him. The Imperial Intelligence Service, not to mention more than a few barons of the Empire, would soon be looking for retired Commodore Gerswin, Shaik Corso, and all the other names and identities he had used. They would turn up the *Caroljoy*, if the search were as diligent as he foresaw, as diligent as it was bound to be silent.

And what about the Foundation?

What about Lyr, sitting dutifully and quietly within minutes of the Intelligence headquarters?

He slowly shook his head. Caroljoy had been right. He had more miles to go, many more, than he had thought.

"Interrogative power requirements and parameters for Aswan."

"Double jump from thirty plus ecliptic possible with point five power reserves remaining. Power to jump will require point one of reserves. Power from reentry jump will require estimated point three from reserves."

Not much leeway, either for the jumps or himself. But there wouldn't be, not in the days and years, hopefully, ahead.

"Break orbit for jump point."

"Breaking for jump point."

No doubt the energy flows would be picked up by the lunar relays, but not analyzed until the questions were academic. Besides, there were no Impie ships in range to do anything.

The pilot leaned back, wishing he could rub his aching forehead.

Rationalization or not, he had a few things more to do. A few things more that might make the galaxy a bit safer for Old Earth, and a debt to one last other gracious lady.

The refuges could wait. They'd waited more than a

century already, and could wait another two if necessary, if he had that much time.

He smiled mirthlessly.

The Empire was slow, but scarcely that slow. His wait, the time until his last return home, one way or another, would not be that long.

XXVI

THE CONSUL AND SECOND SECRETARY OF THE EMBASSY OF Barcelon touched the screen.

"FREE HEIN WADRUP! FREE HEIN WADRUP! FREE HEIN WADRUP!"

He grimaced and lowered the volume before turning to the political attaché.

"What started this?"

The attaché shrugged. "It started on the university grounds. You saw the briefing tape. Wadrup jumped bail. He was never seen again. There is no record of him leaving Barcelon. His body was never found."

"What really happened?"

The taller man shrugged again. "The Police say he jumped bail. Who really knows?"

"FREE JAIME BEN! FREE JAIME BEN! FREE JAIME BEN!"

The Consul winced at the new chant from the screen, showing the scene in the park across from the commercial complex.

"This isn't doing our talks much good. The Sunni government believes in civil rights."

"What can we do? Even if we wanted to, there's

nothing we could do. They've picked people who can't
be found or freed."

"Smart of them."

"Too smart for a bunch of students."

"Can you find out who's behind them?"

"No. We traced one of the leaders, the one who
started the Hein Wadrup movement. Graduate student
from New Glascow studying on New Avalon. He's
definitely from New Glascow. Even his voice patterns
check out. He's a real student, and someone else is
funding him—liberally. Who? How can you trace double blind drops and fund transfers over three systems
and through that Ydrisian commnet?"

"That tells you one thing."

"Right. Whoever it is has money. Lots of it. Like
several thousand commercial magnates in the Empire,
and none of them are terribly fond of Barcelon."

The Consul frowned and turned back to the screen,
half listening to the words of the speakers.

". . . of Barcelon . . . designed to keep control of
agriculture from the people . . . without food, no police
state . . . no accident . . . Hein Wadrup knew agriculture policies . . . what did he know? What did they fear
from Hein Wadrup? . . . nothing to fear, then free him
. . . tell Barcelon . . . prove us wrong . . . PROVE US
WRONG! PROVE US WRONG!! . . ."

"Just a short media incident," observed the political
attaché.

"It's not the single incidents that bothers me. It's
the pattern, the continuing growth of such incidents.
Always around the best universities. Almost as if targeted at the students, and the teachers. And those
students will become teachers."

"Not on Barcelon!" protested the attaché.

"No," answered the Consul, "on Barcelon, they'll
either be jailed or become revolutionaries." He sighed.
"I'd rather have the teachers, thank you."

He touched the screen, which blanked.

XXVII

The gardener whistled a low series of notes as he fin-ished weeding the next-to-last row of his plot in the public garden. Already, the row of dark green plants had shed the first set of blossoms, and the nodules were darkening nearly to purple and beginning to take on the tubular shape of the fruit, if an organic product that tasted like the best hand-fed steak could be truly called a fruit.

The second set of blossoms was another week from bursting into full flower, but the silver-haired gardener nodded as he checked each of the fifteen plants in the first row.

The outside row was a hybrid bean common to Forsenia, with nearly the same dark leaves as the bestmeat plant. The bean plants composed the third and fifth rows as well, while the second and fourth rows were filled with bestmeat plants.

"How they coming, Martin?" questioned a lanky, pointed-chinned, and white-haired woman from the next plot, cordoned off from his by a meter-high snow fence pressed into alternative use as a plot-divider for the short summer growing season.

"Growing. Growing fine."

"Next year, like to try whatever you got there with the beans. Looks interesting. Lots of buds already."

"Give you some seeds if it works."

"See then," grunted the woman. "Got to finish before noon. Get my granddaughter. Long tube ride."

She straightened. "You're always here mornings. Got creds. How'd you qual for public garden?"

"Small pension. Impie service. Work nights at Simeons. No family. Make ends meet."

The older woman shivered. "Say lots of DomSecs at Simeons. Watch yourself."

The man with the short-curled silver hair blinked his dark eyes, trying to flick the gnat clear before the bug got under the tinted contact lenses. Finally, he waved the insect away and returned to his gardening, working his way on hands and knees down the fifth and last row.

"See you, Martin. Off for Tricia."

"See you," he answered without looking up.

Seeing he was alone, he resumed his whistling, the doubled notes softly following his progress.

After a time, he stood up and brushed the soil from the old flight suit he wore, a suit stripped of all insignia, although still with an equipment belt. Some of the original tools were obviously missing, and he had placed the hand hoe in the empty sidearm holster.

His eyes surveyed the small plot registered in the name of Martin deCorso, Interstellar Survey Service, technician third class, retired, and he nodded. Within weeks, the bestmeat plants would be producing, and within days of production he would be sharing his bounty with the other gardeners. Each of the long pods to come would also contain a central seed pod that would allow them to grow their own.

He hoped the Forsenian DomSecs were as indifferent to the retired and elderly as first appearances indicated. If they weren't, then he'd have to try something else.

Fingering the seed packet within his belt, he started back down the plastreet pathway toward the checkout gate, where an older DomSec waited to ensure that no one but approved gardeners entered, and where, when the plants bore fruit, the amount produced was also entered, theoretically, he had been told, for record-keeping purposes.

Since the bestmeats resembled giant cucumbers, Old Earth variety, he did not anticipate any problems to begin with. Forsenia was far enough from Shaik Corso's enterprises and Westmark that the bestmeat furor was unknown to the Forsenian authorities, as were the house tree and a few other biological innovations.

The man shook his head. He was not at all certain about the wisdom or the success of his venture, but he needed time to concentrate on one project at a time, to let things settle inside his own head. He'd told Lyr that he would be out of touch for some time, perhaps more than a standard year. Wise? Probably not. Necessary? No doubt of that.

He glanced around. More than half the plots were being actively tended, even though the temperature was rapidly approaching its midday peak, close to 30°C. The temperature would stay near the high until midafternoon, when the thunderstorms would roll down from the highlands and drop both torrential rains and the temperature, leaving a steamy twilight and evening that would turn progressively drier as the night progressed.

The slender gardener took his hands from his belt and slowed his steps as he neared the guard post.

"ID?" growled the overjowled and near-retirement age DomSec. He peered over the gate at the silver-haired man.

The gardener proferred an oblong card, covered with tamperproof plastic and bearing appropriate seals and a hologram picture.

Creaakk. The gate swung open.

"On your way, oldster."

"Thank you, officer." He did not smile, but neither was his statement obsequious, merely a simple courtesy.

"No thanks. Everything you grow means more for someone else."

The gardener refrained from a nearly automatic headshake and kept moving down the narrow steps toward the almost-deserted boulevard.

The tight control of both urban land and of transportation had made one phase of his project more difficult than he had anticipated.

Nowhere near the city was there any overgrown land. Any abandoned plots were cut regularly by the Forsenian equivalent of the chain gang—citizens required to spend nonworking hours in community service for their overuse of transportation, energy, or food.

Halmia was, as a result, a clean city, a well-tended city. But there were no overgrown corners on which to plant bestmeats or house trees. And the nearest forests and farm areas were beyond easy reach of local public transit. The longer-range public transportation was monitored even more closely by ID scans through a centralized computer system. Private transportation, except for DomSec and military officers, was nonexistent.

Not that such shortcomings had stopped him entirely, but he had experienced more blocks and delays than he had anticipated, and the bestmeats had not been spread nearly wide enough to ensure the success he needed.

The public gardens were another avenue, and he'd passed out seeds quietly to gardeners in other areas, telling them that the seeds were a squash derivative whose fruits were best sliced and then boiled or fried. Once they tried them, he suspected, there would be a substantial increase in the growth of the "squash" derivatives.

He'd also made stealthy forays to garden areas in several other cities, planting his seeds in other plots.

He smiled briefly, before frowning as he remembered that a smile was an automatic invitation for a wandering DomSec to inquire as to one's health and destination. He shivered, despite the heat, wondering why he was going to such lengths for a system like Forsenia.

"Are you trying to establish places where you can't create a revolution?" he whispered to himself under his breath, before pursing his lips as he recalled the use of directional pickups. Rapidly, rapidly, was he beginning to understand the paranoia generated in tightly controlled societies.

He would probably need all three complete identities, if not more, by the time he was through, assuming he didn't have to bail out before then.

A DomSec guard stepped from a wall booth.

"Your card, citizen?"

The retired spacer handed over the oblong that entitled him to exist on the People's Republic of Forsenia.

"Where are you going, Citizen deCorso?"

"Home from the gardens, to rest before I go to work this afternoon."

"You work?" the guard asked as he dropped the card into the reader console.

"At Simeons."

The guard looked at the screen, then at the silver-haired man, and handed the card back. He nodded for the man called deCorso to continue on his way, but said nothing.

The slender man turned the corner with slow steps and even pace until he reached the three-story dwelling where he rented an attic room—a room too warm in this summer season, and probably too cold in the winter. With any luck, he would not be spending the winter in Halmia.

He shook his head as he slipped through the heavy front doorway. Most private homes did not have portals, but old-fashioned hinged doors that the DomSecs rapped on far too frequently.

"Long morning at the gardens, Martin?"

His eyes flickered to the thin and pinched face of

Madame Dalmian. She coughed twice, waiting for his response.

He shrugged. "Warm. Two security checks. Always the security checks."

"We don't have crime here anymore, not the way it was in my grandfather's time."

You don't have freedom, either, he added silently.

"That is true, Madame. All the same, it has changed somewhat since I joined the Service. I do not recall so many guards, so many restrictions. But I suppose that is the price we pay for order and security, and it may become more valuable as I get older."

"Martin, the DomSecs would not think that was exactly the proper perspective."

He shrugged. "Have I said anything against either the Domestic Security forces or the government? No. All I said was that I did not recall so many guards. Perhaps there were. A child would not recall that, and I was scarcely more than that when I enlisted."

She coughed again.

"You should watch that cough, you know," he offered. "I remember when we landed on one planet, a place so far out it didn't even have a proper name. It just had a catalogue number. Still does, for all I know. The air was so hot it seemed to steam.

"Half the crew began to cough, just like your cough, that's what reminded me, and they coughed. Oh, how they coughed . . . airborne bacterials, they said . . . terrible . . . and the shakes . . . even the Imperial drugs . . ."

He slipped into the long-winded personna of the retired technician recalling his glory days, and, as he talked, watched the woman's eyes glaze over, and her efforts to edge away without seeming rude to her boarder.

With her, boredom was his best defense.

XXVIII

LIEUTENANT CATALIN SET THE MUG OF SPIKEBEER ON THE TA-ble with a thud. The mug's impact shook the heavy table, and the remnants of the beer sprayed onto the arm of the passing barmaid.

"Another spiker, lass." Catalin's fingers grasped the woman's arm above the elbow, ready to bite into the nerves should she attempt to leave.

"Right away, Lieutenant." Her husky voice was level, but pitched to carry the five meters from the table to the bartender. Her eyes followed her voice.

The bartender received her unspoken plea, and filled another iced mug. The steam rising from the combination of cool liquid and subzero synthetic crystal circled his face, adding an element of unreality to his sharp features and silvered and curling hair. For a moment, the bartender could have been a ghost.

"It's coming, Lieutenant." The woman tried to disengage the security officer's grip without overtly struggling.

"That's not enough, Lyssa."

This time the woman did not repress the shudder when she heard her name and as Catalin's grip forced her around.

His eyes were perfectly normal brown eyes, but the set of his jaw, and the upward twitch at the corners of his mouth, along with the dull dark brown uniform, revealed the sadistic streak he made no move to conceal or disavow.

133

Lyssa sat down heavily in the chair next to him, forced there by his unrelenting grip. Her breathing was heavier than moments before, her eyes darting back toward the silver-haired and slender bartender as he slowly placed the spikebeer on a small tray.

"Lyssa, your customer's spiker is ready." Despite the man's light baritone and the background noise from more than fifty other patrons, his voice carried easily.

Lyssa started to rise, but sat back with a thump as Catalin jerked her arm.

"Have him bring it here."

"Martin. Please bring it here."

Although her voice was lost in the hubbub, the bartender nodded and slipped out the back side of the bar, carrying the tray in both hands, obviously not in the habit of serving customers from the tray itself.

"Your spiker, ser."

"Lieutenant to you, oldster." Catalin turned to the woman. "Where'd Si pick this one up? From a graveyard?"

The lieutenant picked up the empty mug with his free hand.

"Take this back, pops—if you can!" With all the power he could muster from a near two-hundred-centimeter frame, Catalin backhanded the mug toward the frail-looking bartender's midsection.

Had the mug connected, the impact would have been considerable. Since the bartender ducked backward impossibly quickly, the force of Catalin's blow, aided by the bartender's quick footwork, overbalanced the security officer, and his chair began to teeter. Then it fell and broke under the DomSec's weight. The officer was on his feet before the plastic shards stopped clattering on the tiles.

The bartender retreated several steps, toward an open space, and waited for the towering security officer.

Catalin lurched to a halt as he saw the older man's stance, took a deep breath before he whirled to catch

Lyssa as she tried to ease around the table toward the kitchen entrance.

"Come here. Need to talk, woman."

No one except the bartender even looked as the massive security officer led the dark-haired woman back to his table.

The bartender retreated behind the bar and motioned to another barmaid.

"Take Lyssa's section."

"But—"

"He's Security."

"Poor kid. Her little boy's just five."

"No contract?"

"Dead. Impie spacer. Unofficial. No comp. No status."

The bartender shook his head, but continued to watch the table where the young woman sat, head down, and listened to whatever proposition the security officer was making.

In response to a question, she shook her head. Once, then twice.

Crack!

The sound of the slap penetrated the entire saloon, stilling it for the instant it took for the patrons to see the perpetrator was a security officer. Then the conversations resumed, more quietly, with everyone avoiding the pair at the rear corner table. Everyone except the bartender, who eased out from behind the bar toward the table.

The other bartender watched with a frown.

"Lieutenant? You here on official business? Yes or no?"

"Yes."

"Fine. Could I see your warrant?"

"Don't need one."

"Constitution says you do. I say you do."

"No, Martin!" pleaded the woman. "You don't know what he can do."

Catalin smiled and stood suddenly.

"See you later. Both of you. You'll wish you'd treated me better, Lyssa. Much better."

Both the older-looking man and the woman watched the security officer's broad back disappear through the front entry.

"He'll be back with a full crew as soon as he can round them up."

"And?"

"He'll take us away. Martin, don't you understand what you got me into?"

"Assumed you didn't want to be his property to get used and abused and generally beaten."

"I don't. But I'd submit to it for Bron's sake."

He touched her arm, watched her suppress the wince. "Does he know where you live, or your full name?"

"No . . . I don't think so. Never saw him before tonight."

"Where could he find out?"

"Central payroll, or from Si."

"Will he tell anyone else about you? Or will he come for me as a subversive to prove he can hurt anyone?"

"Uh . . . probably . . . for you."

"Good." He paused. "Go home. Now. Don't argue. You're sick as a dog."

"But—"

"I need to get ready, and Si won't push you. You draw too many customers."

"Martin, you don't understand. Subversion means the Security Farms, and no one comes back from there. Never!"

"I didn't say I was going. Now get home, and, by the way, Lyssa, the name isn't Martin. It's Gerswin. Only tell your friends that. Don't worry about Catalin. He won't bother you again. Or anyone else.

"Now, go."

She gathered herself together, then flounced toward the kitchen, as if offended.

The bartender smiled behind his blank face, and he, in turn, swung around and walked down the side corridor to the back rooms. Once inside the room he wanted, he retrieved a battered and cheap-looking case that nothing short of a field-grade laser could open.

"Leaving, Martin?"

Gerswin caught sight of the stunner in Simon Lazlo's right hand.

"Temporarily. You have some objection? Or are you interested in having me neatly trussed up for the Security Forces?" Gerswin was relieved to find Simon concentrating on him. That probably meant that Lyssa could leave. Gerswin did not set down the case he was holding, but let go with his left hand, leaving it behind the case.

"Let's say I object in practice to my employees alienating Security Forces."

"Then you approved of the way that lieutenant used his rank to force himself on a defenseless woman?" Gerswin edged his hand toward his belt.

Lazlo shrugged. "I don't have to like it, but there's not a great deal I can do about it. Unlike you, I have no illusions and no pretensions. And I have to live with the DomSecs. I just can't run away, Martin."

"Name's not Martin. Call me Gerswin, and I'm not running."

Without raising his voice, Gerswin made three moves simultaneously, hurling the case at the stunner with his right hand, throwing the belt knife with his left, and flinging himself forward and to the right.

Thrumm!

Crunch!

Clank.

The stunner lay on the floor, and Lazlo squirmed to pull himself from the wall where the heavy knife held him pinned.

"Bastard Impie! HELP!"

Thrumm! Gerswin retrieved the stunner and turned it on the saloon operator.

Lazlo slumped.

Gerswin checked outside the door, surveying the narrow hallway. No one appeared, and the noise from the patrons continued unabated. He reclosed the door and retrieved the knife. With the thin door locked, he laid Lazlo out on the floor. The owner's shoulder wound still bled, but not heavily.

After opening the case, he slipped into the black full-fades and strapped on the equipment belt, transferring the knives from his bartending clothes.

He closed the case with a snap and opened the door, slipping down the last few steps to the rear exit. The serviceway outside was dimly lit in the early evening, dimly lit, and empty, with enough shadows for him to leave and take his position without visual detection.

The security squad would doubtless arrive at the front with a flourish after several less obvious troops first appeared to cover the rear.

Gerswin waited in the shadows.

Shortly, he heard the clicking of boots on the synthetic pavement. Three security types stationed themselves at points equidistant from the rear entrance of Simeons.

Gerswin continued to listen, but could hear but a single other set of boots, a single other set of breathing. He checked the stunner.

Thrumm! Thrumm! Thrumm!

The three went down like the sitting ducks they were.

Gerswin did not move, knowing that the fourth guard had been caught unawares and had no real idea from where the fire had come.

Finally, the other guard moved, and Gerswin caught sight of him in the shadows of the nearest parallel serviceway.

Thrumm!

As he dropped, Gerswin hoped that the obvious instructions to maintain comm silence had held. Certainly he had heard no voices, even whispers, from the four. He waited, remaining motionless and silent, listening to see if there were others.

At last, he took out his knives, and did what had to be done.

He left a fair amount of blood with the four bodies.

Fear . . . the only thing those who create it fear is fear.

Surprisingly he felt no remorse for the dead DomSecs, not after what he had seen in the streets and at Simeons.

He moved to the shadows near the front of the building, carrying three stolen stunners and the laser rifle that the last guard had borne.

Lieutenant Catalin had yet to make the grand entrance he had promised Lyssa.

Again, Gerswin waited, straining for the sound of the approaching electrocars, wondering if his judgment of Catalin had been correct, that the man would ignore the silence of his rear guards and plunge ahead.

He was half-right.

Two electrocars purred up. From the first poured five men, who lined up in a rough order, glancing at the facade of the saloon and back at the lightly armored vehicle. One was the lieutenant.

Gerswin shrugged and hefted the heavy laser.

Hisssss.

Thrumm! Thrumm! Thrumm! Thrumm!

Catalin had been the first to fall, with a laser burn through his skull.

Gerswin had missed the fourth guard with the stunner, and the man, with quicker reflexes than his compatriots, had dropped behind the electrocar.

Thrumm!

The return bolt missed Gerswin by more than three meters, but, unfortunately, showed the guard had the general idea of where Gerswin was.

The man in the shadow clothes eased back down the serviceway to the emergency escape and slowly edged upward on it, trying to keep from making any sounds that would carry. Once on the roof, he crossed to the front of the building and surveyed the street below from the facade.

The guard had not bothered to look up, a sign of either poor training or no real opposition.

Hisss.

The exposed guard crumpled, unaware he was dead until the fact was academic.

Still, no one had emerged from the second electrocar, nor was there any action from the slab-sided wagon.

Finally, Gerswin eased away from the facade and to the opposite escape ladder, slipping down it as quickly as possible and edging along the narrow space between the buildings until he was back at the front shadows, on the other side from his first attack. Flattening himself next to the wall, he checked the sights on the laser, then levered the power up to full, enough for two full shots.

Hisss.

The first severed enough of the rear plastaxle for the left rear wheel to buckle.

With such provocation, the side door slid open, and two hulking figures emerged.

Gerswin grinned. The idiots! Both were clothed in riot suits, guaranteed to reflect any laser or stun weapon short of Imperial artillery.

Both carried hand lasers and stunners. Each headed for a different side of the building, the side from which he had first fired, and the side where he now waited.

Gerswin retreated five meters, inching up onto a ledge in a meter-deep recess well above eye level, which, given the darkness and the shadows, should have concealed him until the riot-suited guard was close enough.

Gerswin was wrong. The guard did not even look up or check the sides of the narrow serviceway, but walked through, almost as quickly as possible, firing both laser and stunner at random.

Once the guard was past, Gerswin threw both knives in quick succession.

Thunk! Thunk!

The riot fabric, while proof against energy weapons, was more than vulnerable to old-fashioned throwing knives. The guard collapsed into a sack of muscles and fabric.

Once more, Gerswin clambered up the fire escape after retrieving his knives and taking the guard's most highly charged laser.

It took both knives to stop the second riot guard as the man panicked his way back toward the front street after, Gerswin surmised, finding four bloody bodies. Gerswin swung down and wrenched both knives from the body.

While he would have preferred to have finished off the entire troop, he could hear the distant, but oncoming, whine of more than just a pair of electrovans, and decided to do the prudent thing.

He ran, silently, picking up the case and cloak from where he had hidden them. But he ran, stretching out his strides into the effortless and ground-covering lope of a devilkid ahead of the she coyotes, racing the landspouts and the terrors of Old Earth.

But he ran, real and imagined terrors pursuing.

XXIX

THE COPY EDITOR SCANNED THE SCREEN, FROWNING AS HE read the headline.

"No Need For Protein Restrictions."

"Where did that come from?" he muttered, calling up the full text, speeding through it as he did. Then he reread the first paragraph.

"(INS) New Augusta. 'No system government should need to impose protein restrictions on its people,' claimed D. Daffyd Werlyn, Proctor of Agronomy at the Emperor's College, in his farewell address.

"Werlyn stated that the 'bestmeat' plant, once banned in the Fursine system, could bring about the end of hunger and protein restrictions in any system. 'It's tasty, nutritious, and grows under the most adverse conditions, from poisoned sewage to sand, but produces untainted slices of protein undetectable from the finest organic steaks.'

"Werlyn noted that several systems have banned the growing of the plant because it causes 'agricultural disruption.' The Fursine provisional government just recently revoked such a prohibition and stated that 'bestmeat' was a national treasure, since a small garden could provide enough protein for an entire family of four year round.

"The Novayakin system government recently banned the home cultivation of the plant . . . claiming it provided support for outlawed Atey rebels . . ."

The editor read the squib again, then checked the routing codes, which indicated an Imperial message torp, as opposed to a Ydrisian commercial torp.

He frowned, then tapped his fingers across the board, waiting for the response to his inquiry. The story had already run on two successive netwide faxnews prints.

At that, he smiled briefly before touching the red stud on the console, the special red stud that only a few of the news service personnel had.

The comm screen centered on a man in the dark brown uniform of Domestic Security.

"DomSec, Andruz."

"Pellestri, FPNS. Thought you should see something that crossed the net, Andruz."

"What now, Pellestri? Another subversive headed this way? Another Atey deploring the inappropriate and restrictive technology of Forsenia? Or perhaps another intellectual critiquing the regime from behind the protection of New Avalon's Ivory Towers?"

"I'm sending the squib direct, if you want to receive."

"Send it."

Pellestri touched the transmit stud and listened to the high-pitched bleep. Then he waited, confident that Andruz would not cut him off and that there would be a reaction.

He was disappointed.

"So there's a new food plant? So what?"

"Just doing my duty, Andruz. The regulations say I have to report anything which has a potential of upsetting planetary order."

"So . . . you did what you thought was best. Break."

Pellestri broke. Then he touched the keyboard again, quickly.

"Pelle! And during the day, too."

"Do you have a hard-copy terminal there?"

"Yes. But . . ."

"Take this and see what you can do. All right?"

"Do?"

"Just see if you can track down the subject. Call it personal interest. Might be more than a good story. Might even make life . . . give it a better flavor, if you will."

"Aren't you mysterious. All right." The dark-haired woman nodded slowly, without betraying her understanding of how important the matter was to him. "Send it, and we'll get on it."

Pellestri sent another bleep through the terminal and broke the connection.

Then he went back to editing, although his thoughts did not.

Marta had the old homestead back in the hills, beyond the military perimeter, out beyond where the regime had confiscated private property, and if half of what the squib had hinted were true, it all might be possible, in the months ahead, or at least by next year. But they'd have to be careful. Most careful.

His hands continued to edit the material on the screen as it crossed before his eyes.

XXX

THE MAN IN THE FULL-FADE CAMOUFLAGE SUIT WAITED IN THE shadows for the scheduled DomSec patrol.

Despite the high-intensity pole lights, when the evening fog was thick, as it usually was right after sunset, gloom dominated most of the interval between the circles of light.

A set of footsteps, light and quick, pattered toward the man who lay stretched under the ornamental hedge bordering the public gardens. His eyes followed the thin, middle-aged woman who nervously hurried from pool of light to pool of light toward the tube station three hundred meters farther down the boulevard.

The sound of her steps rang down the nearly silent boulevard long after her image and shadow were swallowed by the yellow-gray of the fog.

The man who waited could feel the vibration coming from the tube buried ten meters beneath him. He quirked his lips and hoped the woman had made it to the station. If not, she had a long wait for the next train this late.

Whhhrrrr.

The purring of an electrovan sounded from the

cross street a hundred meters downhill to his right, then faded as the van continued eastward.

Click. Click, click. Click.

The measured tread of military boots on the pavement continued to increase in volume, although the fog concealed the DomSecs who wore those boots. The man in the depression behind the hedge remained there, flattening himself still farther.

Two sets of steps meant increased concerns. At that, he permitted himself another brief smile. Then he waited. With two guards, there was a good chance one was carrying and using a heat sensor, but sensors were line of sight, and his position was not. He remained hugging the grass behind the hedge as the steps neared.

Click, click. Click, click.

"Scope?" asked a deep voice.

"Negative."

"Waste of time."

"Maybe. You want to be an Atey casualty?"

"Stow it."

Click, click. Click, click.

"Somebody in front of us. See?"

"Small prints. Almost gone. Scope pattern says a woman."

"Who says it's a man after DomSecs?"

"Who says it's one person?"

Click. Click, click. Click.

The steps passed.

The man edged into a crouch, edging along behind the DomSec pair, but well to the side and trailing them, shadowing them, while fitting a small rounded object into a leather sling.

Whirrrrr!

Crack!

Clank!

Hisssss! HISSSS!

The remaining security officer used his laser like a hose, spraying every shadow in sight.

The man in the full-fade blacks had melted back into the ground, behind the hedge and below the line of sight of the laser.

"Fyrdo! Square six, halfway to five. Gerlys down. Ambush! Say again. Ambush. Gerlys is down."

Whirrrrr!

Crack!

Clank.

The man in black, more shadow than the shadows that concealed him, did not wait for confirmation of the second sling, but began the ground-eating strides that would take him through the public gardens. As he ran, he replaced the weapon behind his equipment belt.

What the DomSecs had yet to learn was that in a city, a well-conditioned man who could run quickly, right after the attack, was quicker than their reaction, particularly if his attacks were always aimed at outlying areas and patrols away from the dispatch points. He had made sure they were.

He smiled.

The point was to force retrenchment or repression, or both. Either would do, as would the destruction of the myth of DomSec invulnerability.

XXXI

AFTER STRAIGHTENING HIS TUNIC, THE MAN WITH THE BROWN and gray curly hair and full beard eased out his doorway toward the stairs leading down to the second floor.

He stopped after one step, listening, his acute hearing picking up fragments of the vidfax conversation from the room below, where Carra Herklonn, the woman from whom he had rented the upstairs room, spoke in a voice barely above a whisper.

". . . I'm sure he's the one you want . . ."

". . . said his name was Emile De L'Enver. We are definitely looking for a man named Martin deCorso, who is a Forsenian national formerly in Imperial Service."

". . . same build, and he didn't rent the room until after deCorso, whatever you called him, disappeared. So he has brown and gray hair and a beard. Anyone can color their hair and grow a beard . . ."

"What is the name, Madame . . . Madame . . . ?"

"My name is Herklonn, Carra Herklonn, and his name is Emile De L'Enver. D-E-space-L-apostrophe-E-N-V-E-R. De L'Enver."

"Just a moment, Madame Herklonn."

". . . don't understand why they let people like that run around . . ."

The man on the top step of the stairs began to edge down the steps silently, still listening as he moved.

"Madame, there is also an Emile De L'Enver, with perfectly good credentials and credit, who also recently returned to Forsenia. He has been interviewed several times, as is our practice with returnees, the last being several weeks ago, before Ser deCorso disappeared, in connection for his travel permit. It would seem somewhat unlikely that Ser deCorso would be in Halmia at the same time that Ser De L'Enver was in Varenna . . ."

". . . but he doesn't talk like a Forsenian, not even one who spent years away in the Empire. There's an odd lilt there. You know. You just know. And he doesn't have the right attitudes . . . about DomSec . . . about anything . . . and he's scary . . ."

"What do you mean, Madame?"

"Sometimes I get the feeling he's heard everything I've said. He moves so quietly you can never hear him.

He doesn't act like an old man, even if he does limp a little."

"He limps?"

"Just a bit, when no one is looking, almost as if he were trying to hide it, and that seems strange. And then there's the suitcase. It has Imperial locks on it, the kind Alfred would have called security locks. Not your normal locks, but the kind that look like you could never break them . . ."

"Perhaps we should have another talk with Ser De L'Enver. Is he there now?"

"He's upstairs . . . resting, he said."

"A patrol should be there in the next few minutes, perhaps as long as ten minutes, Madame."

"All right."

"If he is the man we're looking for, he has avoided hurting anyone except security officers. But I would stay out of his way. And I would not mention you faxed us, of course."

"I was not planning on announcing it."

"Good day."

"Good day."

The man known as De L'Enver waited until she had stepped away from the console before walking into the second-floor room.

"Might I ask why you are so intent upon turning me over to the DomSecs, Madame?"

Carra Herklonn started to jab her hand toward the console, but De L'Enver was quicker, and caught her arm before her fingers reached the keyboard.

Despite her greater height and weight, she found she could not break his grip.

"Help!"

"No one else here," he observed with a twist to his lips.

"It was worth a try." She smiled wryly.

"You a former DomSec agent?"

"No. InSec, part-time, before——" She attempted to

twist and drive her elbow into his midsection.

"Ooooo." The expression oozed out as his fingers tightened on the nerves above her elbow.

"Before?"

"Before I met Alfred."

"You don't mind all the social control? The government trying to tell you what to do and when?"

Her reply was another attempt to break away, followed by an effort to smash the bones in the top of his foot with her boot heel.

"I take it you approve of all the repression."

"I don't see it that way. You mind your own business, and neither InSec nor DomSec bother you. They don't torture people, like on Barcelon or Gondurre. There's enough food, and the government doesn't tolerate parasites . . ."

De L'Enver shook his head almost sadly.

"You prize order so highly that you have forgotten freedom."

He cocked his head to the side, as if to listen, then gripped her arm more tightly and moved her away from the console, nearly lifting her off the floor with his right hand.

His eyes caught hers, and despite their muddy brown color, they seemed to flash.

"Do most people share your feelings?" he snapped.

She tried to move away, away from the stare and the force of a personality she had not seen before behind the nondescript facade.

". . . I . . . think so. Very little crime . . . or unrest . . . not that many people in prison . . . not that many emigrants . . ."

He frowned.

"Who would have thought—"

"Thought what?" she parried.

"That so many people would like such a repressive society."

He turned toward her, his left hand coming up like a

blur. She twisted and tried to scream, but the pressure across her neck tightened, and finally she slumped.

De L'Enver laid her out on the carpet and dashed for the third floor.

Within seconds he was up the stairs and back down by the front door, carrying only an attaché case, leaving clothes and what appeared to be personal possessions in the third-floor room.

As he stepped out onto the narrow stoop, he did not hesitate, but adopted the brisk walk of a businessman in a hurry, of a man late for an appointment, but a bit too dignified to rush.

Three blocks from the Herklonn house, he picked up the whine of an overstrained electrovan behind him. Forcing himself not to pick up his pace, he continued toward the tube train station, presenting an alternative credit card, not in the name of De L'Enver, to the gate.

Once inside and down the ramp, he ducked into a private stall in the public fresher and made several quick changes. The beard was replaced, though he left longer sideburns than he had used as Martin deCorso, and the enzyme solution he combed through his hair changed the brown to black, leaving the streaks of gray intact. The brown contact lenses were replaced with a darker shade that left his irises black, and lifts inside his boots added another three centimeters to his height. He reversed the business tunic from brown to a crisper charcoal, and attached a pencil-thin mustache above his upper lip with a skin adhesive that would resist anything but a special disolver. He added a reddish blotch on his cheek below his left eye.

Last, he replaced his identification card as Emile De L'Enver with that of his third prepared identity, that of one Lak Volunza.

After joining half a dozen others on the platform, he watched to see if any DomSecs appeared, but even five minutes later, when he stepped aboard the four-car train to western Varenna, no security types had appeared.

He resisted shaking his head.

Forsenia represented a closed and controlled society, more tightly run than either Barcelon or Byzania, and yet there were few signs of unrest, and the DomSecs were strangely inept as a planetary police force. While the government imprisoned dissidents, the accommodations, according to all accounts, while spartan, were adequate, as were food and medical treatment. Hardcore opponents were sent to the state farms, but there too was the treatment not terribly repressive.

Yet few escaped or tried to, nor were there any underground movements visible. Istvenn knew, he'd looked.

De L'Enver, now Volunza, sat in a two-person seat one seat back from the sliding doors and observed the handful of other riders.

The train slid to its first stop. The doors opened, and another fifteen people trooped into the car, almost silently, as if each individual were wrapped in a blanket of his or her own thoughts.

The man calling himself Volunza studied the car itself.

No litter on the floor. No graffiti on the walls. No tears or rips in the faded upholstery, which appeared to have been recently scrubbed.

The tube trains were scarcely new, occasionally squeaked or swayed, but were well maintained. While some passengers talked quietly, Volunza could see that they were individuals who already knew one another.

His eyes checked the map on the car wall. Three more stops before his destination.

The train squealed as it braked for the next underground station, but only five or six passengers rose.

Once the car halted and the doors opened, the small crowd outside on the platform waited until the departing passengers left before entering. With a hiss, the doors closed, and the train lurched gently as it began to pick up speed.

Lak Volunza continued to study the passengers, the strangely accepting citizens of Forsenia, while the train hummed and hissed along.

When the train slowed in its approach to the next to the last station on the western line, called Red Brook, Volunza stood, along with a handful of others. The majority of passengers remained seated, obviously headed for the end of the line, as he stepped out onto the platform.

While the DomSecs appeared slow, they might be one step ahead, and waiting for him to exit the train at the end of the line—any line. Even if they could track which cards he had used, they would have to wait until he left the station, unless they wanted to stop every passenger on every platform, whether incoming, outgoing, or transferring. He doubted that the DomSecs were worried enough yet to blanket some sixty stations; many of which had much higher traffic volumes and more than one exit.

If their data system were good enough, they could track anyone from the two tube stations that were equidistant from the Herklonn home and compare the names against addresses. That would take a few minutes, but not many, and would certainly narrow the focus of the search.

That possibility was the reason why the credit card he had used did not bear the name or credit codes of Lak Volunza, but those of a newshawk association, the kind of card given to people who traveled on business too frequently to be justified as personal use. Such cards were registered in both individual names and in the names of the organization. His card represented the state news organization, FPNS.

Brisk steps took him up the inclined ramp to street level, where he turned southward along the boulevard lined by squat and oversize dwellings of gray stone, presumably the homes of well-paid functionaries of some sort.

Volunza checked the time. Only midafternoon, far earlier than he would have wished to be less conspicuous.

At the next corner he turned westward, keeping an eye open for uniformed DomSecs and anyone else. He passed a young woman wheeling a buggy, in which a sleeping infant lay, covered with a light, but bright red blanket.

He nodded, somberly, without smiling, as he passed.

Surprisingly he received a tentative smile in return.

He reached the green expanse of the Novaya Park without passing another soul on the broad streets, and with just two or three electrocars humming past.

The park had no gates and presented a series of grassy areas interspersed with dark conifers and the heavy trunks of the ancient and imported oaks. The size of the trees, if nothing else, confirmed the age and stability of Varenna.

As he headed toward the permanent summer pavilions, he wished he had made his hair even grayer. Then he could have joined the group of older men at their endless games of chess.

While the cool breeze felt warm enough for him, he suspected most Imperials would have found Forsenia far too chilly, especially in any season besides the too-short summers.

A whining sound tickled his hearing, coming from the road to his left where it wound toward the common area a hundred meters in front of him. Volunza set his case down by an oak and wiped his forehead, leaning against the tree as if to rest for a moment. Then he sat down.

From the base of the old oak, he had a clear view of the men at their stone tables, as well as of the women playing cards at a second row of tables. His position also kept him shielded from direct observation from the perimeter roads around the park.

The electrovan continued to the common area and the summer pavilions, where it stopped. A uniformed man and woman climbed out and walked over to the men playing chess, stopping by an older man who was watching, standing in the kiosk that sold drinks and dressed in a gray tunic. The seller nodded as the three talked for several minutes.

Then the two security officers walked into the section of tables shaded by the pavilion roof. The woman DomSec pointed to a man, looking back at the man in gray, who nodded.

The white-haired man, the object of her attention, bolted upright. Despite his obvious paunch, he charged the male DomSec, bowling him into another table, and scattering chess pieces in the process.

Both DomSecs turned, but did not draw weapons, as the paunchy man careened off the immobile stone table, pounded past the kiosk, and threw himself through the still-open driver's door of the electrovan. The door slammed closed.

The van began to whine, picking up speed and volume as it whipped back down the road toward the far side of the park.

Wsssh!

The man who temporarily called himself Volunza blinked.

A searing flash of light flared across the grass, so quickly it cast no shadows.

Volunza blinked, rubbing his eyes to regain his vision.

The first thing he saw, when he could see again, was the seething lump of metal that had been the DomSec electrovan. He turned his head slowly to survey the park, but could see nothing else.

"Booby-trapped," he observed to no one in particular.

He watched the group in the center of the park. All but a few of the older men and women returned to their cards and chess. Those that did not merely sat and stared blankly.

The gray-haired kiosk attendant and the two DomSecs strolled casually up the winding road toward the hot metal that had once been a paunchy man and an electrovan.

Volunza quietly eased himself farther down at the base of the oak, nearly invisible to anyone more than a few meters away, and took out a tattered book. Better to wait for the time when everyone was going home before trying to move anywhere farther.

He reminded himself not to borrow any government vehicles. Their rental rate was more than he wished to pay.

He wished the night would come, and with it the shadows that would offer some concealment.

XXXII

THE PURPLE-SHADED SQUARES ON THE MAP REPRESENTED THE territory controlled by the government, territory being enlarged by the DomSecs day by day. The light green represented the shrinking area of rebel control.

Gerswin frowned, shook his head, and folded the latest version of the thin plastic into a small oblong which he stored in the thigh pocket of the shipsuit he wore under the winter furs.

"Forsenia rebel file. Interrogative projections."

"Insufficient data."

Gerswin nodded again. He couldn't expect the AI of

a scout, even his overendowed scout, to have the capability of a tactical AI, but he had hoped.

Despite the advantage of terrain, despite the advantage of surprise, and despite the tactics and stupidity of the DomSec commanders, the rebels were losing, bit by bit, kilometer by kilometer.

Even without the tanks and drones of the security forces, the rebels had more than adequate weapons, and the DomSecs were so careless about theirs and their supplies that neither weapons nor ammunition were a problem. The rebels had, thanks to the bestmeat plant, local flora, and the carelessness of the government troops, more than adequate food. And no one liked the DomSecs.

Gerswin paused in his mental summary.

At the same time, few of the Forsenians actually hated the security forces or the government. They were minor evils to be endured, like the winter, the snows, the continual freezing temperatures.

Did freedom require an inborn hatred of control and government?

He shook his head tiredly.

What in Hades was he really doing? And why? What would a revolution on Forsenia do for either ecological development or Old Earth?

He had had a reason when he started. Hadn't he?

He shook his head again, and stood, gathering the winter furs around him as he walked toward the lock. Regardless of the questions, he could not leave unfinished what he had started, not yet, at least.

Thumbing the lock stud, he waited for the lock to open fully, before slipping out into the darkness, out onto the thin skis, and into a ground-covering pace toward the town ten kilos to the west.

He expected to arrive there before the small DomSec garrison began the day, perhaps in time to liberate quietly a disruptor or two, or something equally effective.

XXXIII

ANATOL SHEFSIN PURSED HIS LIPS AS HIS BROWN EYES PASSED over the two men who stood on the opposite side of the bank of data screens from him.

"Yes?"

"You asked about the Imperial reaction, First Citizen."

"I did. It seemed likely that no quarantine would result so long as the unrest involved neither ships nor heavy weapons. Is that the Imperial position?"

Shefsin's brown eyes were as hard and shiny as the polished brown fabric of his tunic and trousers. He waited without apparent impatience.

"Basically," answered the blocky man in the dark black tunic used in place of a uniform by all senior DomSec officers on Forsenia. "There were words about evaluations and status of the government, but the Imperial office did not seem enthusiastic about recommending a quarantine."

"Refreshing change," observed Shefsin dryly. "Of course, it couldn't have anything to do with the shortfalls in Imperial revenues, could it?"

Neither subordinate ventured an answer. Both stood as if they would stand in the same position until dismissed or forever.

"Of course not," Shefsin answered himself. "The Empire is as it has always been, insisting on our pro-rata share, holding itself as our sole protection against the

157

alien horrors of the galaxy. In the meantime, population pressures around . . ." The First Citizen waved an arm toward the exit portal. "You may go. You have done your duty, and well, and the Republic appreciates it. More importantly, I appreciate it."

Both DomSecs inclined their heads slightly.

"Thank you, First Citizen."

"Thank you, First Citizen."

Shefsin watched and waited until both men had departed before smiling.

He recalled the plans he had studied earlier, the ones for the Republic's first armed jumpships. Before long, before long, the Empire would have to pull back from the Forsenian sector.

The Atey rebellion was fortunate in many ways, he reflected, particularly if he could prolong the conflict until the new heavy weapons complex was in full operation.

While the Empire might need Forsenia and its contributions, the Republic hardly needed the Empire.

Smiling more broadly, the First Citizen looked at the crest displayed on the wall opposite him.

The jagged lightning sword across the olive branch —right now the lightning glittered with promise.

XXXIV

GERSWIN SHIFTED THE HEAVY-DUTY DISRUPTOR TO DISTRI-
bute the weight differently and continued trudging toward the center of the rebel camp, wishing he could shed
the bulky and heavy furs for his thin and insulated
winter whites or grays.

"You there."

Gerswin ignored the voice.

"You with the 'ruptor!"

Turning slowly, Gerswin faced the caller, a bear of a
man who wore the double bands of a force leader.

"Yes, Force Leader," he answered noncommittally.

"Where are you going with that 'ruptor?"

"Back off patrol. To turn it into the armory."

"Not through camp center. Around the perimeter."

"Yes, Force Leader."

Gerswin turned and let his seemingly tired steps
carry him back toward the perimeter, waiting until the
big but junior officer had lost sight of him in the
gathering gloom and increasing snow.

He pursed his lips. Worrying about whether troops
carried disruptors through camp center was scarcely the
priority setting one would expect of a rebel command
facing an approaching DomSec force with the worst of
the winter chill yet to strike.

Whether rebel or DomSec, military or civilian, all
Forsenians seemed to share a concern with procedures

and routine, sometimes to the apparent exclusion of reality.

The man who wore the white furs of a scout sighed. He knew he had learned a great deal from his experiences on the chill planet, but at the moment he was not exactly certain why he had bothered. Not that it would be long before he left, but that bothered him as well.

The armory was a crude bunker whose entrance was shielded from the snow with a small sport tent.

Gerswin stepped inside. A thin and graying man in fraying Imperial winter whites stood inside, glaring at a weapon on a flat bench.

"Log it in, soldier." He did not look up.

"New weapon," offered Gerswin.

The rebel armorer looked up. His eyes widened a touch.

"Where did you get that?"

"The DomSecs were a bit careless."

"Energy level?"

"About ninety percent."

"I don't think I'll ask. Wish we had more like you. Your name?"

"Volunza."

"Oh, you're that one. The scout."

Gerswin nodded.

The older man returned his attention to the disassembled laser, as if Gerswin were not even in the bunker. Gerswin racked up the disruptor, added it to the listing, and used the small stencil gun to etch a number on the butt plate.

He slipped back out into the snowy evening, drifting toward the center of the encampment, listening, occasionally stopping, picking up fragments of conversations.

"When I was with the Twelfth on Herrara . . ."

"Not at all like the Service . . . not at all . . ."

". . . always think the Impies do it best . . ."

He paused, then turned toward the mess tents.

As the smell of burned corbu wafted toward him, he changed direction again and moved toward the command center, easing up toward the guards outside Torbushni's tent.

"Volunza! What did you bring in today, old man?"

"'Ruptor. Guess the DomSecs are getting even more careless. Don't seem to care." Gerswin nodded toward the Commander's tent. "What goes with the Commander?"

The guard looked down at the packed snow, then around the pathways before answering, his voice low. "Now, old Torbi thinks that the DomSecs won't attack, just circle and wait. Circle and wait for us to try to get out. Try to starve us out."

"Might be right."

"Sure he's right. What did they cook tonight?"

Gerswin smiled. "Burned corbu."

"Same as yesterday. And the day before." Salnki spat into the snow to his right. "Except for you scouts, nothing happens. The DomSecs march closer. A blind man could pick off half of them. Torbi says no. Don't get them mad. All the officers agree. Thought this was a revolution."

"Me too."

"Not now. See how many empty tents? Torbi's right, all right. Push comes to shove, and winter really sets down . . . no rebels left, except a handful. Too few to fight." Salnki stiffened.

So did Gerswin.

"Salnki? Who's your friend?"

"Volunza, ser. The scout."

"The one who brought in the case of stunners?" asked the two-meter-high towering figure of Commander-Colonel Torbushni.

"Yes, ser," answered Gerswin.

"Wanted a messenger, but you'll do fine, Volunza. Can you get Senior Force Leader Gruber from communications up here?"

"Yes, ser. If he's in camp."

"If not, get whoever is the senior comm man."

Gerswin nodded as Torbushni retreated back into the heated comfort of his insulated bubble tent, retreated without waiting for an acknowledgment.

Salnki shook his head.

Gerswin quirked his lips and turned back downhill.

Gruber had already disappeared into the hills, but Torbert, remaining comm force leader, would be happy to confer with Torbushni—even if it were an attempt to negotiate a surrender.

Gerswin shook his own head as he trudged through the snow—a snow that represented fall and not winter —the cold beginning to bite into his cheeks as the wind picked up and the temperature dropped further.

XXXV

No sooner had he slipped inside the lock than he began to prepare for lift-off.

"Prelift sequence."

"Beginning sequence."

"Full passive spectrum scan. Put the sequence on screen beta."

"Scan results appearing on screen beta," replied the AI.

By this time, he had the furs and the soiled shipsuit off, and was pulling on a fresh singlesuit, stuffing the used clothing into the cleaner. A full cleanup could wait until the *Caroljoy* was clear of Forsenia.

He strapped into the control couch.

"Interrogative time until lift-off status is green."

"Plus five."

Gerswin scanned the board and screens in front of him.

"Display on main screen the estimated positions of the rebels and the DomSecs. Change to screen delta when lift-off status is green."

The force display showed no marked change from the way things had stood when he had slipped clear of the rebel headquarters the evening before. The DomSecs had the rebels effectively surrounded, but were not using heavy weapons, although they had brought enough to level the rebel encampment, had they chosen to do so.

How could he have so misread the Forsenian character? They might have a tightly controlled society. They might have a few abusive security officers, and they might not like the Domestic Security Forces, and there might be a few malcontents. But few indeed really wanted an alternative, or could have formulated one they would have preferred.

"Nothing to fight for . . ." he mumbled to himself, low enough for the ship's AI not to interpret it as a command or a question.

So? For what had he disrupted three cities, half a planet, and personally killed several dozen DomSecs?

Some, like Lieutenant whatever-his-name-had-been at Simeons, had certainly deserved what they had gotten. Quite a few had not, Gerswin suspected.

"Live and learn . . ." But what had he learned?

What he'd known in theory long before. That people have to have dreams. That they have to believe in those dreams, and that they have to prefer the uncertainty and the risk of seeking those dreams to the security of the present. Without those, nothing could change.

Nothing would change.

"One minute until lift-off status is green."

Gerswin broke away from his questions and reverie to check the screens.

"As soon as possible, begin switchover to orbit monitoring, including all Imperial bands."

"Standing by for lift-off."

"Lift," ordered the former Commodore, his voice cold.

A dull rumble washed out from the lifting and screened scout, a rumble that rained sound into the snow that dropped on the DomSec and rebel encampments, drowning out momentarily the whispering and comm-linked conversation between Commander-Colonel Torbushni of the rebels and Colonel Ruihaytyen of the Forsenian Domestic Security Forces, as a night-black scout older than the Empire raced into the clouded skies toward the deeper night of space.

XXXVI

THE MAN KNOWN AS EYE DRUMMED HIS FINGERS ON THE table, as if he were impatient. The two others, also wearing privacy cloaks, may have smiled behind their own hoods, for the timing of the gesture was off slightly, enough to indicate that the mannerism was contrived.

Contrived or not, it fulfilled its purpose, as the whispers died away and the participants sat up, waiting for the business at hand:

"Do these names break orbit?" He paused, then read from the list projected on the screen flush on the table before him. "Patron L. Sergio Enver, MacGregor Corson, C. J. Grace, Ser Delwood Ler Win, N'gio D'Merton, Commander or Commodore MacGregor Corson Gerswin, Captain M. C. Gerswin, Shaik Corso . . ."

"Eye section has had a watch on retired Commodore Gerswin," answered the figure to his right. "Tracks research projects for some foundation—OER Foundation, I believe. He has a retirement place on New Colora and quarters in the Atlantean Towers here."

"That is what he would like you to believe," answered Eye.

"The other names are not linked to his in the records."

"They are not officially linked to his in any case, and the probabilities are less than point two in some cases. Probabilities aside, Commodore Gerswin is the reason for this meeting." Eye looked around the room, away from the projected list, and silently cleared his throat.

"One of my predecessors twice refused an Admiralty request to have the Corpus Corps target the Commodore. That was after his successful 'transfer' of close to two cohorts of land-dozers to Old Earth. Those actions led to the creation of Recorps, but Gerswin refused Recorps status and chose exile, although he would have been Commandant."

"Why?"

"That is why we are here."

"I don't think I am going to like this." That was from the third figure, the one who had said nothing thus far.

Eye ignored the comments. "The names I listed, plus a number of others without any probabilistic basis, are used by Gerswin in a large number of enterprises spread throughout the Empire. The majority of these enterprises are based in the field of biologics, and in all Gerswin has what amounts to the controlling interests. His *verified* holdings place him above all the commercial magnates in the Empire and above many of the barons. Yet, he has never sought or accepted such recognition."

Eye swept the shielded room with eyes hidden in the depths of the cloak's hood.

"Most important, nothing he has done is in the slightest bit illegal, not that can be traced, not of which there is the slightest bit of proof. But there is a strong suggestion that he is the one who brought down the government of Byzania, and the use of nuclear weapons against one of his suspected holdings on El Lido raises other questions. Unfortunately, we can prove nothing. In the nuclear weapons case, he was ostensibly the victim."

"Why our concern? Gerswin has to die sometime. He's certainly no longer a young man, and rejuves have a limited extending power."

"First, Gerswin has never had a rejuve. He has retained a biological age of roughly thirty standard years for well over a century. His last medical exam by the Service showed superior reflexes and reactions, a neural superiority over the average Corpus Corps member. That was when he was well over a hundred years old chronologically.

"Second, and more important, he seems to have a long-range mission to bring down the Empire."

"Ridiculous!"

"It might be, except he seems to have time on his side. In addition, he understands technology. He was the Commandant of the Standora Base, the one who turned it from an obsolete scrapheap into the best refit yard in the Empire."

"That Gerswin?"

"But his interest seems to have turned to biologics after his retirement. The majority of his holdings and interests lie with ways to replace high technology with simplified biological processes."

"I'm not sure I follow that rationale."

"I am trying to make it simple. But think! The

power in Imperial society is based on the allocation of resources, the use and control of knowledge, and the ability to communicate. If Gerswin is successful in his biologics, the need to allocate resources is decreased, the need for high-level technical knowledge is reduced, and thus, communications control becomes less vital."

"That is rather theoretical, to say the least."

"One example. One of the products reputed to be his is a so-called house tree. All it needs is some simple wiring and power installation, and really not even that in some climates. What does that do to the construction industry, the heavy durables, the furniture manufacturers? What about the raw material suppliers?

"Another product is a biological spore sponge that cleans up anything. Another line of products features high-protein plants that can't be distinguished from meat in content and taste. They also grow anywhere. Who knows what else he may be getting ready to produce?"

"Wait a moment," protested the hooded figure to Eye's right. "That's all well and good, but you don't seriously think that the people of New Augusta are going back to growing their own food, no matter how tasty, and living in a tree house?"

"Of course not. That's not the point. If the outlying planets, or even a large number, take up societies based on biologics, what does the Empire have to offer? Why would anyone want to threaten them? Why would they need protection? Why would they need a large military establishment?"

"Ohhhh . . ."

"You see? Our resource basis is already so fragile that any large erosion of support would be difficult to deal with. But the Emperor and the Admiralty believe in due process, and Gerswin has stayed well within the law. Besides, an all-out effort is likely to make him a martyr, assuming that we could even succeed with a direct application of force.

"His profile indicates that he will revert to total survival, including homicide, if faced with a physical threat. This pattern is likely to dominate more as he gets older. There are some indications that this has already happened in one or two instances, but not that we could prove. Were someone to continue such pressure on him, however . . ."

"I see . . ."

The other deputy to Eye nodded. Once.

XXXVII

PING!

Engrossed as he was, the pilot of the Imperial scout jerked his head up from his Strat-Six battle with the scout's computer at the warning.

"Who could that be?"

"Identity unknown," answered the board.

The pilot glared at the system, which took no notice of the glare, and tapped several plates, then entered additional queries into the system.

"Whew!"

He checked the closure rates again. Then he put them on the display on the main screen, as if he could not believe them.

"Gwarrie," he addressed the computer, "are those figures correct?"

"Assuming the inputs are correct, the readouts are correct."

"Are the inputs correct?"

"The reliability of the inputs exceeds point nine."

The pilot jabbed the transmit stud.

"Hawkwatch, this is Farflung two. Contact. Quad four, radian zero seven zero. Closing at five plus. I say again. Closing at five plus. Data follows."

He shook his head. "That won't do it."

With the incoming alien, and it had to be an alien at that velocity—either that or something the I.S.S. had just invented—the stranger would be past him before he received the return transmission from Marduk Hawkwatch.

The Imperial pilot checked the stranger's indices once more.

The incoming ship, if it were truly a ship, had shifted course, directly toward Marduk. By now, the scout pilot doubted he could have caught the stranger.

He relayed the shift in heading with another data burst transmission, not bothering with a verbal tag.

"How close will she pass, Gwarrie?"

"More than two zero emkay."

"Can we get an enhanced visual?"

"Not within standard parameters."

The pilot frowned for a moment. "Let me know if there's another course shift. Your move."

XXXVIII

HAD IT BEEN VISIBLE TO THE NAKED EYE WITHOUT ITS LIGHT-less full-fade finish, the scout would have looked like an obsolete Federation scout. The energy concentrations within the dark hull resembled those of a miniature battlecruiser, while the screens could have taken anything that a full-sized light cruiser could have delivered.

Speed and power cost, and the trade-offs were crew size (one); offensive weapons (none); gravfield generators (crossbled to screens); and habitability (minimal by Imperial standards).

The pilot checked the signals from the modified message torps he waited to launch. There were three, each adapted to discharge two dozen reentry packets on its atmospheric descent spiral. Each packet contained the same spores and seeds, though the proportions varied.

"Unidentified craft, this is Marduk Control. Please identify yourself. Please identify yourself."

Gerswin smiled, but did not respond to the transmission, instead checked the distance readouts and his own EDI measurements of the Imperials who circled the planet ahead.

"Unidentified craft, this is Marduk control. Please be advised that Marduk is a prohibited planet. I say again. Marduk is a prohibited planet.

"Desct Mardu firet ortley . . ."

The Imperial patrol craft repeated its warning in a

dozen different languages, human and nonhuman.

All of them Gerswin ignored as the *Caroljoy* knifed toward Marduk, his hands coordinating the kind of approach he wanted, with enough evasiveness to make it unpredictable.

Gerswin also listened to the I.S.S. tactical bands as they were filtered through the AI and played out through the console speakers.

"Hawkwatch, Torchlove one, one to launch."

"Torchlove one, cleared to launch. Target course zero nine three, E plus three. One point two emkay."

"Hawkwatch, Torchlove two, one to launch."

"Torchlove two, cleared to launch. Target course, zero nine two, E plus three."

"Hawkwatch, Torchlove three, one to launch."

"Torchlove three, cleared to launch. Target course, zero nine zero, E plus three."

The man who had once been a Commodore smiled and touched the screens' generator status plate.

Satisfied with the readout, he nodded, then tightened the harness about him, and eased himself into the full accel/decel position, the controls at his fingertips, and the critical screen readouts projected before his eyes.

"Hawkwatch, this is Torchlove one. Target locked on EDI, no visual. Say again. Locked on EDI, no visual. Range point nine emkay."

"Hawkwatch, Torchlove two. No EDI lock. No visual."

"Torchlove one, two, three. Opswatch calculates target class one alpha. Class one alpha."

The *Caroljoy*'s pilot grinned sardonically. Class one alpha—high speed, armed, and dangerous. Two out of three wasn't bad for the Impies without even a visual.

"Torchlove one, two, and three. Recommend spread seven, spread seven, with jawbones. I said again, spread seven with jawbones."

Gerswin studied his own readouts.

The Hawkwatch Commander wasn't exactly rolling out the welcome mat, not when he was ordering a tachead spread for the *Caroljoy* to meet.

He also wasn't terribly bright, doing so in the clear. But then, it had been a long time since anyone challenged the Impies, and perhaps they were too slow on scrambles and codes to react. Or, more likely, who cared?

Gerswin touched the full-screen activation button, slumping into his seat under the acceleration as the screens took power diverted from the gravfield generators.

"Hawkwatch, Torchlove one. Lost EDI lock. Lost EDI lock. Still no visual."

"Hawkwatch, Torchlove two. Lost EDI."

"Torch three. No EDI. No visual."

"Torchlove one, two, and three. Launch spread seven based on DRI. Spread seven based on DRI . . ."

Gerswin eased the controls, tensing his stomach as the *Caroljoy* veered slightly—enough to confuse the DRI at his speed and with the screens the modified scout carried.

A sliver of blinding light appeared in the forward exterior screen—momentarily—before all exterior signals were damped to blackness.

The detonation of twenty-one tactical nuclear devices created a glare that would have been observable from the day side of Marduk itself, had there been anyone there to watch the fireworks.

Gerswin edged up his scout's speed, using his own screens and fields to bend the additional energy from the detonations into further boosting his own velocity.

"Torchlove one, two, three, EMP bleedoff indicates target fully operational and extremely dangerous. Probably position two eight five, E minus two."

"Hawkwatch, this is Torchlove one. Interrogative target position."

"Two eight five, E minus two. That's from you, Torch one, at point two emkay."

"Nothing's that fast!"

"Torchloves, interrogative last transmission."

". . . ssss . . ."

Gerswin would have laughed at the obvious silence had he not been pinned down in his shell, but smiling was difficult under the four plus gees.

"Hawkwatch, this is Torchlove two. Probability of contact of non-Imperial origin."

"Probability point eight. Calculated characteristics impute either higher gee tolerance or non-Imperial technology."

"Blithing alien . . ."

"Torchloves, interrogative last transmission."

A faint signal returned. "Interrogative yours."

"Torchloves, mission abort. Mission abort. Estimated target beyond spread range. Return to base. Return to base."

"Hawkwatch, Torchlove one. Stet. Returning to base."

Gerswin scanned the indicators, altered course again fractionally. The *Caroljoy* would skim by Marduk before lifting above the ecliptic for the long trip back to Aswan.

"Three until drop," the console informed him.

The pilot left his ostensibly obsolete scout on course until the three lights winked red in quick succession, then green.

"Torps away. Launch path is clear and green through reentry."

"Hawkwatch, Torch two. Target discharged missiles on reentry course for Basepath."

"Torchlove two, interrogative interception."

"Hawkwatch, that is negative."

"Understand negative."

"That's affirmative. Negative on intercept. Missile

reentry curve will commence prior to intercept."

"Torchlove two, hold data. Say again. Hold data for analysis."

"Hawkwatch, stet. Holding data for analysis. Returning base this time."

Gerswin debated releasing full screens to return normal gravity to the *Caroljoy*, but decided to hang on for another few minutes. It would be just like the Impies to have a few jokers planted around the system.

He altered course again, well within the general departure corridor, but enough to confuse a DRI tracker using the launch curves for the torps as its data base.

His screens blanked again.

"Distance and weapon?" he asked the AI.

"Three triple em cluster at point one emkay."

Nothing like proving yourself correct on the spot. He checked the screens, but they seemed to have held under what had been an extremely close miss.

"Impact near previous course line?"

"Impact less than point zero one from previous track."

Gerswin decided to leave the screens up longer than he had decided a few moments earlier.

"Hawkwatch, this is Turtlestrike. Target evaded DRI line, on high exit course Hawk system."

"Stet, Turtlestrike. Interrogative status."

"Status is red five from EMP backblast."

Gerswin translated. Turtlestrike, whatever craft that represented, had also been too close to the detonation and would be down for at least five stans, long after the *Caroljoy* had made the first of the return jumps toward Aswan.

Gerswin left the screens up, though he dropped acceleration to allow a gee drop to three gees, until he was within minutes of the jump point. Then, and only then, did he return to normal operations for the jump. The switch from three-gee acceleration to near weightlessness nearly cost him the pearapple he had eaten before he had entered the system.

He swallowed hard, gulping back the bitter taste of regurgitated fruit, and plowed through the pre-jump checks.

While the modified message torps carried enough of the spores and seeds to transform Marduk back into a livable planet, given several thousand, or more, years, the Imperial Interstellar Survey Service would still have Marduk as a source of supply for its toxic warheads for several dozen centuries, hopefully longer than the Empire would be around to use them.

He shook his head and touched the jump stud.

The stars winked out; the blackness swam through the *Caroljoy*; and, after a short infinity, another set of stars dropped into place as the scout resettled in real spacetime twenty systems from Marduk.

XXXIX

THE OVERLORDS OF TIME HAVE CALLED UPON THE UNDERlords of Order under the Edict of the West Wing of Chronology.

Listen . . .

Can you hear the whispers of the old papers rustling in the stacks where they were placed by the servators to ensure that the records would be complete?

Can you understand the mumbled words of the languages so old that their alphabets have been lost, so antique that outside of the Library no record exists of them or of those who spoke such soft sibilants?

Do you wonder who filled the Library, for it was neither repository nor refuge by design, but Hall of Destruction, built for the Ancients by the Gods of Nihil?

Do you stand in awe of the Black Gates that no tool can scratch, that not even the Empire could understand, and that the Commonality quietly refuses to see?

Hush . . .

In the silence that falls with the west mountain shadows, you may hear a set of footsteps, if you are in the right corridor, catch a glimpse of the Captain.

The Captain, you ask? That figment of imagination? That illusory paragon of legend? That satyric sire of our long afternoon? That man whom sages deny?

Hush . . .

Three steps, each lighter than the last, a silvered black tunic, and hawk-burned eyes—did you see? Did you dare to see?

Ahhh . . .

You turned your head, away from the sole chance you had to see the Captain as he was. For he was, and is, and will be, as we were, are, and will be.

The Shrine? That time-clouded prison? For now, it holds his body, his thoughts, but not his soul. Not his soul.

His soul is here, along the corridors designed to resist the fires of Hades, where you may see him if you are lucky, when twilight falls from the mountains across the Black Gates. His soul belongs not just to the gentle, nor to the green, nor to the ladies, but to the past, to the storms and the spouts.

One soul, one man, one barrier that separated the Gods of Nihil from the green of the new Old Earth, and you have missed the chance to see.

There never was a Captain, you say?

Are there none so blind as will not see? None so deaf as will not hear? None so alive as will not live?

Speak not of Faith! Faith is but a belief in what cannot be known, and the Captain was, is, and will be.

Knowing and known—the Captain, keeper of the Black
Gates . . .

> *Mystery of the Archives*
> Kyedra L. deKerwin
> New Denv, Old Earth
> 5231 N.E.C.

XL

THE CONTROLS MOVED EASILY UNDER HIS FINGERS, EVEN
though Gerswin had not used the flitter in more than a
year. All indicators were green, and the preflight check
had been clear.

Perhaps he was being overcautious. Even after setting down the *Caroljoy* on his own secluded property on
Mara, theoretically a hunting preserve not directly trace-
able to Gerswin and the Foundation or to his identity as
Patron L. Sergio Enver and the local subsidiary, Enver
Limited, which had taken over the commercial culturing
and production of the biological sponges that could
remove and decompose nearly any organic toxic, he was
skeptical. Skeptical about the workings of a sealed flitter
in a hidden bunker.

On top of the skepticism, he had doubts about the
wisdom of continuing to build biotech enterprises and
continuing to collect ever-increasing income, income he
was having more and more difficulty investing and
handling.

"So why do you keep at it?"

He wasn't sure he knew the answers to his own

questions, outside of the fact that Old Earth wasn't
ready for his return, outside of the fact that stopping
would require some serious thoughts and self-
evaluation. He pushed that away.

The contracts with New Glascow had represented a
nice boost to his personal holdings, besides leading to
the first steps in turning that smelter/manufacturing
planet into someplace livable—not that the New
Glascow Company knew that would be the end result of
using Enver products. All they knew was that if they
dumped the spores into waste piles they got total organic
breakdowns and heavy metals on the bottom of a settling
pond. In short, some water, some oxygen, carbon paste,
free hydrogen, and a gooey mess worth its weight in
metal for easy refining and recycling.

Someday, Gerswin suspected, when the air began to
clear and fish began to appear in all the streams, they'd
discover the overall picture. In the meantime, with a
modest take from the enterprises created from the
application of grant research, all properly licensed, of
course, Gerswin, under close to a dozen names, was able
to finance his own operations with but a token tap on the
Foundation budget, while pouring additional contributions into OERF.

He hoped that his efforts to keep separate from the
Foundation would limit the Imperial scrutiny, or delay it
somewhat.

As far as Enver, Limited, went, he was Patron L.
Sergio Enver, who preferred play to work, but who
occasionally visited the facilities and didn't complain
too much if his senior executives voted themselves
expensive bonuses—provided production and sales continued to increase and provided they kept their eyes
open for new biological technology opportunities.

Already, on Mara and other nearby systems, half a
dozen other competitors were using information stolen
from Enver.

Gerswin smiled as he thought of it. If they knew

how easy he had tried to make such theft! You could offer knowledge on a silver platter, and no one would take it. Once you made money with it, suddenly people would cut throats for it.

He cocked his head as he listened to the whine of the turbines. Despite its inactivity, the flitter handled well, and the engine indicators were normal.

Sooner or later, he knew, the Empire would come calling, and he would have to leave precipitously. Perhaps that was why he avoided worrying about continuing, preferring to leave that decision up to the Empire. The coward's way out . . .

He tapped the signal for the homer as the flitter neared the local Enver headquarters. While he did not announce his visits in detail, he did not want to catch his loyal employees totally by surprise. Usually, he sent a message torp indicating the general time of his next inspection.

Here, on the main continent, the sun had dropped behind the western hills, and the twilight had fled for solid night.

Gerswin dropped the flitter into a sloping descent toward the rooftop pad reserved for the Patron of Enver, Limited. The homer signal remained green on the screen.

As the flitter slowed, he closed his eyes and triggered the flash strobes, searing the roof with a blaze of light. In the following instant, he cut all exterior lights, and the flitter settled onto the hard-surfaced building.

Releasing the canopy of the old-fashioned combat model flitter, Gerswin dropped to the roof on the right side, the side of the fuselage that had no handholds or extended footbars.

With his own unhampered night vision, he could see the watchman rubbing his eyes. But beyond the control bubble . . . was there another figure?

The pilot flattened behind the right stub skid, bringing his stunner to bear.

Two figures with long rods that suspiciously resembled projectile rifles were sighting on the flitter. Their quick reaction to the blinding glare he had flooded the landing pad with meant that they wore night glasses to protect their vision. Night glasses on the roof meant some level of government. Competitors would have used poison, long-range sniping, or some other less violent or more stealthy method.

Government involvement also meant that the pair wore conductive stun armor and helmets.

Gerswin estimated the distance from the flitter skid to the low wall from behind which the two agents waited. Slightly more than thirty meters.

He had to act, and quickly!

In seconds, they would start looking for the pilot, one Gerswin, and, on finding him, calmly riddle his position with whatever projectiles they were carrying —fragmentation, straight shells, or gas.

Thirty meters was too far for the stunner, even without their armor to consider, and certainly too far for the throwing knives.

Gerswin settled on the watchman, who had to be an accomplice, tacitly or otherwise.

A weak distraction, but better than none.

The watch bubble was fifteen meters away, on an indirect line between him and the agents.

Thrumm!

The first stunner bolt flared on the bubble, the second through the open door. It staggered the watchman.

Gerswin sprinted.

He made it halfway to the pair before the taller of the two agents, catching the motion from the corner of his eye, whirled.

Gerswin pumped his mad rush an instant longer, then dived low and rolled to the left, zigging forward, and coming up with the knife.

Scrttt.

Clunk.

The other agent brought her weapon around, hampered by its length, even as the taller one went down, his weapon echoing on the roof.

Whuppp.

Before she could get the barrel toward Gerswin, he knocked it from her hands and swept her feet from underneath her.

The woman tried to bring her legs to play, but he twisted and dropped his full weight onto his right knee, which slammed into the side of her neck. The dull crack and instant limpness of her body signaled her death.

Gerswin followed her down, dropping behind the ledge that had not been sufficient shelter for the agents, and reached for the projectile rifle.

Strummm!

The frequency of the stun bolt—heavy-duty military model—confirmed his earlier impression of the watchman.

Still flat, he glanced at the first agent, wearing a dull marauder-issue camouflage armor and matching helmet, twitching with the knife through his chest, though each shudder was slower and the time between each longer.

Gerswin edged along the walkway, head below the coping level, until he could retrieve the knife. Before he could pull the knife out, the man shuddered a last time and was still.

As the man in business gray checked the long weapon, he discovered it was configured for frag rounds. He squirmed another meter toward the watch bubble, keeping his body well below the wall.

A quick look, and he squeezed off one round.

Crummppp.

He squirmed farther, and tried another.

Crummppp.

There was no answering fire.

Several meters farther, nearly at the corner, he darted another look, then slowly peered once more.

The watchman was sprawled halfway through the open bubble port, and the darkness spread across his shoulders was not sweat.

Now what?

He could leave, if he left immediately, before the reinforcing troops discovered that the wrong man had survived. But then he wouldn't know what was behind it all.

Besides, if the Impies had really known what was happening, they would not have pulled such a weak operation. So it hadn't been organized by the Imperial government.

A good Imperial records check would have resulted in a direct assault or investigation of the Foundation itself, either with more finesse or with overwhelming force.

He would have shrugged as he moved toward the watch bubble and the lift house behind it, but he saw the glimmer of light.

"Once again."

He took a deep breath and charged the portal, managing to cross the ten meters and drop into the darkness behind the side of the portal as the two replacement guards walked out. The portal closed before they were even fully aware that something might be wrong.

The right-hand guard turned toward Gerswin, something in his hand.

Crummpp!

The shot turned the marauder uniform into scraps of flesh and cloth.

Before the second guard could turn, Gerswin reversed the weapon and brought the stock into his diaphragm even as he knocked aside the guard's weapon hand.

Leaving both the dead guard and the unconscious one where they lay, Gerswin scrabbled around to the back side of the lift shaft, looking for the concealed access port he knew was hidden there.

His fingers traced the outline, and he backed away. A snap kick, and the plate fragmented, as designed.

He reached down and punched the three studs in one of the preset combinations and, without waiting, scrambled back to the front of the lift where the remaining living guard was dragging himself toward his weapon.

Gerswin kicked it away, pulled the stunner from his pouch and fired.

Thrummppp!

At that range, even the guard's armor offered little protection. His knees and legs buckled him into an untidy heap.

Keeping one eye on the lift portal, Gerswin picked up the body of the unconscious guard and carried it to the flitter, quickly locking the now disarmed man into the cargo bay.

His return flight was likely to be very quick, followed by an even quicker departure on the *Caroljoy*.

Before he made that flight, he needed to claim whatever he could from the latest of the ongoing work and see if he could determine what exactly had occurred.

Returning to the lift shaft access portal, he pulled a respirator pack from the recesses and pulled it over his nose and mouth, then, stunner in one hand and frag gun in the other, he returned to the lift port and touched the stud.

While the light poured out, no one stood on the lift landing. He crossed the landing and peered down the shaft. Empty.

First things first.

He dropped to the private loading dock where his shipments were assembled, not that they were addressed as such, nor did even the Enver company employees know the real addressee. The official labels announced a destination as Research Center, c/o Drop Five, New Aberdeen.

There were three packages, total weight roughly ten kilos. Gerswin debated, finally dropped the stunner. Anyone who was awake after the dosage of sleep gas that had flooded the building and the others in the complex would be hunting and shooting to kill.

With the frag gun in his left hand and the three packages tucked under his left arm, he eased up the three flights of emergency stairs to his office, officially the office of the Patron, Enver, Limited.

Instead of using the main portal, he walked to the storage closet at the end of the corridor, avoiding the three sprawled bodies in Planetary Guard marauder suits, and opened it, twisting the end of a shelf like a lever, then tapping a code on the plate that appeared.

Inside the spacious office were five more unconscious forms, one in a marauder uniform, two in dress Guard uniforms, and two in civilian dress.

Gerswin studied the office, since he wouldn't see it again, ran his eyes over the Enver seal on the wall behind the wood-paneled executive console, and surveyed the twin leather and chrome couches, the conference table with the underslung recliners, and the Saincleer replica on the inside wall above the low old-fashioned bookcase.

The original Saincleer was for Lyr; she'd mentioned once how she admired the artist. It looked as though she would receive it a bit sooner than he had thought, provided he finished up and stopped meandering.

Gerswin turned his attention to the older of the two civilians—the one with the short blond hair and square chin, with the incipient potbelly.

The planetary premier—the same man who had taken the credit for landing Enver, Limited, as a major new employer—had apparently regretted his action.

Why?

Gerswin frowned. He would love to know why Alerio had decided on or accepted such strong-arm tactics.

He shook his head, glanced back at the Saincleer

replica, then at the premier. The only possibility was the Empire—the only possibility.

He gathered a few small items from the console as he considered the implications.

Item—if the Empire had actually decided to move against Gerswin and the OER Foundation, then there would have been some rumors on New Augusta.

Item—if the Empire were to move, then the I.S.S. or the Corpus Corps would have been involved, not the Maran Planetary Guard.

Item—Alerio could not have had access to the Privy Council or the Emperor.

Conclusion?

Gerswin laughed once, silently, behind his respirator pack.

Eye Corps had set up Alerio to set up Gerswin, to give Eye the excuse to declare him an enemy of the Empire.

The decisions were all already made. All he had to do was to move faster than the Empire.

He stood by the executive console and tapped in a series of numbers, waiting for the acknowledgment. When the confirmation came, he tapped in another set of numbers on a tight beam to the *Caroljoy*. Those would begin the evacuation options for Lyr. Once he returned to the ship and broke orbit, the message torps would take care of the rest. At least in that area, he had anticipated the need.

He waited, then tried to access Enver data. The screen remained blank. He tried the most urgent priority codes, but the result was the same. No data.

Finally, he entered the last code.

The data in the files was gone—entirely gone. Within twenty-four hours, the buildings of Enver, Limited, on Mara would cease to exist. That might even buy his competitors, and their stolen techniques, some time before the Empire realized their enemy was not Gerswin, but the changes in society bound to occur as his biologics became more widely accepted.

Gerswin took a final glance around the office he used perhaps fifty times and left through the storage closet.

The corridor was still deserted, but he used the emergency steps to the roof—three more flights.

Once in the open air, he could hear the distant sirens converging. After sprinting to the flitter, he dumped the guard from the cargo bay onto the roof, then scrambled into the flitter, beginning the take-off sequences even as he strapped in.

The fading scream of thrusters on full power, four dead and one unconscious guard, and dust swirling over them were all that the Maran backup force found on the roof.

The Maran Planetary Guard's atmospheric strike force—thirty assorted flitters and skitters—arrived at a dusty field in a distant corner of the remote hunting preserve of the Count de Mermont just in time to feel the concussions created by the hasty departure of a high-powered and unseen spacecraft.

Orbit control tracked, but failed to intercept, the streaking ship that ignored all departure procedures and conventions.

XLI

THE SCREEN CHIMED, AND SHE ACKNOWLEDGED.

At the blond hair and yellow eyes, she smiled, but her smile was wiped away by his first words.

"Are you all right? Is there anyone with you?"

Normally, he launched into whatever he had in mind.

"Yes, I'm fine. And there's no one here except the normal staff. Why?"

"You have reservations on the luxury transport *Empress of Isabel* from the Imperial shuttle port tomorrow morning. Take only what you would take on a short vacation. Everything else has been arranged. The necessary documents and itinerary are in your name at the normal Halsie-Vyr drop."

"In my name?"

He ignored her question and continued onward.

"The *Empress* is an Analexian ship operated for profit, and the human quarters are quite opulent, I assure you. I thought the change would be beneficial."

"Why? I just can't drop everything and run off on a vacation." She brushed a gray hair off her forehead.

"You'll understand once you're aboard. I can't explain further. Take too much time, and time is short."

"Can't it wait?"

"No. Get your itinerary from Halsie-Vyr and get on the *Empress*." Although he did not raise his voice, his eyes seemed to leap through the screen at her, and in all the years she did not recall such intensity directed at her.

Perhaps she was tired, for she found herself saying, "Of course. Will I see you there?"

Instead of answering directly, the image softened.

"Take care, Lyr. Take care."

And the screen, with the background of the scout, blanked as suddenly as he had called.

As she stared at the vacant console, she began to worry. After the first conflicts, the Commander had almost never ordered her to do anything. While going on an expensive vacation was not an onerous order, there had to be more to it than met the eye. With him, there always was.

Then, too, he had seemed rushed, almost as if he were trying to complete a long list of tasks without enough time.

Finally, unlike him, about whom she knew more than he realized, or at least more than he let on she knew, Lyr was not the adventurous type once the subject got beyond financial management.

And he was promising an adventure.

XLII

"CAN YOU EXPLAIN IT?"

"No, ser. I can measure the changes, but that's about all."

The Commandant of Recorps, Old Earth, cleared his throat. "Environmental improvements suddenly occurring, and we haven't any explanation?"

He glared around the conference room, ignoring the

blotches on the walls that indicated all too clearly the age of the building. "So what are we doing? Why are we holding together antique dozers with Imperial castoffs? Why are we risking lives day after day on the offshore purification pumps? Why are we working nights to educate shamblers?"

"Commander." The voice came from the woman, but it was cold and deep enough to chill the conversation.

"Commander," she began again, "whatever biological processes are involved are localized cases, at least so far. We cannot track the cause, only the results, and so far they have shown up in the Rhyn River effluent. There may be others, of course. While there are changes in the forest patterns near the river, with increased undergrowth, these are so far inconclusive.

"In the meantime, Recorps has reclaimed nearly thirty percent of the most arable land left in Noram, plus nearly all the High Plains area. We have similar successes, albeit on a later time line, in Norcan and the Brits. No one else has even tried so much."

"Except the Captain . . ." That unspoken thought loomed. Or had someone voiced it?

"You're right, Mercelle," observed the Commander with a tired shrug. "Hard to keep things in perspective. We'll keep at it, keep track, and see if nature will at last give us a hand. Istvenn knows we deserve it."

"We forget," added Mercelle, "that biological cleaning is a gradual process. Sometimes, you can't tell it's even taking place. Besides, until an entire region is clean, it really isn't complete. In the meantime, we finally have an increasing population that needs the new ground we reclaim every year.

"For the first time, we're actually making an export surplus from the luxury items. Not much, but it's positive."

"And," added the Executive Officer, "we need to keep that progress up to justify the budget from the Privy Council."

"Right. The budget, always the budget," concluded the Commander sardonically. The logic was clear. With all the increasing pressures on the Imperial Treasury, and the decreasing revenues from the associated systems, unless Recorps could show continued numbers of hectares reclaimed annually, as well as an increased amount of resupply goods for visiting fleets, Recorps would be cut to what it could subsist on from foreign exchange from its minuscule exports, and that was nothing by comparison.

What else could they trade on but tradition —tradition, reclamation, and sentiment?

He pushed aside the thought that someday, someday, sentiment would not be enough. Nor would the tradition of Old Earth be sufficient.

That was when they would need the mythical Captain!

XLIII

THREE MARINES, CLAD IN FULL BATTLE ARMOR, WHEELED THE laser cutter up to the portal.

A combat squad deployed behind the three technicians in the corridor of the building which had been sealed off. All the other offices had already been evacuated, silently, and one by one.

The senior Marine technician gestured. The deployed troops dropped their visors, and the two other techs began to bring the laser on line.

The bright and thin purple lance of the cutter was

nearly invisible as it knifed through the endurasteel casement of the portal, a reinforced structure designed to resist anything less.

Thud!

The tiles of the corridor carried the vibration as the entire portal assembly fell inward into the office it had served and guarded.

More than a dozen Marines sprinted into the office —a space totally empty of people—sweeping the area with stunners to ensure that the smoke caused by the abrupt rise in temperature created by the use of the laser did not hide anyone.

Their duty completed, the assault squad returned to their deployed positions as the I.S.S. technical specialists who had been waiting behind the barricades trooped forward into the office.

The most senior technician, white-haired, thin-faced, sat down at the main console, the one with the finish below the keyboard dulled with age.

He frowned at the unfamiliar layout of the symbols.

"Logart, this is an old Ferrin model, updated with Usart couples."

"Ferrin? Never heard of it."

"Ferrin Symbs hasn't turned out anything since the twenties, maybe earlier."

"What was this place?"

"Some Foundation. According to the offreq scans, used as a cover for some of the Atey rebs. OER Foundation, I think the name was."

The third tech, a dark brunette who was inventorying records, decorations, and other loose items not actually in the databanks, looked up with a puzzled expression.

"Jocham, this is original equipment."

"So?"

"So," answered the white-haired tech, "that means this place has been around a lot longer than the Atey movement."

"How do you figure that?"

"Simple—"

"Techs," interrupted a fourth voice, one belonging to a figure wearing a privacy cloak over full-space armor, "all speculations are better confined to your official report, and backed by specifics."

The senior tech saw the woman about to complain, not realizing the organization the armored man represented, and cut her off.

"Geradyn, official reports, as the Eye Service has requested. Official reports, with all relevant data."

Geradyn blanched. "I didn't . . ."

She broke off her statement and returned to her inventory under the shadowed eyes of the Intelligence Service officer who paced from one side of the OER Foundation offices to the other.

The white-haired technician almost smiled, but replaced the expression with a more appropriate frown as he began to attempt the indexing job, based on the fragmentary codes provided by the Intelligence Service.

The screen remained blank, but the energy levels indicated it was functioning.

Somehow, he did not know how, though he could have devised an equivalent method, the use of force had resulted in the entire data set being destroyed.

Outside of hard-copy reports, the Eye Service wasn't about to find out much new about whatever the OER Foundation had done, or what it had been.

He did not voice his opinion, but, instead, continued to try all possible methods for discovering or recovering the dumped information, but, suspected, based on the codes already provided, that neither he nor the best from Eye Service would have much luck.

These conclusions, of course, he would reserve for the official reports, submitted after all efforts had failed.

The Intelligence officer continued to pace as the Marines waited outside.

XLIV

"LORD ADMIRAL, WE DO NOT HAVE THE RESOURCES TO KEEP this up much longer."

The silver-haired Admiral silently studied the figures on the inset screen before him, his lips quirking.

"You realize that, ser?"

The silence resumed as the Service chief refused to comment.

Teeth chewing at his lower lip, the Commodore glanced back at his own screen, wondering if the Admiral was studying the same simple projections his own screen held, wondering why it took so long for the man to respond.

"What is interesting, Ambester, is what is not on the screen."

"Ser?"

The Admiral glared at the Commodore, momentarily ignoring the other two more junior flag officers.

"We can provide the more detailed backup information, if you would like."

"More data never solved any problem, Commodore. Hades few, anyway." He paused, then inquired, "Has anyone investigated *why* there are more quarantines? With the relaxations on local armed monitors and greater local autonomy, one would expect fewer quarantines, not more. None of your information addresses that."

"Political problems are followed by the Ministry of Internal Affairs."

"Have you contacted them?"

"No, ser."

"Then I suggest you do. Your data is clear on one point. We cannot continue to enforce quarantines at this rate. It's also clear on another. The conditions creating unrest and local political breakdowns are increasing. Any of you could see that."

His hard gray eyes raked the three other officers.

"So why didn't anyone ask the reasons? You all know the resource pressures on the Service."

There was no answer.

"Last question. Does anyone else have this synthesis?"

All three heads nodded in the negative.

"I doubt that either, but maybe not very many people know yet. Now get me that information. We'll probably need to get together with Internal Affairs."

The Admiral pushed back his swivel and stood. Nodding abruptly, he turned and left the small conference room.

XLV

AS SOON AS THE FLITTER TOUCHED DOWN AT THE LANDING PAD above the chalet, she jumped out, feeling twenty years younger, or more, in the cool, light mountain air.

The chalet was just as she had imagined, from the wide balconies that jutted from three sides, from the view overlooking Deep Loch to the crags both behind the chalet and across the Loch on the far side of the valley.

Her steps felt lighter than they had in years, not surprisingly, considering the treatments she had received, and she smiled as her feet touched the wide wooden planks of the balcony.

After a long look down at the crystalline green of the loch, she took slow steps down to the rear portal of the chalet, which the land agent had opened for her.

Inside, the spaciousness was more than she had anticipated. The off-white rough finish of the walls, the light wood beams, and the expanse of lightly tinted armaglass all added to the openness while retaining a feeling of warmth.

In the main living area stood a stone hearth and fireplace with real wood to burn, and off from the fireplace was the study she had always coveted.

She stepped inside the study, and her mouth dropped in an amazement she was not sure she could have felt. Above the simple desk, which she admired in passing, was an original oil by Saincleer, one she had never seen, and one which probably cost more than the chalet itself.

Whoever had furnished the chalet, and she could guess but did not want to speculate, yet, had known her tastes.

Some of the pieces she might move slightly, and perhaps one or two she might not have chosen, but the overall effect was spectacular; exactly the sort of home she had wanted, but one which she had never spent the time to discover or to have built, had she been able to afford such a place, let alone in such a location.

"You approve?" The agent was a young local woman who had met her at the Vers D'Mont shuttle port and who had presented a card that had matched the directions included with her itinerary.

"Approve . . . approve? It's magnificent!"

"There is a message."

Lyr saw the envelope, sitting alone on the desk under the Saincleer

Lyr.

That was all that was on the outside, and she wondered if the script were his. She shook her head. To think after all the years that she had never seen his writing.

She did not open it immediately, but held the envelope in both hands.

There was so much she had not known, had not anticipated—from the impossibly expensive rejuve treatments reserved for her aboard the *Empress* to the star-class accommodations, to the flowers every night, and the personally tailored wardrobe.

She wondered if she dared to open it, or if she dared not to.

After her years of priding herself on being the type not to be overwhelmed, she asked herself whether the Commander had set out to overwhelm her. First, the star-class passage on the *Empress*, then the identity as Baroness Meryon Von Lyr, with all the supporting documents, and the sizable credit balance with Vinnifin-Yill, and now a chalet retreat on Vers D'Mont that might be the envy of most commercial magnates of the Empire.

So why did she feel something was missing?

She took one deep breath, then another, and brought the envelope up to her eyes, not that she needed to now. Her eyesight had been restored to what it had been more than fifty years earlier, along with her figure, muscle tone, and hair.

After a time, she opened the envelope.

The single, plain cream-colored sheet was folded in half, and she unfolded it. His message was half-printed, half-scripted, looking more childish than she would have thought.

Again, she looked away, lowering the message without reading it, and stared without seeing at the loch glistening in the white gold of the early afternoon sunlight.

The faint cry of a circling soareagle roused her, and she looked back down at the black words.

Lyr—
As you may have guessed, Lyr D'Meryon no longer exists. She died in a tragic fire in her Murian Tower dwelling. Only the Baroness Von Lyr remains.

She brushed back a stray hair, a lock which, with all the others, had been restored to its original sandy blond shade, and which, she had been told, would retain the natural color for at least another half century. Still holding the envelope in her right hand, she glanced out through the armaglass at the crags across the loch and then back inside, not wanting to open the envelope.

She settled on the vidcube library, filled with cubes, and the antique built-in bookshelves, overflowing with neatly arranged volumes.

She blinked back a single tear, and looked down at the envelope, then at the land agent.

The other woman apparently understood.

"If there is anything you need, let me know. Your own flitter is hangared underneath. There is some food, as well."

Lyr swallowed hard before speaking.

"Has anyone . . . lived . . ."

"No. It has been kept for you. No one, not even the man in gray, has ever spent the night here. About that, he was quite adamant."

Lyr could feel her eyes beginning to fill, turned away from the other, and sank into the corner of the long white couch that had been placed exactly where she would have placed it.

She still clutched the envelope.

Through the swirl of her feelings, she could hear the

rear portal close as the other left, hear the whine as the
flitter lifted, and the silence that dropped around her like
a cushion.

After a time, she looked back down at the envelope.
The top of the *L* was blurred where a tear had fallen on
the black ink.

> First, cold details. In addition to the
> Vinnifin-Yill account, you have an account with
> the local trust, Gerherd, Limited, and another
> account on Ydris with Flournoy Associates. Sun-
> dry other assets to match your background are
> listed in the console memory under your personal
> key.
>
> The chalet is yours, fee simple outright in
> perpetuity, and there is a townhouse in New
> Mont'plier if you yearn for a more urban exis-
> tence at times.
>
> The Empire will fall, perhaps in your life-
> time, which should be long, perhaps not. It is one
> reason for the diversity of your holdings. But
> stand clear of New Augusta.
>
> By now, the Empire has seized the Founda-
> tion and the remaining assets, although there is
> no data left to track, and has an alert out for me,
> both for crimes against the Emperor and other
> offenses. I intend to avoid the Empire for a time,
> until it will not matter.
>
> I wish I could have told you more, or that I
> dared now. You trusted me, made my future
> dreams possible. I have given what I can, poor
> repayment. Knowing you, it is poor indeed.
>
> Knowing me, it is for the best.
>
> G

Lyr finally rose from the perfectly placed white
couch, though she could not see through the cascade of
tears, and walked toward the armaglass door that
opened as she neared the balcony. Her shoulder brushed

the casement as she stepped onto the wooden planks.

Though she shuddered with the weight of more tears than she could ever shed, her eyes cleared, and she clutched the letter in one hand and the smoothed wood of the rail with the other, and stood on the shaded balcony, with the breeze through her hair.

In the afternoon quiet, in the light and in the cool of the gentle wind, the shudders subsided, and so did Administrator Lyr.

As the breeze died, the Baroness Von Lyr wiped the last tear, the very last tear ever, from her eyes and turned back toward her perfect chalet.

She did not notice that the darkness behind her eyes matched what she had seen behind her Commander's eyes.

XLVI

EACH MAN EXPECTS HIS DAY IN THE SUN. EACH GOD RAISED BY a culture may expect not days, but centuries in the brilliance of adoration and worship.

On men and gods alike, in the end, night falls. For men, that darkness comes with merciful swiftness, but for gods and heroes, the idols of a race, the darkness may never come, as they hang suspended in the glow of an endless twilight, their believers dwindling, but unable to turn away, their accomplishments distorted or romanticized, and their characters slowly bleached into mere caricature.

Under some supreme irony, the greater the hero, the greater the power attributed to the god, the longer and

more agonizing the twilight of belief, as if each moment
of power and each great deed requires more than mere
atonement . . .

> *Of Gods and Men*
> Carnall Grant
> New Avalon
> 5173 N.E.C.

XLVII

"... RELEASE ALL FURTHER INTEREST IN YDRISIAN UNITED
Commuications for other good and valuable considerations, as outlined in the addendum."

The pilot paused and reread the lines on the data
screen. Possibly not as legalistic as it should be, but the
Empire would hesitate to take on the Ydrisians, and the
release of his interests would deprive them of their
strongest pretext. That was the best he could do. Had he
been wise enough to divest himself of the residual ten
percent interest in the network, the question would have
been moot a century earlier.

His eyes blurred. The text was the last in the series,
and the AI had already programmed the torp. He had
earlier loaded the necessary physical documents.

Isbel's granddaughter would be surprised to receive
actual documents from the torp, but there was no
helping it. The Empire was not about to try to intercept
even a single incoming torp to the Ydrisian hub station,
not with the outlying systems wanting their own pre-
texts.

"What is the girl's name?" he mumbled, aware that

his words were slurring from the mental effort of trying
to wind up all the financial angles of his businesses.

"Inquiry imprecise."

"Well aware my inquiry is imprecise . . . not directed at you. Directed at my own confused memories."

Isbel—that was the old Port Captain, and her
daughter was Fienn. But Fienn's daughter?

That was the trouble with all his enterprises and all
his contacts. After nearly three frantic centuries, the
faces, the scents, and the names became harder and
harder to separate. Not when he saw people face-to-face
—that wasn't the problem, because the reality sorted out
the recollections—but when he was by himself trying to
sort them out.

Fienn's daughter?

Murra? Had that been it?

"Interrogative destination code, Ydrisian Hub, for
Port Captain Murra Herris Relyea."

"That is affirmative. Code on screen delta."

The pilot sighed. "Stet. Torp two to destination
code for Port Captain Murra Herris Relyea."

He tapped the complete block for the material on
his data screen, the message to Murra that would explain
her obligation.

Simply put, in return for the ten percent interest she
was receiving from him, she had to transmit the transactions and instructions packed into the message torp to
their addresses—all various Gerswin enterprises. He
had done his best to divest himself of such interests, if
only to keep the Empire at bay. Some of those concerns
would survive. Some would not, but most of the techniques they had brought into commercial acceptance
would survive, along with the increased levels of biologic
technology.

He wished he had left himself the time to conduct
the last steps of divestiture himself, but he wasn't about
to try, not with three Imperial squadrons reputed as
committed to find him.

Far safer to leave the remainder to the Ydrisians.

They owed him, and they knew they owed him. And
Ydrisians paid their debts. No matter what the cost.
Always.

That brought up another question.

Debts.

"And have you paid yours?"

He did not bother to shake his head, knowing the
answer. Like an insolvent institution, he had not rendered full repayment on each credit. Like a chronic
gambler, he had bet more than he had, using other
people when he could not cover his bets. Other people,
like Lerwin, and Kiedra, like the poor altruistic
Ydrisians, like Lyr. Especially like Lyr.

Her whole life had gone to the Foundation, nothing
more than a charade and a cover for his determination
to reclaim Old Earth. She might guess, but would never
know, could never know, how successful that real mission had been.

While he had given her back some of those lost years
through the extensive medical therapy and rejuves he
had arranged for her, he had led her on with promise
after promise . . . and had never delivered.

"Will I see you there?" Those had been her last
words, and he had not even answered them.

For a time, his eyes looked beyond the views on the
screens before him, beyond the exterior view of the
uninhabited system where he orbited while he completed his last Imperial-related business. He saw neither
sun nor stars, recalling, instead, a sandy-haired woman,
earnest and intense, and the warm wood of an exclusive
private club.

How many trusting souls had he led on? How many
had there been, particularly women, each thinking he
had given them something, when he had no more than
given them a glimpse?

Caroljoy . . . Faith . . . Kiedra . . . Allison . . . Lyr . . .

Those were the ones it had hurt for him to hurt. But
had it stopped him?

And what of the others, the ones he had blazed past in hours or days, never turning back, his eyes on a future that might never come to pass?

"Interrogative dispatch instructions," asked the AI, the cool tones of the disembodied intelligence cutting through his memories.

"Dispatch torp two."

"Dispatching torp two."

With another sigh, the pilot turned his attention to the controls, and to the jump-point plots.

"Time to jump point?"

"Two point five."

He touched the controls and began to plot the coordinates and course line manually, rather than letting the AI do it, understanding that he did so not only to prove his abilities, but to avoid the memories that seemed ever more ready to spill out and to draw him into endless self-debate.

He frowned, pursing his lips, as he watched the plot, wondering how quickly the Empire would act, or whether it would bother, for all the rumors, for all the speculations reported so far.

There were arguments for every possibility.

He shrugged. One way or another, he was going home. Although it was no longer the home he had known, there was no other place that could or would claim him.

He sealed the course, leaning back in the couch.

After a time of keeping his thoughts blank, he dozed, trying to push too many shadowy figures back into his subconscious, half waiting for the time when the AI would sound the chime that signified that the jump point was approaching.

Cling!

"Jump point approaching."

"Stet."

He scanned the board, twice, then ran through the parameters . . . feeding in three possible post-jump courses, probably unnecessary, since the odds of an

Imperial patrol being within an emkay of his reentry were minuscule. If the odds, however long, were wrong, he needed to be ready.

"Ready for jump."

The pilot scanned the screens and the data board one more time, his survey still conforming to the military patterns he had learned so well and so long ago.

"Jump."

The familiar black-white flash that seemed instantaneous and endless enfolded the ship and its pilot, then deposited them on the outlying edge of the arrival/departure corridor for a G-type sun, one no different than any other from the distance at which the scout emerged.

"EDI traces toward system center."

"Interrogative distance."

"Beyond one standard hour at standard reentry velocity."

"Interrogative closure."

"That is negative."

The pilot frowned at himself. He should have realized after all the years that there would be no closure —not yet. His instruments were picking up EDI traces that could have been hours old. It would be several minutes more, at least, before the Impie patrol, if that was what the traces represented, picked up his reentry.

"Full screens. Commence acceleration at one gee toward contact."

"Commencing acceleration. Full screens in place."

As the *Caroljoy* began the inward trip, the pilot began to study the information as it built upon the screens before him. Given the angles and the placement, and his own energy reserves, there was no way to avoid some confrontation, and the straight-line approach he had picked would minimize his exposure.

He continued to study the data, sometimes nodding, sometimes frowning, but mostly waiting. Waiting until the pattern and the distances became clear enough for his actions.

As the ancient scout slipped in-system, the silence in the control cabin remained unbroken except for the hissing of the ventilators and the occasional click of the pilot's fingers on the control board.

The numbers on the data screens changed, as did the locations of the contacts on the representational screens, but the pilot said nothing as he watched those changes, as he watched his ship as it neared the Imperial patrols.

Finally, he touched the control panel, and the speakers hissed into life.

"Double eye, this is Longshot one. Jump entry wave at one eight five, plus point five."

"Interrogative characteristics."

"Negative this time. Negative EDI trace. Could be mid-jump. Sending data track."

The pilot of the incoming scout smiled, relaxed as his course curved him above the normal reentry plane path. Transecliptic courses used more energy, but he wasn't planning a return.

"Longshot one, this is Double eye. Data track indicates incoming is target. Probability exceeds point eight. Suggest optical distortion scan. Track against standing wave. Target screens capable of EDI block."

"What in Hades else does he have?"

"Target capable of higher acceleration than standard scout."

"Ist—" The rest of the transmission was cut off.

Gerswin smiled. The fact that the Intelligence-ordered intercept group did not have all the information on the *Caroljoy* made it possible—just possible—that he could get almost on top of the outlying pickets before they realized his speed.

What he would do when he got close to Old Earth was another question, since he could not attempt atmospheric entry without deceleration. Not if he wanted to arrive planetside in fragments larger than dust particles.

His hands continued to flash across the controls, more from habit than from necessity.

Cling!

"Contact, zero zero five relative, thirty emkay, minus one," observed the AI.

"Stet. Continuing present course," returned the pilot.

The *Caroljoy* would pass nearly one emkay above the corvette.

"Interrogative probability of detection at ten emkay. Assume contact has optical distortion scanners."

"Probability of detection by contact is point two at ten emkay."   .

Gerswin checked his harness, then rechecked the scout's energy status and the projected reaction times.

At the moment of detection, he would have twenty-two seconds before the Imperial ships' optical distorters would register a change in his speed or acceleration. The lag time was critical. For Service torps to travel faster than ships, they had to make mini-jumps, and such jumps did not allow course adjustments in flight. When both combatants were moving slowly, around orbital speeds, the torp drives were most effective. At higher speeds in deep space, the torps lacked maneuverability and required good predetermined target positions.

Gerswin shook his head. He couldn't remember the maximum gee acceleration for Service ships. After so many years in Service, he couldn't remember?

Rather than voice his inquiry, he put it through the data console. Number in hand, he set the *Caroljoy*'s first acceleration burst for thirty seconds at ten percent above the Service maximum. Then he programmed in a series of course changes, applied at differing intervals than the acceleration changes, that would lead his scout back toward the normal reentry channel, but behind the picket line.

"Interrogative range to contact."

"Nine minus emkay."

Gerswin's gut tightened, and he tapped the preprogrammed acceleration/course sequence into action, grunting as the gentle pressure pushed him back into the shell. While he had hoped to wait until he had been closer, his instincts had insisted he not delay.

As if to confirm his feelings, the screens flared and blanked, and the speakers relayed the tactical Imperial frequencies.

"Contact. One eight zero, system orient, at *plus five relative*. Spread one away."

Gerswin shivered. Even with his experience, it was unnerving to have the detonation arrive before the announcement of its dispatch.

No sooner had the *Caroljoy*'s screens cleared than they blanked again, despite his course changes.

"Longshot two, this is Double eye. Interrogative target acquisition."

"Double eye, Longshot two. Negative this time."

"Double eye, Longshot one. Negative on spread. Target undamaged. Second spread away."

Gerswin pursed his lips, waiting for the AI's report.

"Detonation patterns ranging from one five zero to two one zero relative. Point zero five emkay."

Gerswin changed heading, nearly at right angles, and triggered another acceleration burst.

Once more, the screens cleared, only to blank with the flash of another detonation.

"Double eye, Longshot one. Spread three away. Interrogative instructions on spread four."

"One, Double eye. Fire on best track data."

Gerswin grinned. With luck, all he had to worry about was whatever the Eye Service had managed to deploy around Old Earth itself. His grin faded as he reflected that what he had just evaded would be a short and easy exercise compared to what awaited him.

The ship's screens cleared and blanked briefly a fourth time.

Gerswin made another small course change and boosted the acceleration, but negated the rest of the programmed changes.

"Double eye, this is Longshot one. Scanner information indicates target is continuing Old Home."

"Stet, one. Understand. Regroup Double eye. Regroup Double eye."

Gerswin set the alarm and leaned back in the control couch, finally dropping the acceleration to normal gee force to conserve the most possible of his remaining energy. Further acceleration would not help, and could only require more power to kill at destination.

More than a standard hour passed before the alarm chimed softly.

Cling.

"EDI traces in destination area."

"Display on main screen. Note deviation from system plane."

From what the sensors could pick up, there were three corvettes and a light cruiser orbiting Old Earth.

"All for poor old me?"

"Inquiry imprecise."

"Stet. It's very imprecise."

"Please reformulate."

"Disregard."

"Disregarding imprecise inquiry."

He wiped his forehead with the back of his right hand. Would the same general strategy work twice?

He smiled. If it did, it would certainly play Hades with Imperial tactics manuals. And the reentry path he had planned would leave communications a bit ragged. Ships weren't supposed to split the planetary polar force lines.

He touched the command keyboard to put the Imperial frequencies back on the ship's speakers.

". . . negative on incoming this time . . . verify reported velocity . . ."

". . . can't be human at that . . ."

"Please restrict transmissions to tactical objectives, Hotshots one and two."

"Stet, restricting."

Gerswin boosted the ship's angle to the system plane. In-system, paradoxically, it was easier, with less dust. Too bad you couldn't jumpshift that close to a sun.

Given the ship dispersion around the planet, and the position of the lunar relays, the three corvettes, but not the cruiser, might have a shot at him. But not as much as they anticipated, not unless they wanted to have tacheads detonating in Old Earth's upper atmosphere. Gerswin doubted that the Emperor, even the current Emperor, would approve of the uproar that could cause.

"Eye Cee, this is Hotshot three. Tentative target acquisition through optical distortion scanners. Bearing two seven five relative. Mean radian seven zero."

Gerswin swung the scout another ten degrees and began deceleration.

"Hotshot three, cleared to fire."

"Range to contact." Gerswin swallowed.

"Seven emkay."

His fingers ran over the console. For all practical purposes, he was going to have to decelerate from his present velocity to damned near nothing if he wanted to get down in one piece. With the corvettes on station, the simple business of establishing orbit, then determining descent, was shot to Hades.

That meant the distances he was now covering in minutes would take more like a half an hour, giving the Eye group more chances, and requiring more evasion than he would have liked.

He keyed in a near-random deceleration schedule and waited, listening, as the scout began to slow.

Abruptly, the forward screens flared and blanked.

"Range and distance?" inquired Gerswin, feeling the sweat on his forehead, and waiting for the transmissions that would tell him, because of the transmission lag, after the fact.

"Spread pattern, three detonations. Nearest approximately point zero four emkay at one seven zero."

The pilot wiped his forehead, still waiting for the Imperial transmissions.

"Eye Cee, Hotshot three. Target acquisition remains tentative. Deceleration pattern not within analyzer parameters."

"Hotshot three, fire when possible. Use best approximations."

In the static between transmissions, Gerswin adjusted his course "downward" and away from a direct intercept with the corvette, increasing the deceleration more steeply than on his original plan. He shifted his weight to get more comfortable in the two gees riding on him.

The screens cleared, only to blank with another flare.

"Eye Cee, spread one missed. Estimate error of point zero three emkay. Reassessing track."

"Hotshot three, fire when able."

"Hotshot two, this is Eye Cee, interrogative arrival point delta."

"Eye Cee, two here. Estimate arrival delta in ten plus."

"Four estimates arrival in one five."

Gerswin calculated. If point delta were where he estimated, then neither of the other corvettes would be that much of a problem. Hotshot four might not be a factor at all.

"Eye Cee, spread two away."

Gerswin grimaced. The Captain of three was delaying his reports to throw Gerswin off by more than the transmission delay lag.

"Range and distance?" he asked the AI.

"Point zero three emkay. Zero one zero relative."

For the third time, the screens blanked. This time the scout shivered.

Gerswin wiped his forehead and frowned, ignoring the extra effort it cost him under the gee load. The Captain of Hotshot three was better, far better, than he would have liked. He turned the ship farther from the corvette than he really wanted to, and increased the deceleration further, squinting at the increased flow of sweat from his forehead.

Gerswin gambled and eased the *Caroljoy* all the way

back to a head-to-head course with the corvette, but left the deceleration untouched.

"Eye Cee, spread three impacted near target, but prior scanner data indicated target still on possible reentry course."

"Stet, three."

"Hotshot two, Eye Cee. Interrogative target acquisition."

"Eye Cee, negative this time."

Gerswin squared himself in the shell and keyed in three minutes of maximum deceleration, trying to keep his mind clear and picturing mentally the changing relative positions.

"Eye Cee, this is Hotshot three. Reported lost optical distorter scan. We may have reacquired. Say again. May have reacquired. Target managed to obtain decel below tracking parameters."

". . . what in Hades is that scout? . . ."

"Please restrict transmissions to mission!"

Gerswin stopped the deceleration totally, breathing deeply in normal gravity, and hoping that the corvette had managed to lock in at maximum deceleration. He watched the seconds unroll on the tactical clock.

The exterior screens blanked. The interior lights flickered and dimmed, before resuming their normal intensity. A series of red point lights flared on the systems status display, then faded. All but two.

"Damage report!"

"Screen shock impact at two. Auxiliary power buffer inoperative. Secondary screen generator status delta."

Gerswin scanned the systems board, rechecked the *Caroljoy*'s relative and absolute velocities, then squared himself for another two minutes of maximum deceleration. If he had calculated correctly, *if*, then he would need only another two-minute maximum decel just before the near right angle polar reentry path he had plotted.

"Eye Cee, this is three. Report final spread impacted

target screens. Target screens held to plus five."

"Plus five? Interrogative plus five."

"Affirmative, Eye Cee. That is affirmative."

". . . what that thing riding . . ."

"Please restrict transmissions to target net."

"Hotshot two, this is Eye Cee. Interrogative target acquisition. Interrogative target acquisition."

"Acquisition negative. No EDI tracks. Optical distortion scanners down. Down as reported two days previous."

Gerswin smiled as the deceleration load lifted. The bitterness in Hotshot two's transmission told more than the words used in the transmission.

He recalculated. From his plot, Hotshot four would not be in intercept position, except for less than a ten-second window, and two had no way to track him, provided he did not remain on a steady course.

With that self-reminder, Gerswin tapped in a series of random length zigzag course changes to position the *Caroljoy* erratically over the next several minutes.

Finally, he fed it into the AI.

"Suggest changes as noted on the data screen," the AI commented.

Gerswin studied the changes and nodded, then incorporated them into the reentry codes. While he would have liked to make the final descent personally, the timing was too tight. So the AI would have to handle it, until the *Caroljoy* was well within the atmospheric envelope.

"Hotshot two, this is three. Data indicates target will be zero one zero relative to you at point three emkay in one minute from mark. Fire spread delta . . . MARK!"

"Damn him . . . too damned good," muttered Gerswin as he changed course again and keyed in twenty seconds of acceleration at half max.

Wheeeeeee . . .

Before the acceleration ended, the ship staggered,

and the cockpit dropped into the red gloom of the emergency lighting system.

Thud . . . thud . . .

The two jerks of an EMP shock wave slammed Gerswin against his harness.

The status board was half-red. As Gerswin focused his attention on the systems, ignoring the ringing in his ears and the throbbing in his head, some of the lights turned green. A good ten shifted to amber, and five remained in the red.

"Damage and status!"

"Secondary screen generator omega. Primary and secondary power buffer systems omega. Grav systems delta. EDI omega . . ."

Gerswin ignored the rest of the damages. The *Caroljoy* was sound enough to make it down, provided nothing else was thrown at him.

He shook his head slowly, afraid to move suddenly.

"Eye Cee, this is two. Fired on mark from Hotshot three. Detonation, but no instrumentation."

"Eye Cee, three here. Impact at less than point zero zero five emkay. Target screens held to plus seven."

". . . holy Istvenn . . ."

Gerswin ignored the Imperial byplay, since neither corvette could fire again without risking planetside damage, and strapped himself more tightly than before.

"Eye Cee, this is Hotshot four. Have target acquisition, but unable to deploy without possible damage orbit control."

"Stet, four. Hold until able to fire."

"Three here. Four cannot hold. By the time orbit control is clear, target will be in reentry."

Gerswin smiled reluctantly under the gee force at the Captain of Hotshot three. He never seemed to give up.

"Four, continue to hold until you can deploy without damage to Old Home or orbit control."

"Four, holding."

Gerswin looked at the controls as the gee force went from half maximum to more than seven gees, jamming him back into the couch.

"Commencing reentry program."

"Eye Cee, this is Hotshot three. Target commencing reentry on max-gee curve through main mag-field taps."

". . . said scout wasn't human . . ."

". . . one squadron not enough . . ."

eeeeeeeeEEEEEEEEEEEEEEEEEEEEEE!!!!!!

Gerswin winced at the high-frequency static pouring from the speakers, the noise created by his own unique reentry path.

For the following five to ten minutes, most atmospheric communications in the northern hemisphere of Old Earth were going to be difficult, if not impossible.

Instead of fighting the sound, he shifted his attention to the readouts, ready to override the AI if necessary.

The pressure across his chest began to ease, as did the screeching on the comm bands, replaced with a deeper and less intense growling that began to fade as he caught scattered fragments of the Imperials' communications.

". . . unique reentry . . ."

". . . alert Eye Cee . . . possible planetside follow-up . . ."

". . . nothing like . . ."

". . . orbit control . . . track . . . interrogative track . . ."

". . . negative . . . this time . . ."

". . . lunar relay . . . position inaccurate . . ."

The transmissions became fainter and fainter.

"Reentry complete," announced the AI.

Gerswin sat forward and checked the coordinates against those for the Euron retreat, nodding at the relatively short distance remaining. His head ached, and his ears still rang.

Then he tapped in the last courses, monitoring both

the course line and the far screens as the scout edged toward the hidden bunker that had waited so long. The bunker from which the *Caroljoy* could never rise.

"Time to touchdown?"

"Estimate five plus."

He watched the waves beneath on the screen, and then the blotched land that alternated between golden grass, scattered trees, and purple clay and its matching scraggly purple grass.

"Homer is on."

"Descent path clear."

Gerswin mumbled the landing points to himself, slowly easing the black scout through the concealed bunker door and down the tunnel and into the hangar. Scarcely a fitting grave for the scout.

"Gates closed."

He sighed, letting his muscles relax for a moment before releasing the harness.

"What now?"

"Inquiry imprecise. Please clarify."

"What do I do now?"

The AI said nothing, as if it had not heard his clarification.

"About the ship, about you . . . doubt I'm coming back. May use the flitters . . . no energy left . . . not to speak of . . . nowhere to go . . ."

He wondered why he was talking as he did, but it seemed almost as if he were trying to justify what he said, what he was going to do.

"Terminate."

Terminate? The single coolly feminine word hung in the control room. Had the AI actually said terminate?

"Please clarify." This time, the pilot asked for the clarification.

"Energy reserves insufficient for continued full-status operation. Pilot has expressed no further need for ship and AI. Therefore, suggest full shutdown and AI termination."

"Why?"

"No further purpose for ship. Ship cannot be lifted. Cannot be repaired."

He swallowed hard. How could he feel sentimental about a chunk of metal and electronics? Even if he had built it? Even if it had been home, on and off, for a century?

"Request AI recommendation for optimal outcome for AI."

"Termination optimal outcome for AI. Pilot has expressed no further need for AI. Ship cannot use AI. No remaining function for AI."

How could he do otherwise, practically and in fairness?

"You left everyone else, didn't you?"

Neither he nor the AI answered the question, as, hands trembling, he began the series of codes that would fulfill the only request the AI and ship had ever made. The only request.

XLVIII

TOUCHING HIS TONGUE TO THE SIDE OF THE SPECIAL TOOTH, the gaunt man, the rail-thin man who had carried the title of Eye for too long, sighed. Sighed again, and touching the side of the tooth with his tongue again, read the cryptic message a second time.

"Devilkid home. Exact location unknown. Energy consumption indicates probability of lift less than five percent."

Eye frowned. No probability involving Gerswin

could be that low, not with the resources and ingenuity involved.

He tried to relax the muscles in his face, but failed.

Despite the power squandered in the deployment of three squadrons, despite the continuing use of energy such deployment required, and despite the sacrifices and efforts of the overstrained Service as a whole, Gerswin had gone home. Just as the man had done whatever else he wanted. Gone home and left a devil's brew behind. Gone home, brushing aside the Service as an inconvenience.

Although he had left the Foundation behind, the administrator was dead in a strange fire, and the records were blank, except for scraps that confirmed Eye's worst fears. The bank records, those few that Eye could reach, only confirmed the confirmation.

The gaunt man touched the golden call button.

Unlike his predecessor, he would not wait to be called by the Emperor. He had already waited too long.

Then again, it had been too late before he had taken the reins. Calendra had known, but neither he nor the Emperor had believed Calendra.

The Earl of Selern touched the call button and began to wait.

XLIX

Onull crouched at the base of the largest boulder between her and the demon. She shivered in the fog that had swept in off the northern sea, the fog that the doc had said would come because of the black demon that twisted eyes.

She had not seen the demon when it had flown over the huts and into the hills the day before. Devra had, and now she would not speak of what she had seen. Devra had seen and refused to come back to tend the southern flock.

That was why Onull was there, crouched into as small a ball as she could make herself, hoping that the demon would not notice.

Like the other youngsters from Wallim's village who had been in the forest, gathering, she had smirked behind her hand at Devra's tale, and at the visions seen by the old women who sat in the square by the well. She had even volunteered to watch the flock the next day, until Wallim decided who the new shepherd would be. Watching sheep was far easier than grubbing and gathering in the muck of the woods.

Then, just moments before, the ground had trembled beneath her feet, and she had run for the rocks, her mouth agape as the flat cliff had split in two and revealed a dark cave down to whatever depths the demon had come from.

She shivered again, waiting for the demon to come and take her, afraid to move, for fear any motion would call her to the attention of the monster.

The fog continued to swirl in from the not-too-distant sea, wrapping itself around the hillocks and dropping from the higher hills as it flowed inland.

Onull hoped its grayness, and the tattered gray garment that was her cloak, would shield her.

Click, click, click, click.

She shuddered at the metallic sounds, drawing herself closer to the boulder, wanting to look, and afraid to look.

Rurrrrr . . . clunk.

The ground vibrated under her feet, and she glanced upward.

Through the mist, she could see that the gray cliff

face was smooth, totally smooth, as it had been through all her life.

She shuddered.

Who else but demons could make caves appear and disappear in solid rock?

Click.

She finally peered around the boulder.

At the base of the sheer cliff stood a figure, seemingly in black, looking out toward the sea, though it could not be seen, Onull knew, except from the very top of the hill above the cliff, and then only on a clear day.

She darted another look, ready to duck her head behind the stone that sheltered her should that black-clad figure turn her way.

It looked like a man, a slender man with golden hair, but with demons, doc said, you could never tell.

The demon man turned toward her, and she flashed behind the stone before he could see her.

Click . . . click.

Her heart began to pound as the terrible steps moved toward her, and she wanted to run. But her feet would not move, and she curled into a ball at the base of the stone that had not sheltered her enough.

Click, click, click. Click, click.

She could hear it coming around the boulder, as if it knew she were there, searching her out.

Click. Click.

The footsteps paused, and she could feel the burning gaze of the demon as it penetrated her thin and ragged cloak. But she did not move.

"So much fear. So much. Best not . . ."

Then its voice deepened.

"If you wish to live beyond the instant, promise yourself you will not speak of this moment and this meeting."

Though the words sounded strange, she understood. She shuddered, but said nothing. Knowing she would never, could never mention what she had seen, even if the demon had not bound her.

Click, click. Click. Click.

The awful steps died into the fog, echoing ever more faintly through the stony hillside, until at last the demon was gone.

Onull scraped herself into a sitting position, shivering, wondering if she would ever feel warm again, and wrapped her cloak more tightly about her as she stumbled back to the village.

L

THE MAN WHISTLED AS HE WALKED SOUTH ALONG THE DUSTY trail above the river, pausing at times to stop and to listen, but always resuming his steps toward the southern mountains.

The patches of lifeless ground were fewer in the higher reaches, as were the twisted trees and stunted bushes. Occasionally, as he viewed an area where house trees flourished or where the ecological recovery seemed well along, he nodded.

Before him, the trail veered left abruptly, away from the river. He stopped.

The reason for the path's change of direction was clear enough from the purpled ground, the scraggly growths, and the tumbled bricks and stone. He peered over the low rock and rail barricade at the desolation.

After completing his cursory study, he paused again, letting his ears and senses take in the environment around him, alert for any sounds or indications of movement. The waist-high undergrowth that surrounded the path was silent, and from the forest that began a good hundred meters up the hill, he could hear only the distant sounds of a single jay. Farther away, there was the intermittent caw of a croven.

The dust of the path showed day-old scuffs of a wide-tired wagon, the kind pulled by the traveling peddlers who brought Imperial and Noram goods into the back reaches of the continent.

His right hand on one rock post, he vaulted the rail barrier and landed lightly on the purpled moss. In a dozen quick steps he was down the hillside and in the shadowed hollows of what he assumed had been some sort of factory or commercial establishment. Farther downslope he could see the cracked pavement of the old highway, the sterile strip that hugged the eastern bank of the river, without even the traces of that scruffy purple grass that struggled up in all but the worst polluted areas.

Off came the backpack, and from it two thin canisters.

Picking spots with shelter and soil, no matter how contaminated, he planted two minute seedlings. Next came the pouch with the capsules.

He lifted his head and estimated the area. Three capsules, one of the spores and two of the virus. He pricked the first, the catalytic virus, and scattered the contents with a practiced motion. Within weeks the improvement would be dramatic.

After repacking and reshouldering the black backpack, he took another dozen long steps and scattered the contents of the second capsule, the spores. On the far end of the sundered complex, he released the contents of the third and last capsule.

Although his journey was more survey, more for personal satisfaction and knowledge, while his supplies lasted, he would try to provide an additional boost to the most blighted spots.

As he had suspected, once he crossed the factory site, the path returned to its previous course paralleling the river. Again, he vaulted the makeshift rock and rail barrier to continue his southward trek.

"Just a regular jonseeder," he murmured as he stepped up his pace.

In time, the slender man in the dark olive singlesuit reached a junction where a larger trail, nearly a road, emerged from the forest and met the river path to form what appeared to be a major route southward.

He wondered if he should have donned his black cloak as he caught sight of another traveler. A heavyset man, who had appeared from a shadowed section of the wider trail shadowed by the overarching trees, waddled down the gentle slope toward the river and the man in olive.

"Yo!"

The waddling man, who resembled the extinct walrus in his brown leathers and flowing mustache, hailed the man with the pack.

The slender traveler waited.

"Yo!" hailed the bigger man again.

The slender man who waited returned the greeting with a wave vaguely akin to a salute, but said nothing until the other was within a few meters.

"Beg your pardon, but I speak the local tongue poorly."

"No problem," exclaimed the overflowing man. "No problem. Panglais, then?"

"That would be better," returned the other in Panglais, "if you do not mind."

"Fine! Fine! All the same to me. Language is language, I say." He shivered and looked at the faint sun, strong enough to cast shadows, but struggling nonetheless to disperse the high gray haze.

"Would that words could warm as well as the sun should. And you, a peddler of some sort, I bet. That or a pilgrim, heading south and over the deadly mountains to the fabled southern shrines."

"No. Just a traveler, seeing what I can see." His ears had picked up the rustles in the underbrush. He gestured generally as he spoke and placed his hands so that his thumbs rested on the wide equipment belt.

The walrus man gestured in turn. "Werner D'Vlere, at your service. Minor magician, basso profundo, and bon vivant." He carried but a small satchel of scuffed brown leather that, in general terms, matched his jacket and trousers.

The traveler inclined his head. "Magician?"

"A bit of sleight of hand, a few jokes. Enough to guarantee a meal or two from the small clumps of cots that call themselves towns."

The traveler said nothing, but nodded, as if to ask the magician to continue.

"And you, my friend the traveler, how do you pay your way through these backward reaches?"

"Somehow, I find a way. Usually I perform services." He shifted his weight and stepped to the left a pace. The rustlings continued, though more quietly and slowly.

"Services? Well, I would suppose that a traveler such as you would have some skills that they would not have."

"I manage. Better some places than others."

While the sounds from the underbrush had stopped, the traveler was aware that the individuals who had created them were alert, quite alert. Either the pair in hiding had no energy weapons, or deigned to use them on a lone traveler.

He stepped toward the heavy man, stopping less than a meter away.

"Will you introduce me to your friends?" He gestured toward the underbrush.

"Alas, you have seen through my sleight of hand." A small projectile pistol appeared in the left hand of the leather-clad man. He gestured with his right hand, and from the shoulder-high brush rose two youngsters, both in leathers stain-darkened in blotches to create a camouflage effect.

"May I see your pack, if you please? And gently, please. If you would put it—"

Like a spring wound nearly to the breaking point, the traveler uncoiled, his hands blurring from his waist, and his body moving sideways at the same speed.

Thunk! Thunk! Thunk!

Three silver flashes creased the heavy riverside air, and the traveler crouched beside the body of the walrus man, the projectile pistol in his own hand.

He stood.

The two youngsters looked down, openmouthed, at the heavy-weight knives buried in their shoulders, knives that had struck with enough impact to force them to drop the long knives they had carried.

The traveler nodded at the two.

"Come here. Leave the knives on the ground."

As they edged toward him, he studied the pair, still listening for the telltale sounds that would indicate reinforcements.

He realized that the one on the left, as they converged from their spread positions, was a young woman, and that they were related, probably brother and sister. Their eyes differed from earth-norm, not like the hawk-searching of the devilkids, but more catlike, with a reflected luminescence that suggested night vision.

"Sit down."

He pointed to a spot for each. Then he tucked the gun into his waistband, and eased the pack off, ready to drop it and disable either or both if necessary.

He pulled out what he needed and set the pack on the ground, out of the way.

"Speak Panglais?"

"Yes." That from the woman, scarcely more than a girl.

He nodded at the other youth.

"Yes."

"I'll take the knife out and treat the wound. If either of you moves, I'll kill the other."

He smiled at the confusion his remark caused, knowing instinctively that each would want to protect the other.

He started with the young man, not out of reverse chivalry, but because he couldn't count on the brother's good sense if he began with the woman.

The knife came out simple enough, since it wasn't barbed. The weight and design were for initial shock value and reusability, not for cruelty.

Next, he sprinkled some bioagent into the wound and covered it with gel.

"That's it. Muscle tear is pretty bad. Should start healing immediately. Won't have any infection if you don't mess with the gel. Don't touch it."

The youth twitched when he pulled the knife from the sister, but said nothing as he treated her wound as well.

Then he retrieved the third knife from the body of the dead man, cleaning all three quickly and replacing them in the sheaths hidden in his belt.

Standing and stepping back, he surveyed both siblings.

Dressed identically, with black hair, cut roughly at shoulder length, pointed jaws, cat-green eyes, smooth chins, and virtually no body hair, he guessed. The man's features were marginally heavier than the woman's, and his legs, under the loose leather trousers, indicated thicker muscles.

"What should I do with you?"

"Don't turn your back," suggested the man.

"Do you really think you could move faster than I can? Heard you all the way down the hill. Remember, you had your knives in hand. I did not. Also, I chose not to kill you. Could have."

"You sleep," observed the girl, ignoring the implications of his statement.

"Bad assumption." He paused. "What about your defunct friend?"

"No friend."

"Pardon. Former employer."

"We had no choice."

"Oh? And you talk about surprising *me*?" The

traveler raked them with his eyes. "What do they ca
you here? Devilkids? Nightspawn? Devilspawn? Fire
eyes?"

The two looked at each other from their cross
legged positions on the dusty flat where the three path
joined, then back to the slender blond and curly-haire
man, seeing for the first time his own hawk-yellow eyes

Their glances dropped away from the intensity o
his gaze as he pinned first the man, then the woman.

"Here?" she asked. "There are others?"

"There are always others."

"Will you take us to them?"

"Not now. My path does not lie in that direction
Might call me a pilgrim. The heights." He pointed up th
river toward the unseen mountains that lay over the hill
and beyond the horizon, beyond the seemingly endless
young forest through which the deadly river flowed.

Both shivered.

Finally, the woman spoke. "The trees disappear in
the distant hills. No one lives there now. Not with th
cold and the poisons."

"I know. But that is where I travel. There and
beyond."

Silence stretched between the three.

The traveler pointed. "Stay here until you canno
see me. Then do what you will. But do not try to surprise
me again. I know your step."

Both dropped their heads, though they still watched
him. The traveler knew they would wait until his steps
had taken him clear and out of sight.

While he had time, perhaps forever, he did not like
delays on his road to nowhere.

With that, he shouldered his pack. With quick
strides he was close to fifty meters up the river path
before the pair looked at each other.

Shortly, the two were lost over the hill and behind
the gray haze that had dropped onto the region.

He wondered what their names were, or if they had
any, and whether they would follow.

He began to whistle another of the newer double-toned songs he had composed as he crossed the continent. The older ones he tried not to remember too often.

After a time and a number of songs, he looked back over his shoulder, down the winding stretch of trail, for it now had narrowed so greatly it could scarcely be called a path, toward the two figures who marched as effortlessly as he himself.

He shook his head.

"Damned fools."

But he stopped and waited, and as the light began to dim, they approached the scrawny tree under which he sat. Both walked slowly now, showing open hands, palms up as they neared him.

Finally they stopped.

He stood.

"Yes?"

"I am Tomaz. My sister is Charletta."

"You may call me Gregor. Close as anything these days. Now that the pleasantries are over, what do you want?"

"We would like to travel with you. Or until you find others. Others like us." The woman's voice was light, with an odd huskiness he found appealing.

Careful there, he told himself.

"How do you know I'm not an evil magician?"

"You are not."

"If you say so."

He spread his hands, palms up.

"Onward, then. For a place to sleep."

"There are caves farther up," offered Tomaz.

"Best offer so far. Lay on, McTomaz."

"McTomaz?"

"Let's go."

He shook his head.

Always trying the singles game, and always someone seemed to come along and join up. Not that it didn't work out, but never quite as he had imagined.

No, never quite as he had imagined.

LI

"From the viewpoint of those of us in Stenden, Commander, under the Imperial presence, things have been all downhill since the days of the Commodores Gerswin and H'Lieu."

Nodding solemnly in response to the Stenden official, the overweight man in the dress uniform cleared his throat.

The skies were clear, but with the thirty-kay winds from the east, the Commander had tucked his dress visor under his left arm. Regulations forbade it, but regulations were not what they had been. His balding forehead gleamed in the afternoon light. He cleared his throat again before speaking.

"The Empire understands your concerns, Ser Mayor. In turn, I am sure you understand the fiscal pressures, especially with the increasing commitments facing the Service, and the reduced maintenance requirements of the current Fleet . . ."

"We understand, Commander. Believe me, we understand. Fewer ships need fewer repairs, and Standora is far out on the Arm. That is why we made our proposal." The Stenden official's voice was even, his crisp dress shirt as formal as his diction.

"Ah, yes . . . about the proposal . . . the proposal . . . you understand that the Empire has always attempted to live up to its commitments . . ."

"That was certainly true of Commodore Gerswin."

"Ah, yes, Commodore Gerswin. Quite a . . . really

228

larger than life . . . that is . . . I understand he was rather impressive . . . according to . . ." replied the I.S.S.
Commander.

"I am not always certain that Stenden Panglais is
the same language as Imperial Panglais," observed the
Stenden Mayor. "Commodore Gerswin observed all the
protocols. He made Standora Base a most highly regarded repair and refit facility, and he won the respect of
his peers in the Imperial Service and the admiration and
respect of the people of Stenden. His example has
become, for better or worse, a local legend."

"Quite. Much larger than life, but times change, Ser
Mayor, and with these changes we all must change."

"Regrettably," answered the Mayor. "And what
about the proposal?"

"The Empire has considered your generous offer to
maintain the facility and to offer services and preferred
treatment to Imperial vessels. Quite a generous offer, I
might add. Unfortunately, the Base now represents quite
an investment in resources . . ."

"The Base or the refurbished ships in the museum?
Those that have not been recalled to duty?"

"As I indicated, Ser Mayor, the times do change."

"You may certainly have the ships, all of them, since
they were Imperial ships before the Empire declared
them scrap and sold them to the museum. And the
museum has always operated under Imperial charter.

"While Stenden would have preferred to retain the
ships here, we would still like to maintain the Base itself,
and we would still provide preferred maintenance for
Imperial vessels."

"The majority of the basic facilities could not be
moved, we all know, Ser Mayor, and the Empire would
certainly be remiss in not opting for the best possible use
of the facilities. Stenden has certainly made an offer
which should be considered, although, as I indicated
earlier, the times have changed."

"I take it that means you want the ships and the few
remaining fusactors."

The Commander's eyes darted toward the aging plastarmac under his polished shoes, then to a point beyond the Mayor's shoulder. Finally, after clearing his throat, he spoke. "You have a solid grasp of the situation, Ser Mayor."

"Fine. We'll take the Base over, and you take the remaining museum ships and fusactors. You have such an agreement, I trust?"

The Commander nodded without meeting the Mayor's eyes.

LII

TIRED, THE MAN LIMPED ALONG THE ANCIENT PAVEMENT toward the wall surrounding the settlement. Behind him a pair of youngsters trudged. All three moved so slowly that their feet raised scarcely any of the fine and dry dust that kept drifting back across the pavement.

To the west, to the right of the trio, the sun peered through the haze and dust with an orange light strong enough only to cast eastward-leaning shadows barely darker than the dust itself.

On both sides of the dirt road stretched fields filled with stunted plants and weeds, sprinkled occasionally with patches of purpled grass.

The man shook his head and stopped, rubbing his forehead.

The wall was nearly a hundred meters away, but the pair of guards at the gate had shouldered their shields and stood, waiting.

"Shields," he muttered, tossing the black cloak back over his shoulders and straightening.

"These the people the forest people fear, you think?" he asked the girl.

She shrugged.

The boy said nothing.

The man glanced over his shoulder at the distant mountains behind them before confronting the sentries. Then he, in turn, shrugged, and walked toward the wall and its sentries, the tiredness seemingly gone from his step.

As he approached, he could see that the wall was constructed more like a stone fence than a true wall. While the stones were fitted together roughly and rose to nearly three meters, the construction included chunks of crumbling and ancient concrete, smooth blocks of odd-sized ferrocrete, bricks, and assorted stones cut ages before for differing purposes.

"Halt!"

"Of course."

"Your business in Gondolan?"

"Travelers passing through. To have a good meal and some rest."

"How do you propose to pay?"

The young man and woman exchanged glances, their expressions puzzled. So far, everywhere the man had stopped, he had been welcome. Greeted and fed for the knowledge and information he brought. And he had often repaired devices or offered suggestions to solve problems.

Travelers were few indeed, and to be welcomed in a marginally hospitable land.

"What do you suggest?"

The guards now exchanged glances, as if unsure how to answer. Finally, the taller one, dark-haired and dark-skinned, with a full beard, looked back at the traveler, staring at the slender man in a black cloak who traveled with two who seemed scarcely out of childhood.

"Weapons. Service to the King."

The traveler laid down his wooden staff and spread his hands.

"Weapons? You have weapons, not a poor traveler such as myself. All I can offer is knowledge. Some information the King might find of value."

"He knows what he needs to know," offered the shorter and stockier sentry, spitting into the dust.

The traveler reclaimed his staff.

"Then I can offer little, and we must travel around your wall."

Once more the youth and girl exchanged glances, as did the two guards.

"Then you may not pass."

The traveler shrugged. "What would you have us do?"

"You're young enough. Serve in the Guard; so could the boy. As for her"—leered the tall dark guard —"there's always a place for young women." He reached toward the girl, awkwardly, spear in his hand.

The staff in the traveler's hands blurred.

Crack!

Crack!

Both soldiers lay on the fringe of cobbled-together pavement that reached but a few meters outside the closed gate. The blond man dragged one body, then the other, into the guard shack.

He pounded on the gate.

"Gerlio?"

The traveler pounded again.

"All right!" the gruff voice exclaimed, and the gate swung ajar, pushed by a single wide-bellied man, wearing the same leather uniform as the two dead guards. His shield and spear leaned against the town wall, and a sheathed sword hung from his soiled leather belt.

His unruly brown hair was streaked with gray, and his mouth gaped soundlessly as the traveler slipped inside the gate before he could remove his hands from the rachet wheel.

Crump!

This time the traveler's hands struck, and the third guard dropped, merely unconscious.

The blond man motioned to the two outside the gate, and as they entered, he used the wheel to close the gate behind them.

Then he walked toward the central square, hood back over his head and cloak down around him like a robe, staff in hand, trailed by the two youngsters.

The girl glanced down at the uneven pavement, then behind herself, but the boy jerked her arm, as if to remind her not to look back.

As the blond-haired man passed one, then two rough-sod inns, the boy's face screwed up in puzzlement.

While several women peered from glassless and half-shuttered windows at the trio, the few men and children in the dusty streets looked away.

At the central square, little more than an open space with a handful of peddlers' tents surrounding a statue dragged from some forgotten city, another functionary in dirty leather confronted the three.

"Your passes, travelers. Your passes!"

"Passes?"

"Who let you in? You're supposed to have passes."

"No one let us in. The town gate was open."

"Open?"

"Yes, open. How else would we have gotten in?"

"Open? Open, you say?"

"That's what I said. Open. How else would a poor traveler and two children enter a walled town?"

"This is not a walled town. This is Gondolan, home of King Kernute."

"Which way to the palace?"

"That way," answered the constable. "But you don't have passes."

"You'll be able to find us, I am sure, should you need to."

With that, the traveler swept past the man and headed down the slightly wider alley that passed for a street toward the only three-story building in the town, and one of the few not built of either dried sod or crumbling local brick.

A wall two and a half meters high surrounded the royal residence, and four guards stood at the open gates.

"A traveler to see the King!" announced the black-cloaked man.

"King Kernute said he'd see no one."

The traveler shook his head sadly.

"And to think he would miss the weapons he has searched the entire continent for . . ."

He turned, as if to go.

"Hey, let's see those weapons!"

The traveler looked back.

"The King asked. The King should see."

"So you say."

The traveler shook his head, holding his staff one-handed. "If I were to reach for them, you would misunderstand."

"You got weapons, beggar man, and I'm Kernute's sister," announced the senior guard, whose position seemed verified by the metal arm gauntlets he wore. "Ought to send you to the barracks, you and the boy. Send *her* to Kernute. He'd like that."

The three other guards laughed, roaring as if the comment were the best joke in days.

As they did, the traveler took the leather straps from his sleeves and the smooth stones from his belt.

"Behold!" he declaimed. "A miracle."

Whhhrrrr. Whhrrrr.

Crack!

Crack!

The whiplash sounds echoed through the gate and back.

"You! You . . ."

Crack!

"Piggut!"

Crump!

Fast as the guards had moved, the sling and staff had

been faster. Before the last body hit the ground and
rolled, the leathers had disappeared into his sleeves.

"Guards! Guards! To the gate! To the gate!"

The boy turned as if to run, but the hawk glare of the
traveler held him, and the three waited.

The traveler stepped over and around the bodies
and moved inside the gate into the courtyard, where he
stopped. Stopped and again waited. Waited as another
four guards charged from the northern palace gate
toward the eastern gate where he stood, where two
youngsters stood behind him.

He watched as the guards came around the base of
the palace thirty meters away. One was waggling a spear,
and two had already drawn their short swords.

The leathers reappeared and began to twirl.

Whhrrr . . . whhrrr

"Behold the fist of God!"

Crack!

"The fist of God!"

Crack!

The traveler blurred sideways to avoid the thrown
spear, and the two behind him moved with nearly equal
speed. He returned with another sling cast.

Crack!

Two guards were down, but the last two were within
meters.

Crack!

Thunk!

A brief silence descended upon the courtyard as the
traveler slipped the heavy knife from the body of the last
guard, wiping it clean on the dead man's none-too-
spotless uniform before replacing it in its sheath.

"Might as well go find his royal and majestic majesty," he suggested to the open air as he began to walk
toward the palace.

The boy behind him moved the forefinger of his
right hand in a circular motion as it pointed at his own
head, then leveled it at the head of the traveler.

"Crazy, that one."

The sister looked from the youth to the man and back again.

"No."

They followed him as he marched briskly around the corner of the first floor of the palace, giving it a wide enough berth to avoid thrown objects of any sort. The presumed royal residence was nothing more than an overgrown villa without any openings on the first floor. The second floor had narrow balconies, although each balcony was walled, as if to provide a platform for soldiers or guards, though none appeared.

The northern face of the building presented a staircase, on which soldiers/guards congregated, milling into a rough formation even as the traveler approached.

"Close up!"

"Swords!"

A muscular and scarred man in blackened leathers stood at the foot of the staircase, bellowing up the wide stone stairs.

Three younger men, dressed in smooth and better-cut leathers with ornamental chains around their necks, half stood, half lounged around the pillars at the top of the stone steps.

The traveler nodded, sighed, and pulled the slender gun from his pouch.

Thrumm!

The burly man dropped like a stone, crumpling into a sack of sinew and bone on the clay below the first step.

"Kill him!" screamed one of the younger men at the stairs top.

Thrumm!

He too dropped, rolling down the steps and scattering some of the now more-disorganized guards.

Thrumm!

Clank!

Although a second attacker had thought himself hidden as he raised a spear for a cast, both his body and the spear followed the first man down the steps.

"Hold it!"

The traveler stepped out of the shapeless black cloak, standing back from the foot of the stairs in an Imperial-style singlesuit without insignia. Insignia or not, it looked like a uniform.

Radiating authority, both with his eyes and the black weapon in his left hand, his eyes swept the score of ill-armed soldier guards.

"You tired of this dung? Tired of marching through dust? Tired of other men's women? Tired of no fire of your own?"

"Kill him!" The screamed command was shrill, from one of the two remaining "officers" on the landing under the pillars at the top of the stairs.

"You come down here and kill me, if you can." The total contempt in the traveler's voice silenced all the guards. The men on the steps shuffled and turned to look behind them.

"Come on . . ."

". . . see you do it . . ."

". . . always orders . . . no piggut . . ."

The traveler let the grumbles mount, then casually aimed the weapon.

Thrumm!

"You? You!" His voice cracked up the steps toward the remaining officer. "You challenge me?"

There was no answer. The man looked one way, down at the troops turning upward toward him, then back the other way, moving toward the nearest pillar. Too late.

Thrumm!

Clank!

"All right! You want a change?" charged the slender man. "Fine. Go in there and bring me King Kernute. I'll fight him hand to hand, or sword to knife. Whatever he wants."

The guards did not move, but shuffled their feet.

"You're scared of Kernute?"

Thrumm!

Another soldier dropped.

"Better be more scared of me."

Several figures looked up the stairs, but did not move.

Thrumm!

"Get me Kernute!"

One guard looked down at the last casualty and started to run for the gate.

Whhhrrr.

Crack!

His body pitched forward onto the clay.

"Get me Kernute."

The thirteen remaining guards began to shamble up the stairs, slowly at first, then more quickly as they disappeared into the palace.

The traveler smiled, but moved up the steps to the top, selecting a pillar near the far left end of the row of mismatched and discolored columns. He leaned against the stone, out of view of anyone within the palace's upper stories.

The sounds from within were mixed.

Several feminine shrieks, male shouts, were followed by the clashing of swords, clanging, and bellowing. Then a few muffled voices.

Finally, the traveler heard footsteps, and swords clanking.

"Who comes to challenge the great King Kernute?"

By this time, an entourage had spilled out onto the stairs. A handful of more highly armed guards, dressed in blackened leathers and mismatched breastplates, surrounded a single man, a man who stood a full head taller than the tallest of the guards.

Beside the guards and the King stood three women, one older, her hair streaked with gray, but her face and figure still that of a young woman, and two younger women but a few years out of girlhood.

Separated from the official entourage were the soldiers prodded into the palace by the traveler. One clutched a bloody arm, and there were nine others holding swords awkwardly, as if unsure of what to do next.

The traveler counted. Less than twenty armed men —about what he had expected. He stepped around the column and down the steps toward Kernute, avoiding the bodies still sprawled where he had dropped them.

"I challenge, Kernute."

As he neared the King, he could see some of the personal guards shake their heads. The ruler was clearly of greater stature, strength, and girth. The traveler appeared slim, dusty, and comparatively unarmed.

"You?" bellowed the monarch. "I wouldn't soil my sword . . ."

As if his outrage were a signal, the tallest of the personal guards charged from beside the King, spear in one hand, sword in the other, shield dropped on the clay.

This time the traveler did not use the slender black weapon which remained hidden, but waited, motionless, until the guard was nearly upon him.

Then he moved, and like a bolt of lightning blurred in the vision of those who watched.

Clank!

The guard lay on the clay, unbreathing, his neck at the odd angle that indicated it had been broken.

"I challenge," answered the slim stranger. "And if you keep putting it off, you won't have enough guards left to protect you, let alone your miserable little town." He gestured toward the bodies lying across the stairs and courtyard.

"What weapons?"

"You? Whatever you want."

"None of your magic."

"Only my hands, a rock or two, perhaps my knives."

"Your hands and knives against my sword and shield?"

"Why not?"

The traveler motioned to the personal guards. "Stand back." He looked at the soldiers. "You! There!"

He gestured them toward the base of the steps.

The boy and girl who had accompanied the traveler watched from beneath the exterior wall of the grounds, twenty meters distant, as if they could still not believe that the traveler would topple King Kernute.

Kernute advanced slowly, letting his shield cover as much as possible.

The stranger watched, hands on his belt, his eyes taking in not only the King, but the four remaining personal bodyguards and the ruler's apparent wife/consort.

His hands flicked once, and a silvery knife appeared in his left hand. Twice and another appeared in his right.

Kernute was more than two meters away from the man in the dark olive singlesuit when he jumped and his sword licked out quickly.

The traveler did not seem to move, but he was not where the sword was.

". . . magic . . ."

". . . quick . . ."

Another sword probe followed, and another. Both missed.

"Stand still, you . . ."

"Sorry, Kernute," said the traveler as the knife streaked from his left hand.

The four members of the personal guard stiffened as they watched the King tumble face forward over his shield.

"Ohhhh!" One of the girls buried her head in the arms of the older woman with the gray-streaked hair.

"Stop!" snapped the traveler as one of the black-leathered men lurched a step toward him.

The guard stopped.

"You four, get moving. Out of Gondolan. Not long before the townspeople will start to take you apart."

One looked at the traveler, then at the guards on the steps, before dropping his shield and scuttling toward the gate. A second shook his head as he dropped shield and followed, but more warily, as if he expected the town to be waiting outside the gate for him.

"You're the new King, I suppose?" asked the older woman as she cradled her daughter.

"No. Could care less." The traveler's hawk-yellow eyes raked the mismatched group. "This happened because the King did not welcome travelers. Strong-arm tactics don't work, not for long.

"But me . . . I have a long way to go . . . miles to go."

He had walked over to the heap which was composed of the black cloak and his pack, picked up both with a quick motion, still watching the remaining soldiers, and noting that the guard with the bloody arm had also slipped away.

"What you decide to do with your town is up to you. Suggest a bit more friendliness. Might stop terrorizing the neighbors. The Empire doesn't like that sort of thing. More important, I don't, either."

He shook the thin black cloak and folded it into the pack before hoisting it back onto his shoulders. Last, he walked over to the deceased ruler and retrieved his knife, wiping it quickly on the dead man's tunic and replacing it in its sheath. He stood, surveying the small crowd.

"Up to you. Try to do better next time."

He began to walk toward the gate, his pace so quick that he had passed through the northern barriers to the palace and into the small town before there was any reaction at all from the stunned group.

Belatedly, the boy and girl who had watched from next to the wall, squatting, scurried to their feet and after him.

"Devilspawn follow him . . ."

"Devilkiller . . ."

". . . watch for the traveler . . ."

The soldiers looked at each other in the chaos that dropped on them in the stranger's absence, then at the bodies strewn across the palace grounds as if by a lethal wind.

The King's widow sought to console one daughter, while an amused smile played around the lips of the older girl as she watched the remaining bodyguard strip off his black leathers and edge toward the widow.

Several hundred meters to the south, a shopkeeper parted with a few items, and thereafter, a few minutes later, a town gate opened, but did not close.

LIII

"WE ARE NOT PLEASED WITH YOUR RESPONSE TO OUR INquiry," stated the thin man behind the antique wooden desk and the double energy screens.

"I understand that, Your Majesty." The speaker sat quietly in the narrow and straight-backed chair. His tunic and matching trousers were a somber blue, darker than his piercing blue eyes, and almost as black as his boots.

"Then why do you not act?"

"If Your Majesty wishes, I will send a full squad of Corpus Corps troops to Old Earth. That will leave two full squads to handle what has historically taken four or five squads. Training for replacements will proceed at half schedule, and once it becomes known that we have lost a squad on Old Earth, you will have double the unrest on the outer rim systems. But, if you wish, I will dispatch a squad."

"Morren, are you telling Us that this . . . this antique relic . . . this broken down ex-Commodore . . . can destroy a full squad of the best Corpus Corps troops?"

"No. But no one on Old Earth is likely to turn on a local legend, from what I know. Since no one knows where on Old Earth he might happen to be, a squad would be necessary just to locate him."

"Why not locate him with regular Service personnel?"

"The last effort to find and stop him took three squadrons filled with regular personnel. I might remind Your Majesty that the efficiency ratings of those squadrons were considerably higher than the current averages. We could locate Gerswin with regular personnel, if Your Majesty wishes to pull at least one squadron from the rim patrols. But to pin down Gerswin would still take half a squad, and the probability of success would be less than sixty percent."

"If that is the best you can do, then perhaps We should find a new Eye."

"That is Your Majesty's choice. The failure to stop Gerswin has brought down the three previous Eyes, who, frankly, had a great deal more to work with, and considerably fewer internal problems to resolve for their Emperor."

"Are you telling Us that you cannot find and terminate this relic who has caused the Empire so much unrest and loss?"

"No, Your Majesty. I am frank in telling You the cost of such an operation. The choice is Yours. I can only serve."

The thin man who wore the title of Emperor and who sat behind the antique desk of his predecessors frowned. Finally, he looked back up at his chief of Intelligence.

"Did you know this when you accepted your position?"

"Not for certain, Your Majesty, but I did suspect it might prove to be the case."

"Why?"

"Gerswin couldn't destroy the results of his first physical examination, the one before he became cau-

tious. He also built the biggest commercial barony ever
put together in a single lifetime—without anyone understanding its extent until he walked away and let its
collapse ruin the economies of more than a dozen
systems."

"So what is the man, an immortal genius with the
talents of a dozen Corpus Corps types and the soul of the
devil?"

"That might overstate the case, Your Majesty. Then
again, it might not."

His Imperial Majesty continued to frown.

"Might I have your leave to depart, Your Majesty?
You can always request my termination."

"Go . . . go, Morren. Let him rot on Old Earth, and
preserve what you can for Your Emperor."

"As Your Majesty wishes."

LIV

THE WIND COMING OFF THE INLAND SEA STREAMED THE
once-black cloak from his shoulders like wings, and the
red sun perched on the western horizon outlined him
like a black marble statue above the angled stones and
marble columns that remained.

The oldest of the old cities, that was all the cat-eyed
people had called it, but ruins were ruins, whether they
were buried beneath the purpled clay of the high plains,
or but half-buried and standing on a hillside above the
Inland Sea.

The lower edge of the crimson sun touched the

water, and the gray and wispy high clouds melted pink. The dark water took on a maroon tinge. Once it had been called a wine-dark sea, and now it was again, though it was neither sailed nor crossed by the scattered peoples along its shore. That, too, was as it had been in the first beginning.

He had stayed too long, too long after he had helped them found and defend their settlement, too long indeed, for even the children, incredibly quick, bright, bowed as he passed.

He turned until the sun was at his back, not that the fading light carried much warmth, and began to walk upward toward the row of fallen columns for another look at the statue.

His boots clicked on the stone underfoot, the steps fractured and cracked, but still in place.

He nodded a greeting to her, her face already in shadow.

Without further gestures, he sat on the column to her right, squinting as the last rays of the sun cast a glow at the base of the fallen goddess. Her face was beautiful, in the old style, the style of a Caroljoy, but remained expressionless. Her arms were long since gone, but neither she nor he looked to hold or to be held.

He studied the white lines, the unblinking eyes, while the light dimmed.

Soon, the fog would creep in, climbing the hill toward the fallen pillars and tilted white stone blocks.

Glancing down at his cloak, no longer crisp black, but worn, faded almost into olive, with the use of the past years, worn and patched, the last patches those provided by Charlotta, who had patched it while complaining that Berin would let her do nothing strenuous until their child was born, until her time had come.

He snorted as he looked at the stone goddess.

"Your time has long gone, and mine also."

If you say so.

"Already, this continent is reawakening. Was the

worst of all. I belonged to the dead times."

You cannot die.

"Nor can you."

I lived only while people remembered.

"Remember? Soon I will remember little."

You do not want to remember.

"Don't want to forget either. Where does that leave me?"

She did not answer, and he looked away from the perfect white face of the recumbent woman and watched the upper tip, the last crimson slivers, of the sun drop below the watery horizon, watched the long shadows lengthen, dancing from slow wave to slow wave.

"Well, my lady, we had our times."

It is early for self-pity.

"I forget. You have watched more centuries than I have."

I have seen nothing.

"Have I? Tell me I have seen. Watched while others lived, loved, and died. Watched and killed, killed and watched. Pulled strings, played god, and for what? For what?"

You have lived, if not how you wanted. You have lived.

He could not refute her last statement, and did not try, as he sat on a ruined column, keeping company with a statue, as the twilight became night. Knowing that the next day—the next day, for he had waited too long—he must begin the trip to the place of his beginning.

LV

Above the faded olive singlesuit, patched and dusty, hawk-yellow eyes glittered beneath tight-curled blond hair. The jaw remained elfin, and the skin smooth, but there was a tiredness behind the youthful features reflected only in the lagging steps, where each stride stopped short of briskness, each step mirrored more than mere fatigue.

The afternoon sun glared down at the solitary figure on the empty road as he trudged westward, staff in hand, pack on back.

The gently rolling hills to his right sported an uneven growth of assorted bushes and trees, none more than twice the traveler's height, and all less than a pair of decades old.

Nodding without pausing, he contemplated what would one day be a forest, recalling when the area had boasted little beyond purpled clay, land poisons, and a few clumps of the purple grass that had been all that could grow.

Glancing to his left, he observed the recently tilled soil, and the dark green tips of the sponge grains beginning to peer through the soil that retained a tinge of purple.

A faint rumble whispered from the west.

With a sigh, the traveler turned from the packed clay road less than five meters wide and marched northward into the underbrush, finally halting underneath a small oak and seating himself to wait for the road roller to pass on eastward to the newly developed coastal settlements.

Not that anyone expected him, nor wanted him, but meeting even a roller crew in the middle of the piedmont would raise questions, and there would be enough of those when he reached the high plains. Time enough for the questions then.

He stretched out his legs and waited, listening for the faint sounds he hoped were there—the twitter of the insects, the chirp and rustle of remaining or returning birds, as well as the reintroduced species, those few that had been preserved on New Augusta, New Colora, or in reserves throughout the Empire.

The insects resumed their twitters immediately, even before he stopped moving, but the heavy and moist air brought no sounds of birds or other larger species.

As the rumbling of the roller grew from a whisper into a grumbling, the cargo vehicle topped a hill and gathered momentum to plunge down its slope on its eastward route.

Within minutes, the grumbling roar had dwindled back into a whisper.

The traveler stood, flexing his shoulders as if to remove the tightness, reshouldered his backpack, and picked up his heavy, but well-worked staff.

Soon, he would need to refill his water bottle, and to see what he could find to supplement the food he carried. Soon—but not for another five or ten kays, at least.

His steps were even as he returned to the road, where the heavy red dust had already settled back to blur the wide traces of the cargo rollers where they had flattened the right of way even more smoothly than before.

The respite had refreshed him, and his steps were brisker. He began to whistle one of the newer tunes he had composed in the last few years. Although he recalled the older ones, and whistled them now and again in his

blacker moments, he usually avoided them and the
memories they brought back.

At the top of the next hill, he paused to survey the
gentle hills that rose into the eastern Noram mountains.
He could see the darker green of their forested slopes,
where the ecological recovery had been quicker than on
the slower draining and clay-based hilly plains where he
stood.

How long had it been since he had overflown this
area?

He pushed the thought away and started down the
western slope of the hill, his booted feet leaving barely a
trace on the shoulder of the packed clay road.

Three kays westward, he paused again upon a hilltop, when he saw a single man standing beside a machine
—a locally built tractor type pulling a tilling rig.

He shrugged and continued downward, until at last
he stood beside the machine, observing the man who
struggled with an assembly that controlled the tilling
bars dragged by the tractor. The tractor, obviously of
local design and manufacture, bore more patches than
the traveler's singlesuit, but appeared clean and in good
repair.

"Hades . . ." muttered the operator, refusing to pay
any attention to the traveler.

In turn, the traveler seated himself in the midafternoon shade of the large wheels and waited, taking a sip
from his nearly empty water bottle.

"Hades . . . double Hades . . . grubbin' Impie design . . ."

The blond man finished the water and replaced the
bottle in the harness attached to his pack, stretching his
legs out to wait for the other to complete the repair or
surrender to the need for assistance.

Clank!

Plop!

A large hammer dropped beside the traveler, who
looked up without curiosity.

"Perfectly good machine . . . useless because some idiot tech decided it was easier to copy from a stupid Imperial design . . ."

"That bad?" asked the blond-haired man as he watched the operator clamber down from the tractor.

"Wouldn't be hard at all if I had Imperial tools, three hands, and a graving dock to immobilize the whole stupid assembly!"

The operator had the long-armed and narrow-faced look of shambletown ancestry, but wore a relatively new jumpsuit, which carried only recent dirt and grease. His black hair was short, and he wiped his forehead with a brown cloth, which he replaced in a thigh pocket of the jumpsuit.

"Mind if I take a look?" asked the traveler.

"Be my guest. Not scheduled for a pickup for hours yet. Don't seem to have the tools to fix it."

After nodding sympathetically, the traveler climbed up to the assembly with an ease that spoke of familiarity with both equipment in general and repairs in awkward locales.

The man in the olive jumpsuit frowned as he surveyed the jammed assembly. In one respect, the operator was correct. The Imperial design, obviously adapted from a flitter-door system, was far too complicated.

Still—Imperial designs usually had more than one solution.

He bent over the assembly, looking at the far side upside down. A wry smile creased his face as he straightened and checked the small tool kit which the operator had left.

Not ideal, but he thought what he had in mind would work. Even permanent connections could be removed, if you knew their structure.

Click. Click.

With the right angle, the hidden releases, and an extreme amount of pressure, he managed to get the "permanent" coupling released.

The loss of pressure on the line allowed the assembly to drop into place. With the pressure off the line, he was able to release the other end of the connector.

As the operator had probably known, the check valve was jammed with debris and hardened fluid. Within a few minutes he had it clean again, and ready to reconnect. Doing the best he could, he cleaned out the tubing and the fittings before he reassembled them.

Finally, he closed the tool kit and climbed back down to the puzzled operator.

"Think it should work now. Want to try it?"

The operator shook his head, wiping his forehead once more with the brown cloth.

"How did you do that?"

"Had some familiarity, once, with that sort of design. A few tricks I happened to remember."

"That Hades-fired assembly gives us more problems than the rest of the equipment put together. I've never seen anyone fix one that quickly."

"Luck, I suppose."

"Where are you headed?"

"West."

The operator surveyed the traveler, looked from the patched and faded singlesuit to the western mountains, taking in the backpack and staff resting against the tractor wheels.

"On foot?"

"Simpler that way. No hurry. Feet don't break down if you rest them now and again."

The operator shook his head. "Still a few wild Mazers loose. I wouldn't recommend going much beyond the next check station. Better to catch a ride with one of the road rollers. They'd be happy to take you. They like the company."

The traveler nodded. "Appreciate the suggestion."

"You sure look familiar. Swear I saw you someplace."

"Not likely. Been a long time since I passed this way."

"Well . . . whatever. I appreciate the help. Appreciate it a lot. Anything I can do for you? Like to give you a lift, but . . ." The Recorps operator surveyed the half-tilled field.

"Understand. You've got a job."

The operator nodded. "Stet. Beats running the hills. Even if I don't see the lady more than once a week. Kids always have enough to eat. Not like the old days, bless the Captain."

"Pardon?"

"Not like the old days, I said."

The traveler smiled faintly, nodded, and bent to pick up the pack and staff. Straightening, he twirled the staff one-handed and inclined his head momentarily toward the Recorps tech.

"Good luck," he called to the operator as he set out toward the road and the mountains toward which it led.

"Sure not like the old days . . . Captain and all . . ." He could hear the operator murmuring as the tech began to check out the equipment before returning to his tilling.

The traveler waited until he had crossed the next hilltop before resuming his whistling.

LVI

THE COMMANDER RAN HIS EYES OVER THE SCREEN, TRYING TO focus on the words, finally letting them settle midway down the text.

". . . mysterious traveler on the Euron Continent has been blamed for the overthrow of two local rulers, at

least, for the death of a score of bandits, and for the
establishment of a 'devilspawn' settlement on the inland
sea . . .

". . . settlement verified, location on grid three,
named Stander, allegedly founded in memory of the
traveler who departed in a wagon of fire . . .

". . . not all events reported can be verified, but all
verified references fall within a three-century period . . .
some evidence to indicate traveler was real Imperial,
perhaps a wandering scholar of some sort . . . but . . .
would not explain ability with weapons . . . particularly
with native arms . . ."

The Commander bit his lip. No sooner had he
managed to purge the superstitious gobbledy-gook from
the main base records than it was turning up elsewhere
on Old Earth.

Reclamation was a serious business, dependent far
too much on worn-out equipment—equipment modified so much the original specs were useless—too few
supplies, and too few trained personnel. As the Empire
continued to shrink, with each subsequent cutback,
there were fewer replacement parts, fewer visiting ships
of any sort with which to trade for the needed technical
equipment the Empire failed to supply.

With all the drawbacks, there was less and less
incentive to push back the landpoisons.

His hand touched the screen and sent the report to
the system files.

Bad enough that the early Captain, whoever he had
been, had been turned into a godlike legend. Now he had
to contend with other magical forces and legends.

How could he explain the improved environmental
monitoring reports from places where Recorps had
never been? It had been hard enough to justify the
limited Imperial support with the bad reports from the
out-continents.

Despite his efforts, and the efforts of the comman-
dants before him, Recorps was shrinking, and the rate of
progress slowly but surely declining.

The records showed that four centuries earlier, Recorps had been operating the now-closed Scotia station, and that two centuries before that the Noram effort had crossed the Momiss River. Yet they still had not completed the eastern sections of Noram, despite the efforts in the Brits and on the fringes of Euron.

There never were enough techs, let alone enough officer-grade types, to fill the positions necessary. The Admin complex was filled with empty offices, empty quarters, empty labs.

Still, the spouts were less severe, and far less frequent, and there hadn't been a stone rain in Noram in over a century, and summer ice rains were a rarity, rather than the norm they had once been.

"Hard work . . ." he muttered. Hard work, that was what had caused the improvement, not the magic of some traveler in mysterious Euron, or some long-dead Captain.

Even that Captain, he rationalized, had worked hard. *He* hadn't used magic, no matter what the old locals insisted, no matter what the Corwin tapes had said, no matter what the old songs said.

It would be so easy to give up, to assume things would still get better without Recorps. But until the Imperial and Recorps effort had begun, what had there been? Savages and shambletowns, a declining local population, and despair. Who wanted to go back to that?

He ran his fingers through his thinning hair, then touched the centuries-old console, the once-gray plastic sheathing now nearly black, not with dirt, but from the continued exposure to the radiation of the interior lights, designed so long ago to supplement the sunlight that had been virtually nonexistent.

Would there be a time when Recorps would not be needed?

He hoped so, but was glad it would not be soon, would not be in his time.

He flicked off the console, and stood, stretching,

before he straightened his uniform and headed for his empty quarters. Unlike his predecessor, he lived in quarters, not in New Denv.

He frowned and shook his head as he went out through the open portal.

LVII

THE SLENDER BLOND MAN HALTED HIS WORK ON THE PAINSTAK-ingly squared golden log and stood up as he watched the agent vault from the flitter with the grace of the trained hunter.

The uniformed man moved with an easy stride from the flats where he had landed the flitter, a narrow space requiring more than mere skill, more even than reckless-ness or nerve.

The blond man nodded. He recognized the step of the other. He did not bother to touch the knives hidden in his wide belt, knowing that the other could not have immediate violence on his mind or hands.

He continued to wait until the agent, wearing a sky-blue uniform he did not recognize, with the Imperial crest that he did, halted several meters from him.

The woodworker smiled and set down the tool with which he had been smoothing the log.

"Commodore Gerswin?"

"Answered to that once." He nodded at the uni-form. "Corpus Corps?"

"Yes. But not on official business—not the kind you mean."

"No uniform on those missions."

The agent smiled faintly and half nodded in acknowledgment.

"Nice location here."

"For me . . . under the circumstances."

The agent looked around the partly built structure, noting the perfect joint where each golden log had been fitted into place, the dark stones that seemed to fit precisely without mortar, and the way the home-to-be nestled against the cliff behind it.

"You do good work, Commodore, not that you always haven't."

The blond man smiled wryly, dismissing the compliment.

"One way of looking at it."

The agent looked down at the stone underfoot, then back at the man who looked no older than he did.

"Why did you put in the change of address for your retirement pay with the Recorps base here? And why did you use coded entries?"

"Why not? No sense in the Empire having to keep searching. Waste of resources. You either get me, or decide it's not worth it. Too tired to play god much longer."

"You? Too tired? Why didn't you use those tacheads? There were nine left . . . somewhere . . . wherever they are. Not to mention the hellburners."

"Assuming I had any," sighed the thinner man. "Just wanted to get home, not that it is, you understand."

"It isn't? Thought you were from here."

"Was. But you know better. You can't really go home. So long no one really remembers. Why I used codes. Be worse if they knew for sure I was the Captain. Won't matter someday. Doesn't matter to the Empire already, I suspect."

The agent frowned, started to shake his head, then stopped, fingering the wide blue leather belt, centimeters from the stunner in the throw-holster.

"You win, Commodore, just like you always did." The words carried a tinge of bitterness.

"Didn't win. Lost. You lost. We both lost. Lerwin, Kiedra, Corwin, Corson—they won. So did the children, those lucky enough to have them . . . and keep them."

"That may be," answered the agent, "but you won. The Empire is coming apart, and the Ydrisians, the Ateys, the Aghomers—you name it, you're their patron saint."

The slender man pursed his lips, waiting.

The Corpus Corps agent studied the wiry man in the thin and worn singlesuit, but kept his lips tightly together.

"You drew the duty of having to tell me?"

"No. I asked. I wanted to see a living legend. I wanted to see the man who single-handedly brought down the Empire."

"I didn't. May have hurried things. But not me." He smiled wryly once more. "Disappointed?"

"No." The agent's tone said the opposite.

The slender man's hands blurred.

Thunk! Thunk!

Twin knives vibrated in the temporary brace by the agent's elbow, both buried to half their length.

"Does that help?"

"A little . . ." The agent took a deep breath. He could not have even touched his stunner in the time the Commodore had found, aimed, and thrown the heavy knives. ". . . but how—it couldn't have just been the weapons skills."

"No. Helped me stay alive. Any man who cared about Old Earth, about life . . . any man could have done the rest . . . if he sacrificed as many as I did . . ."

The man in the blue uniform nodded.

"Now. A favor."

"What?" asked the agent cautiously.

"Better that the locals know I'm just a retiree. Don't know more, and they don't need to. Your records will go when the Empire falls."

"Should I? Why? Let you suffer in notoriety . . ."

The hawk-yellow eyes of the Commodore-who-was caught the agent, and in spite of himself, he stepped back.

"Why?" he repeated, more softly.

"Because, like the Empire . . . out of time . . . out of place . . ."

The agent watched as the Commodore's eyes hazed over, looking somewhere, somewhen, for a minute, then another. He waited . . . and waited.

A jay screamed from a pine downhill from the pair, and a croven landed on the rock above the flitter, but the Commodore noticed neither the birds nor the man in blue.

Finally, the Corpus Corps agent stepped forward.

Thunk!

A third knife appeared in the brace, and the former I.S.S. officer shook himself.

"Sorry . . . reflex. Hard to keep a thought. Too many memories," apologized the Commodore, who still looked to be a man in his middle thirties.

The agent, despite his training, shivered.

"I understand, I think, Commodore." He paused, then saluted, awkwardly. "Good day, ser. Good luck with your house."

He turned and slowly descended the even-set and smooth stone steps, then walked along the precisely laid stone walkway, still shaking his head slowly as his strides carried him back to the flitter.

"We all lost. Him, too."

He was yet shaking his head as the flitter canopy closed and the turbines began to whine.

Behind him, the blond man picked up his tools and returned to smoothing the golden log, smoothing it for a perfect fit, a perfect fit that would last centuries.

LVIII

WEARY. OLD. EITHER ADJECTIVE COULD HAVE APPLIED TO THE still-buried building that served as the landing clearing area for the few travelers to visit Old Earth.

The historian/anthropologist took another step away from the shuttle-port entry before stopping. Her recorder and datacase banged against her left hip as she halted to survey the hall. Compared to Imperial architecture, the ceiling was low, and despite the cleanliness of the structure, a feeling of dinginess permeated the surroundings. That and emptiness. There had been two passengers on the annual Imperial transport—most of the space was for technical support equipment for Recorps.

She debated taking a holo shot of the receiving area, then decided against it. She squared her uniformed shoulders and stepped up to the console.

A bored clerk in a uniform vaguely resembling hers waited for the lieutenant to present her orders.

He took the square green plastord and eased it into the console.

"Your access code, please, sher."

"I beg your pardon."

"You have special orders, Lieutenant. Service doesn't trust us poor cousins. For me to verify your arrival, you have to punch in your own access code." He pointed to the small keyboard built into the counter. "Right there."

259

The lieutenant shrugged. Her precise features, thick, short, and lustrous black hair, and an air of command gave her more of an "official" presence than the Interstellar Survey Service uniform.

Stepping over to the keyboard, she tapped in the access code and waited.

Several seconds later, another console beside the clerk beeped. He retrieved the plastord square and handed it back.

"Welcome to Old Earth, Lieutenant Kerwin."

"Thank you. What's the best way to reach the old Recorps Base?"

"Old Recorps Base? Didn't they tell you? You're in it. There's never been more than one main base. Outside of the work ports in Afrique and Hiasi, this is it. Oh . . . we have a few detached officers in Euron and around the globe, but here's the center."

Lieutenant Kerwin looked around the open gray hall, again, even more slowly.

"You want base quarters . . . go to the end of the hall. Take the left fork. That leads to the tunnel to Admin. Plenty of room these days."

"These days . . ." she murmured.

"Days of the Captain are gone, Lieutenant. Lot of nostalgia, especially with the big Atey report," added the suddenly loquacious rating. "Their Institute sent a team last year, but haven't seen a report. May not have one, Captain Lerson says. Lots of nostalgia. Sensicubes all romance it. Don't believe it. Never was a Captain, not like that, anyway . . . if you ask me. You'll have to make your own decision."

"Who told you that was my job?" asked the officer softly, with a touch of ice in her tone which pinned the man back against his console.

"Told you what?"

She smiled, and the smile was a cross between sudden dawn and the pleased look of the reintroduced hills cougar sizing up a lost beefalo calf.

"Surely you're joking?" she asked with a laugh, and the laugh had a trace of silvered bells in it, with steel behind.

In spite of himself, the rating failed to repress a shiver.

"Just around, Lieutenant. Someone from the Empire coming in to study the myth of the Captain. To check our records. Two passengers, and the other was a hydrologist recruited from Mara. Had to be you."

"Around? That's interesting." She pursed her lips before continuing. "Don't put down myths, Reitiro," she concluded, picking his name off the tag on his tunic pocket, "they all started with reality. You might think about the reality of the Captain."

Reitiro frowned as the Survey Service officer turned and left, moving with an easy stride down the hallway toward the tunnel to the Administration building, the tunnel a relic from the days when the environment had been totally out of control.

From before the days of the Captain, if the myths were indeed correct.

LIX

THE FACE IN THE SCREEN WAS GRAY. WHETHER GRAYED BY THE age of the tape or whether the gray reflected the actual physiological age of the man could not be answered.

The tape itself came from a databloc out of the sealed section of the Recorps archives, from a tape that should have been blank, and was not. The exterior had

contained neither date nor other identifiable informa
tion. Why it had been left remained as much of
mystery as what it contained.

"Commander Lerwin said I ought to scan this an
leave it in the back of the Archives. Someone shoul
have it."

The silver-haired man had an unlined skin, an
neither beard nor mustache. His voice was so soft, eve
with maximum gain, that the I.S.S. officer and the bas
archivist/librarian had to strain to catch his words.

"Already, people are doubting what the Captai
did, or what we all did. As the land improves and ther
are fewer spouts, they forget the days of the stone rain
and the ice that could strip a flitter bare in minutes. Th
old crews are scattering, dying, having children, and th
Captain's not here to hold it together. Soon, no one wil
remember that there was a Captain. They'll doubt th
records, or change them."

The narrator looked down, blinked, and lifted hi
head to face the viewers.

"But there was a Captain. And he brought the eart
back to life when it was dying.

"Am I mad? I suppose I am. But a madman ha
nothing to tell but the truth. Who designed the rive
plants? The Captain. Who commandeered the dozer
when the Empire wrote Old Earth out of the Emperor'
budget? The Captain. Who forced the creation o
Recorps?

"I could go on, but already none of this shows in th
histories. How could it? Only a devilkid could hav
carried it off, and none of them knew he was a devilkid
or what a devilkid was. *We* knew—"

The man's face was replaced with a swirl of color
and then by an even gray.

"Is the rest of the tape like that?" asked the lieutenant.

"I've run it through twice. That's the only fragment
left intact. It was deliberately scrambled, and probably
in a hurry."

"Why did they leave the beginning?"

"They didn't know they had. The man who made he recording didn't understand the recording limits. On hese older blocs, you were supposed to run twenty to hirty centimeters before beginning the recording. This tarts with the first millimeter. Everything beyond thirty s blank."

"But wouldn't a scrambler catch it all anyway?"

"No. The outer layer of the tape expands against the casing. The reason for the procedure is that you can't blank the first lead of a bloc without actually running it."

"Why would anyone want to erase something like hat?" Why indeed, wondered the historian.

"It's a pity," observed the librarian. "Now that the days of the Captain have become a myth, it would be helpful to have firsthand reference material. Amazing how quickly the process took place. Less than four centuries, and no one knows what really happened back then. Would be nice to know."

"Someone didn't think so."

The rating shrugged. "What can I say, Lieutenant? I finished training less than a year ago, and it's pretty dull. Most of the reclamation here on Noram is done, and they say the natural processes are taking care of the rest.

"No minerals, and with the Empire almost gone —excuse me—with the Empire taking a less aggressive position, we don't get much interest in the archives these days.

"Everyone else just wants to know if we've gotten any of the Imperial sensitapes. Probably have to close Recorps before too long. Not much Imperial funding, and the export trade is down. Two-thirds of the old quarters are already empty."

"Can you tell when the erasure was done?" asked the lieutenant, bringing the issue back.

"Could have been done a hundred stans ago, or two. That swirl pattern doesn't happen when you use what we have now, and our stuff's at least fifty years old. Besides, you saw the dust on that rack."

The officer rose. "You mind if I just browse throug
the rest of the old blocs?"

"Regs—but who cares. Just don't blow it around."
She smiled at the young rating.

"Thank you. I won't."

The librarian scratched his head as he watched th
lieutenant head for the master indices for the archives

He rewound the old cube and closed down th
viewing console before he picked it up to carry it bacl
into the storage area. After that, he'd have to go back t
the main console, not that there would be much busi
ness.

The word was already out that the Imperial shij
hadn't brought any sensitapes.

LX

STARK—THAT WOULD HAVE BEEN THE POLITEST WORD SH
could have used to describe the interior of the dwelling

Neat it was, and light enough, though age ha
darkened the golden wood that comprised the walls and
matching roof beams. But there were no hangings on the
walls and no coverings on the floors. The air was coo
and clean, but the starkness made it seem almost chill.

The hawk-eyed man turned in the antique swivel
but did not stand as his eyes ran over her. The direct-
ness, the blaze, of his gaze sent a chill down her spine.

He added to that chill with an odd two-toned
whistle so low that she could barely hear it even as she
felt its impact.

"First time someone like you has come looking for me."

His eyes flickered as he took in the uniform.

"Service. Don't recognize the specialty insignia."

"Research. I understand you might be able to answer some of my questions."

"Doubt it."

"Would you try?"

"So what does the wonderful and crumbling Empire want with me?" He looked away from her and out through the circular bubbled window that she recognized as having come from an alpha-class flitter, despite the painstaking custom framing that made it seem an integral part of the structure.

She frowned, letting the fingers of her left hand wrap around the styloboard more tightly than she intended. Shaking her right hand loosely to relax it, she hoped she would be ready to use the stunner if she had to, but that it would not be necessary. The whole idea was not to upset someone as unbalanced as he was reputed to be.

His head snapped back toward her.

"Forget about the stunner. You couldn't reach it in time. Too close."

Automatically her eyes gauged the distance from her feet to his relaxed posture in the antique recliner/swivel. More than three meters.

She lifted her eyebrows.

"Could prove it. Will. Maybe. Later."

He glanced back out the bubble window, the only outside view from the dwelling.

The Imperial officer took the time to study the structure, noting the fit of the native logs, squared so evenly that there seemed to be no space at all between them. The wide plank flooring showed the same care, despite the hollows worn by years of use. There was more than enough light, thanks to the four skylights. The more she studied the structure, the more she began to realize the effort and design that had gone into it, an effort and design that seemed strangely out of place on Old Earth.

She shook her head. There were so many strange examples, as she was learning all too quickly.

This hideaway south of the Recorps Base was yet another, a seemingly rustic cabin whose design, orientation, and construction demonstrated more expertise and knowledge than she had expected, far more.

Her attention drifted back to the man, now regarding her with an amused smile, as if he had read her thoughts. He was clean-shaven, and the faded gray tunic and trousers, once probably of Imperial issue, were spotless, though worn.

"It's said you're native to Old Earth," she began.

The amused smile remained, and she did not realize she had stepped backward until her shoulders brushed the wood behind her.

"It's also said that you were an Imperial officer for a long time. One rumor is that you once commanded the Recorps Base."

"Who would say anything that fantastic? Never commanded the Recorps Base."

"The Maze people . . . some of the older New Denv families . . ." She tried to match his light tone.

He sat upright, leaning forward. "Every place has its stories. When it doesn't, it's dead. Nearly that way here once. Now they tell stories."

In a silent flash, he stood upright, next to the swivel, which slowly returned itself to a position not quite upright. His feet, wearing Imperial-issue boots, had not made a sound as they hit the wooden floor.

"What do you really want?"

What did she want? To track down a rumor? To chronicle the debunking of a myth to put the Service at ease? She shook her head again. Her mission seemed less and less clear.

"Your thoughts, your recollections about how things really were," she said, trying to recapture the sense of purpose that had driven her to Old Earth, back to a forgotten corner of a world the Empire would just as soon forget.

She took a step sideways, as much to remind herself that she would not be backed into a corner as to get closer to the former officer, and waited for his response.

His eyes raked over her again, as if he could see beneath the undress tunic and trousers. She could see his nostrils widen, as if he were drawing in some scent.

Hawk or wolf . . . or both?

"You smell familiar."

"Familiar?" Istvenn! He's got you off-balance and keeping you there. "I don't see how. I've never been here or on Old Earth before."

His lips tightened, and his eyes narrowed.

"Could be. But somewhere . . ."

"Is it true you were an Imperial officer?"

"True as anything else you'd hear." The intensity with which he had regarded her subsided, and he turned so that he faced neither her nor the bubble window, but a narrow tier of inset wooden shelves that reached from ankle height to the base of the roof beams.

Her eyes followed his. She could see that a number of the antiques on the shelves were actual printed publications, which indicated their age. Printed pubs were used only on frontier worlds or in remote locations where the use of energy for a tapefax or console was not feasible, and there had been sufficient energy on Old Earth since the rediscovery.

Without being able to read the faded letters on the spines of the volumes, she knew that most were Imperial manuals.

"Why did you leave the Service and settle here?"

He gestured toward the wall behind her, then laughed a short laugh.

"Nowhere to sit."

"It's not really necessary—"

He brushed past her and did something to the wooden panel behind her.

The lieutenant stepped aside as the blond man

lowered a double width bed from the wall and pulled a quilted coverlet, red and gray, from a recess over the bed, and spread it over the Imperial-issue colonist's pallet.

She could see his nostrils quiver as he straightened and motioned toward the couch/bed.

"Still familiar." His low statement was made more to himself than to her.

He frowned, but with three quick strides returned to the swivel and dropped into it, turning toward her as he did.

"Two questions. One asked. One unasked. Last first. The Imperial supplies? Maintain some credit balance at the Base. Lets me buy what I need. First last. Why here? Nowhere else to go."

His words answered one question, but not the other. Only a retired or disabled member from Recorps or one of the Imperial Services had Base-purchasing privileges. But he had not answered why he had settled on Old Earth.

"Why did you settle here?"

"Why not? Didn't settle. Born here. Not that anyone would remember. No place for me in the Empire. No place for me in Recorps, either. Not when all the barriers are crumbling."

"Barriers?" The single word question tumbled from her lips. Why did she sound like such a simpleton? Why? Why? Why?

"You can take the stress so long. Had to be civilized. That meant barriers . . . if I wanted to survive. I built them, but not strong enough. Time wears down all walls. Remember. Grew up when the shambletowners hunted the devilkids."

"Shambletowners?"

"Old Mazers . . . what they called them then."

She could see that the hardness was gone from his eyes, the terrible intensity muted, misted over.

The lieutenant waited for him to go on, wondering why he was so obsessed with age. He had to be a mental case, or disabled. He didn't look much older than she was, and she certainly wasn't ready for retirement, not just five years out of the Academy. But the dwelling was undeniably his, and the locals called him old. Why?

"Watch out for the old devil," at least three of the reclam farmers had told her. "He knows everything, but he moves like the lash of the storm, like the *old* storms."

She studied his face, the so-short and tight-curled blond hair, the tanned and smooth skin of his face, trying not to stare, waiting for him to go on.

The afternoon wind whined, but the cabin did not shake, unlike some of the town buildings. While their native wood bent, it never broke, not with the local design.

"When the Empire rediscovered, they were lucky. Between storms of summer and howlers of winter. No landspouts that day.

"Could be we were lucky. Time should tell. Couldn't see the sky then, just the gray and gray of the clouds, and purple funnels of the landspouts. Screaming and ripping through the hills and plains. Rock rains all the time. Sheerwinds could cut rivers in half.

"Silver lander. Went hunting and found a devilkid."

He laughed, a short hard bark of a laugh that contrasted with the soft penetrating intensity of his light voice.

"That was six centuries ago. You act like you were there."

He ignored her interruption. "Great Empire decided they had some obligation to poor home planet. Guilty conscience. Decided to fix us up. Till the local budget got tight, and they decided to recruit locals. Couldn't find anyone, except a devilkid. Others couldn't hack it. Devilkid ended up in charge. Called him Captain. Still a devilkid in soul. Scared the Impies until the day he walked out. End of story."

"You haven't told me anything."

"Who are you?"

"Me?"

"No matter. Told you everything. Now listen. My turn."

She frowned, then leaned back as he began to whistle in the strange double-toned sound she had heard him let out momentarily when she had arrived.

The song had a melody, a haunting one, that spoke of loss and loss, and yet somehow each loss was an accomplishment, or each accomplishment was a loss. The melody was beautiful, and it was nothing.

Nothing compared to the off-toned counterpoint, which twisted and turned her.

The tears billowed from her eyes until she thought they would never stop, and his song went on, and on, and on.

When the last note died, she sat there. Sat and waited until he sat beside her and stroked her cheek.

As he unfastened her tunic, she shivered once before relaxing in the spice of his scent, before letting her arms go around him, drawing him down onto her.

The song was with her, and with him. Nor did it leave until he did, and she laid back on the coverlet, shuddering in the rhythms of music and of him, her movements drawing her into a sleep that was awake, and a clarity that was sleep.

She woke suddenly.

Her clothes were where they had dropped, next to the bottom edge of the bed, and her stunner and equipment belt had been moved to the highest shelf, the one without the old books on it.

She rolled away from his silent, and, she hoped, sleeping form gently, until their bodies were separated. She waited, half holding her breath, to see if he moved.

Next, she eased into a sitting position, a position she hoped would not wake him. Again, she waited.

An eternity passed before she edged to her feet, and silently padded across the smooth and cold wooden floor.

First, to get the stunner.

By climbing onto the bottom shelf, she reached the

belt and eased it down. Her fingers curled around the butt of the weapon, and she drew it from the holster.

"Wouldn't."

She brought the firing tube up and toward him, but before her fingers could reach the firing stud, his naked form of tanned skin, hair-line scars, and blond hair had struck across the room like the flash of coiled lightning he resembled. His open hand slashed the weapon from her fingers.

Ramming her knee toward his groin, she drove to bring her right elbow toward his throat.

Before she could finish either maneuver, she found herself being lifted toward the bed, her right arm numb from the grip of his left hand.

"NOOOO!"

"Yes."

She could feel her legs being forced apart, his strength so much greater that her total conditioning and military training were brushed aside as if she were a child, and she could feel the hot tears scalding down her face, even as his heat drove through her like hot iron.

You were warned, a corner of her mind reminded her. You were warned.

But they didn't know. They didn't know!

When he was done, this time, again, he kissed her cheek, ran his hands over her breasts. But he did not relax.

Standing quickly, he went to the hidden closet and pulled out a loose, woven gray robe and pulled it on before sitting at the end of the bed, his hawk-yellow eyes exploring her.

She wanted to curl into a ball, to pull into herself and never come up. Instead, she took a deep breath and slowly sat up, cross-legged, and faced him.

"Was it necessary to hurt me?"

"After a while, need the thrills. Beauty isn't enough. Neither is scent. With you, it's almost enough." He frowned. "Shouldn't have tried for the stunner. High-minded lady. Sexy bitch. Changed her mind and tried to zap old Greg. Hard to resist the instincts. Don't have many barriers left, and fewer all the time. Happens over the ages."

He straightened, leaning back with his eyes level with hers, for an instant before he stood. She could see the blackness behind the yellow-flecked eyes, a blackness that seemed to stretch back through time.

She shook her head to break away from the image.

After crossing the room with a slight limp she had not noticed before, he turned and walked back, picking up her clothes, and sorted and folded them, putting them on the foot of the bed. Next he put the equipment belt down, without the stunner.

He shook his head, hard.

"You had better leave. Not exactly sane, not all the time, anymore. Never sure which memories are real, which are dreams."

She dressed deliberately, afraid that undue haste would be construed as fear, which seemed to be a turn-on, or that slowness would be a tease.

By the time she was together, boots and belt in place, she realized that he had also dressed, though she did not remember him changing from the robe back to the gray tunic and trousers.

The late afternoon light was flooding the cabin with the dull red that preceded twilight when she stepped outside the door.

In another quick move, he was at her side.

She looked down. The stunner was back in her holster. Neither acknowledging the weapon's return nor flinching at his speed, she took a deep breath and opened the door.

His right arm held her back, went around her shoulders, and she found herself against him again, face-to-face, the strange spice scent of his skin and breath still fresh.

His fingers relaxed as he kissed her neck and brushed her cheek with his lips.

"Goodbye, Caroljoy. Thought you'd never come. Goodbye."

He released her, standing there, face impassive, as she slipped out and onto the wide stone slab that comprised the top step on the long stone staircase down to the old highway and her electroscooter.

The tears she could not explain cascaded down her cheeks, a few splashing the dust from her boots, a single one staining the last step of the stairway.

Her carriage perfect, she did not look back, but felt the door close, felt that as it closed it sealed away a forgotten chink in the past as surely as though she had destroyed the sole copy of a priceless history text.

Eyes still blurring, she started the scooter back toward the Base.

LXI

"INCOMING. EDI TRACKS. CORRIDORS TWO AND THREE."

The senior lieutenant relayed the report from his screen to the Ops Boss, both on the audio and through the datalink. He did not altogether trust the ancient and patched-together equipment, but there was no new equipment and nothing left to cannibalize.

"Understand EDI track. Incoming Cee one and Cee three."

"That is affirmative."

"Interrogative arrival at torp one range."

"Unable to compute," the lieutenant responded. "Synthesizer is down. Data fragmentary."

The lieutenant wiped his forehead.

"Interrogative arrival estimate," repeated the disembodied voice of the Ops Boss.

The lieutenant ran his thick hand through his thinning hair, wishing he could undo the brevet that had jumped him from senior tech to full lieutenant, wishing he were back in the old days when the Service had really been the Service.

"Data is fragmentary," he repeated. "I say again. Data is incomplete."

"Understand data limitations. Interrogative *estimate* of incoming at torp one range."

The lieutenant sighed to himself. "*Personal* estimate, based on trace strength and standard incoming combat closure. Personal estimate of incoming ETA at torp one range in less than point five stans."

"Understand arrival in less than point five stans. Interrogative incoming classification. Interrogative incoming classification."

"Data incomplete. *Personal* estimate of incoming is uniform three delta."

". . . damned Ursan cruiser . . ." muttered the rating at his elbow, ". . . coming in for the kill . . ."

"Understand Ursan heavy cruiser."

"That is current estimate." The lieutenant wiped away at his damp forehead, unable to keep the sweat from the corners of his eyes, with the building heat in the orbit control defense center. The station's internal climatizers were just as old and patched as the nonfunctioning synthesizer and the unreliable defense screens behind which they all waited for the inevitable.

Two red stars flashed on the display panel. The lieutenant swallowed. Both corridor control centers destroyed—more than an hour ago, with the data only arriving at light speed, not all that much ahead of the incoming Ursans.

"Control Alpha and Control Delta. Status red omega. Status red omega this time."

"Interrogative . . ."

The audio request and the display panel before the lieutenant blanked. The lieutenant sat gaping as the lights overhead dimmed, then went out. The hiss of the ventilators whispered into nothingness. Only the dim red glow of the emergency light strips remained.

The orbit control center had been the last functioning base between the Ursan raiders and New Augusta itself. The last, and it no longer functioned.

". . . raiders . . . just damned raiders . . . not even a fleet . . ." muttered the sour-faced rating.

"Begin evacuation plan delta. Evacuation plan delta . . ."

The lieutenant, out of habit, touched all the shutdowns before easing himself from behind the screen, shaking his head in the gloom as his fingers slipped across the age-faded plastic surfaces.

LXII

THE TEN MONTH WINDS CAME. CAME WITH THE BLACK CLOUDS that whistled death, as those clouds had whistled death through all the centuries they had struck the easternmost hills of the continent-dividing mountains. Came and whistled death for those who ventured out into the violent gusts, bitter cold, and ice arrows that attacked with the force of a club.

None of the hill people, nor the high plains farmers who lived downside of the hills, left their dwellings while the ten month winds blew, but huddled inside their well-braced homes. The hardy might dart forth in the lulls between storms, but always kept an eye toward the

west and an ear cocked for the low moaning that
preceded the devilstorms.

Cigne, from neither high plains nor hill stock, had
waited, and waited. This time she had played coy,
forcing down her nausea, then, as her chance came, she
had bolted from Aldoff into the low wailing that fore-
shadowed the winds. Praying that the killer gusts would
arrive in time, she had scrabbled from the tiny cottage
Aldoff had acquired for them. Clawing, stumbling, falling and staggering up, stumbling again, she had scrambled into the hillside trees before he had managed to get
his other leg back into his trousers and his heavy boots
back on.

Cigne hated those heavy brown boots. To think she
had once thought him rugged and handsome!

Less than two hundred meters into the trees she fell
headlong.

"Oooohhh." A stone gouged into the purpled bruise
on her left thigh.

"Cigne! You bitch! I find you . . ." Aldoff's voice
carried above the low wail of the dark winds sweeping in
from the west.

She jerked herself back to her feet, ignoring the
shock that ran from her hip to her calf, and tottered
uphill, willing herself toward the taller spruces and the
darkness beneath them. Moving uphill, her breath leaving sharp white puffs, Cigne staggered on, winced at the
sharp small stones that had invaded her shoes and had
sliced even her callused feet. Blood welled out of a dozen
cuts, leaving the thin town shoes she wore slippery from
within, and making each step less and less certain.

Whhhppp!

The first ice missile crashed through the spruce
overhead.

The cold air chilled further, as if winter had arrived
instantly with the ice. The afternoon gloom deepened, as
though twilight had descended. The wind's low whistle
lowered into a deeper moan, rattling the branches above
and around her on the hillside.

"Bitch! Bitch! Cigne! Get self down here!"

She had put more distance between them, for his voice, even at full bellow, was fainter.

Just because she had not been able to conceive —was that any reason to turn against her? With every other woman having the same problem? It was not as though she were some freak. And Aldoff refused to believe it might be his problem—not big, bull-strong Aldoff.

Stumbling again, she reached out instinctively. Her hand touched a boulder nearly waist-high. With a sharp breath of cold air, she halted and looked around. She looked up. Looked up and took another, fuller breath, in an effort to repress a shiver.

The overhead sky boiled black, black as night, as it erupted gouts of ice and flung them at the earth and forests below.

Cigne steadied her grip on the rocky outcrop and glanced around her, searching to see if she could find a better shelter than the pair of upthrust boulders no higher than her waist. The two slanted toward each other and would provide some protection.

Whhhpppp! Whhhppp!

With the sound of the ice missiles, she scrabbled under the outcroppings, burrowing as far under the larger as possible, huddling with her left leg, the still one, as covered as far as she could stretch the leather skirt.

Aldoff had sold her leather trousers, the ones provided by her family. Then, she had not known why, she had not protested the cavalier actions of her rugged husband.

Whhhpp! Whhhppp! Whhhppp!

The ten month winds struck the trees, struck from the black clouds with ice and gusts that splintered branches and ripped bushes from exposed hillsides. Struck from the black clouds that represented destruction, that condemned all those unsheltered to near-certain death.

Whhhp! Whhhppp! Whhpp!

With and through the winds flew the ice spears, whistling death from the blackness above, as they had for all the centuries since the Great Collapse.

Cigne flattened herself still farther into the depression under the outcropping. Already the spruces were bending in the shuddering gusts of the winds. In the distance she could hear the wailing moan of a devilmouth spout as it raced through the heavens toward the high plains east of the hillside where she lay.

The spouts never touched the hills. But the killer winds did, pulling spruces and golden trees out by their roots, smashing entire stands of trees flat, hillside by hillside.

After the winds lifted, before the snows drifted across the desolation, the woods crafters would come, picking the best of the downed timber for furniture and for the vans and simple machines that could be fabricated without metal, or with minimal use of metals. Then would come the builders, to take their timbers and planks from the second cull. Then, finally, would come the fuelmakers, to salvage what remained for alcohol and stoves. Even the chips would be put to use, for paper and kindling blocks.

At last, in the spring, when the snows melted, months after the annual devastation, would come the planters, armed with seedlings and the spores and knowledge to rebuild the hillside.

Cigne huddled under the rocks, shivering with each ice chunk that rebounded from the trees against the thin jacket that had been all she could grasp as she had fled. Each impact would leave a bruise, she knew. More bruises. As if a few more would matter now.

"Cigne! Bitch-woman! Down come! . . . Freeze until spring, bitch!"

In the lull between gusts, she could hear Aldoff's bellow, as he stood at the base of the hillside.

Whhppp! Whhppp! Whhppp!

Another wave of ice missiles clipped smaller branches from the upper limbs of the spruce. The wind shrieks peaked momentarily, then dropped off.

"Hope you die! . . ."

Cigne shuddered between the rocks as she listened to Aldoff's parting words.

She likely would die, lying on a hillside she scarcely had seen from her confinement in the hut Aldoff had called a cottage, lying in the chill of the ten month winds. But go back to Aldoff and his rages?

Snap! Craaaaaccckkkk!

A spruce uphill from her broke at the base, and she winced, waiting for the tree to fall into the narrow space between the boulders and crush her.

Crack! Crack! Crack!

Trees were now falling like lightning around her, one after the other as the winds scythed the hillside with nearly the precision of the ancient lumberjacks.

Whhhppp! Whhp! Whhhppp! Whhhppp!

Without the taller trees to intercept the ice chunks, more of the smaller missiles and ricocheting fragments began to strike Cigne's exposed back and left leg, the one Aldoff had kicked so hard she could not bend it to get under her.

She shivered continuously as the ice pelted her, as the wind whipped around her, and as the darkness swallowed her. Dragged her into the night she knew would be endless, the night she fought even as she wondered why. The chill seemed warmer, but as she drifted toward the darkness, she tried to move immobile muscles, tried to push away the seductive warmth of that darkness.

When she woke, half-surprised, Cigne could not feel her hands, nor her feet, but she was moving, being carried.

"NO!!!!" she croaked.

She jerked, trying to get out of his arms, for it had to be Aldoff, carrying her, carrying her back to . . .

"Gentle . . ."

At the sound of the voice, a light baritone, and because she could not move against the steellike arms

that held her, she collapsed, half in shock and half in
relief that her rescuer or captor was not her husband. She
let the darkness reclaim her.

An unaccustomed warmth woke her the second
time, that and the pain of having the bruises on her legs
being touched.

She could smell a bitter, but faint, odor, the one she
associated with the visiting medical teams from her
childhood.

"Oooohh."

"Tried not to hurt, but could be some infection
here."

Although she tried to sit up, Cigne found a firm but
gentle hand on her shoulder, holding her down.

"Don't move. Concussion."

"Concussion?" The word meant nothing, and the
subtle lilt in his voice told her that he was from somewhere else, certainly from no district she knew.

"Head bruise."

After forcing herself to relax, Cigne waited until his
hand left her shoulder. Then she shivered.

Without lifting her head, she shifted her eyes
around to see where she might be. The eye movement
alone left her head throbbing.

The muted roar of the wind and the warmth told her
she was sheltered. The first savage onslaught of the ten
month winds had passed. A steady yellow illumination
meant a glow lamp, and a glow lamp meant her rescuer
was no ordinary farmer or woodsman.

She hoped the man was her rescuer, and not something worse. With that thought, she shivered again.

She appreciated the warmth of the coverlet that he
drew up to her chin, although she did not try to look at
him, not with the pain behind her eyes.

"Relax . . . quiet . . . you need to sleep . . ."

"No. Aldoff. He will find me." Her voice was no
more than a raspy whisper.

"No one will find you. No one will take you."

The chill certainty in his tone made her shiver, even

as she slipped back into sleep, as she realized she had yet to see his face.

When she woke, for the third time since she had bolted from Aldoff, Cigne did not move, but slowly opened her eyes, waiting to see if the throbbing resumed within her skull.

The place where she lay was no longer lit by a glow lamp, but by the diffuse, grayish light of afternoon, of a ten month afternoon. She could still hear the background hum of the wind, as low as it ever got during the tenth month.

Slowly . . . slowly, she inched her head sideways, toward the strongest light. Overhead, she saw the vaulted ceiling, one composed of beams supporting fitted planks, all of golden wood. While she was not a crafter, she recognized the workmanship as the sort that only skilled crafters or the merchants who sold and traded their works could afford.

Her eyes focused on the strange oval window, framed carefully within golden wood as well.

Through the clear off-planet glass, she could see trees, not the brittle bud spruces, but firs with heavier and darker trunks and, between the dark spruces, heavy bare-limbed trees. She had heard of the trees that had leaves that shed like the scrub bushes, but had never seen any so large before.

Click.

Her head jerked toward the sound. She winced as a muted throbbing began behind her eyes.

The man who stood inside the heavy door he had just eased shut could not have been much taller than she was. Slender, wiry, with golden hair curled tightly against his skull, he studied her without stepping toward her, without moving a muscle.

"How do you feel?"

"Not good." Her voice rasped over the two words.

"Thirsty?"

"Yes."

He turned toward a narrow alcove.

Cigne heard the sound of running water. Running water—she thought she had left that luxury when Aldoff had insisted they leave the Plains Commune for the woods beneath the mountain hills.

"Here."

She had not heard him, nor seen him move, but he was kneeling next to her, offering a smooth cup.

Cold—that the water was. The chill eased the soreness in her throat, a soreness she had not felt before.

As close as he was, she could smell him. A scent of spice, a clean scent, so unlike Aldoff, and so different from the odor of sweat and dirt that had cloaked her farmer father and brothers.

Rather than dwell on his scent, she fixed her thoughts on the smoothness of the cup, with its simple yet elegant curves, and comfortable handle. A handle heavy without seeming so.

The glazed finish of the pottery held within it a web of fine lines, indicating it was hardly new.

Cigne had not realized how tightly she had gripped the cup until her fingers began to tremble.

"You can have more later . . ."

She surrendered the cup reluctantly and tried to keep from tensing her muscles as he eased her head onto a single thin pillow.

"Shouldn't lift your head at all, but your eyes are clear." He spoke softly, as though he were talking to himself, rather than to her.

With the pillow under her head, she took in the room more fully.

She lay on an elevated double width pallet, under a soft gray and red coverlet. On the far side of the large central room were two of the strange oval windows, wider than any she had seen—one opposite her. Before the other stood a desk. From the simple lines and the flow of the wood, Cigne saw it was the work of a master crafter, just like the rest of the woodwork she could see.

Even the grains of each plank in the wall between the twin off-planet windows seemed identical. Her mental efforts to compare the planks intensified the throbbing in her head. Cigne closed her eyes, still listening.

She could feel the man moving away from her, although she could not hear footsteps. When she eased her eyes back open, he was setting the old cup upon the desk.

She shivered, despite the warmth of the coverlet. But she could feel her eyes getting heavier.

The dwelling remained silent except for the moaning of the ten month winds.

LXIII

THE WOMAN SAT ON ONE SIDE OF THE NARROW DROP TABLE AND picked up the empty cup one more time, studying the webwork of lines underneath the porcelain-smooth glaze. A simple cup, heavy, with a handle ample for a man, finished in a uniform off-gray. On one half was a golden diamond, faded. On the other was a stylized spruce tree, green and brown.

When she studied the two designs closely, she could see precise brush strokes, finely done under the heavy and clear glaze. Both the cup and the two designs were unique in small ways, almost in the feel of the cup and the sense of the designs. Both the object and its decoration had been produced by a skilled hand.

Cigne shook her head. The man who had rescued her from the ten month wind and storms, winds and storms which still were striking the surrounding hills periodically, had produced both house and cup. Or so he had said.

If he had, he was extraordinarily skilled. If he had not, he was rich, or a thief, or both.

Greg—that was the name he had offered. But she had refused to use it. So far she had avoided any form of address.

Click.

Cigne kept her eyes on the cup as he walked to the other side of the table.

"Feeling better?"

She nodded, but did not meet his eyes. The old legends had been dismissed by most, but she remembered to be wary about "the old man of the hills" with the demon-yellow eyes. Still, he had been nothing but gentle when easily he could have taken advantage of her.

He had not pressed when she had refused to discuss why she had been out in the storm or from whom or what she had fled.

In turn, she had not pressed him on how he could so easily dare the gusts that felled bigger men.

"Still don't want to go back?" He waited for her answer.

This time, this time, she shook her head.

"What about Denv?"

"I have no money. No goods. No trade. Besides . . . a woman who cannot . . . without . . ." She stopped and looked up to see his reaction, but the smooth face with the near-elfin face remained impassive.

Finally, he spoke slowly.

"Forget money. Never a real barrier. Nor goods. You know enough."

Her chin moved as if to nod, but she halted the movement almost before it started.

"Real problem elsewhere."

She did not have to nod.

"No children?"

She looked down at the smooth inlays of the table, taking refuge in the abstract design of the dark and the light wood. Wondering how he had been able to set such intricate and curving strips of hardwood within the boundaries, and to match the repeating pattern so identically time after time.

"He blames you."

Cigne could not trust her voice and continued to study the inlaid pattern of the table.

"Wondered about the bruises. Figures. Need population. Fewer children, but no recognition yet. Macho types. So far."

His laugh, while gentle, was mirthless, and chilling, as if he understood something that no one else could possibly see.

Both his words and laugh had not been addressed to her, and she did not answer. Not that she had understood all that he had said, but the tone had been clear. He had not sounded pleased.

Cigne shivered.

Although "Greg" had not raised his voice around her, she could not forget how he had carried her through the winds that had staggered and stopped Aldoff, those winds that the strongest of the hill runners feared. She recalled the unyielding strength of his arms, a strength that made Aldoff seem childlike, and she reflected on his speed and the silent way he moved, so quickly he seemed not to cast a shadow.

"Money and a child—what a good widow needs . . . " he mused.

Cigne frowned, but looked up at the amused sound in his voice. He stood between the table and the nearer portal window.

As she glanced toward him, his eyes caught hers, and she was afraid to look away.

"Do you really want your heart's desire, lady?"

Cigne looked down at the table, afraid to answer, afraid not to.

"Be careful with wishes, lady. Certain you will never return?"

"I am sure. I will never go back."

"Suppose not. Not if you were willing to try the spout winds." He turned halfway toward the oval transparency before his desk. "And the other makes sense. Especially if you could get to Denv. Not that it would be a problem."

"Denv? Not a problem? It is kays and kays away."

"No problem."

He sat down in the strange leaning chair by his desk and pulled off the light black boots.

"Listen for a time, lady. Just listen."

The lilt in his voice seemed more pronounced, and she looked toward him, but he was gazing into the window.

"Listen?" she asked.

"Just listen." He turned back toward her, but she would not meet his eyes and stared at the dark spruces in the afternoon light.

"A long time ago, in a place like this, the people were dying, for each year they had less food, and each year there were fewer of them. The winter lasted into the summer, and the summer was cold and short and filled with storms. And the summer storms were like the ten month storms, while the winter storms hurled boulders the size of houses and ripped gashes the size of canyons into the high plains.

"In this old time, a young man escaped from the cold and storms in a silver ship sent by the Great Old Empire That Was. And he went to the stars to learn what he could learn. He wished a great wish, and it was granted. And he came back to his place, and it was called Old Earth. And he broke the winter storms of the high plains. And he taught the people how to grow the grains and make the land bear fruit they could eat. But the storms elsewhere still raged, and the people in those places away from the high plains sickened and died, and the ten month storms raged through all the year but the short summer. And still the trees would not grow.

"The young man wished another great wish, and it was granted. But the price for the second wish was that he must leave his people forever. He climbed back to the stars, and in time he sent them the Rain of Life.

"The trees grew once more, and the people no longer sickened, and the summers returned. And the people were glad. In their gladness, they rejoiced, and as they rejoiced they forgot the young man and the two great wishes.

"As the great years of the centuries passed, the young man climbed back from the stars and returned to the place he had left. But it was not the same place. He was still young in body, but old in spirit. And his people were gone, and those who now tilled the soil and cut the trees turned away when they saw him. For they saw the stars in his eyes and were afraid.

"The women he had once loved had died and were dust, and those who saw him feared him and would have nothing to do with him.

"But his wishes were granted."

Cigne shivered at the gentle voice telling the fable that she knew was not a fable. She said nothing, but looked back down at the inlaid pattern on the table, endlessly repeating itself.

"There is a danger in wishing great wishes."

She lifted her head, though she did not look at him, and spoke. "There is danger in not wishing."

This time he nodded. "True. All wishes have their prices, and the price we agree to pay is the lesser of the prices we pay. Are you certain you wish to pay such a price? For you will pay more dearly than the spoken word can tell."

Holding back a shiver, she nodded.

"Then listen again."

He stood and turned toward the window. A single note issued from his lips, lingering in the late afternoon gloom like a summer sunbeam trapped out of season.

A second note joined the first, both singing simultaneously, before being replaced with a second pair, then a third.

Though she had never heard of the songs of an old

man who looked young, she listened. Though she feared
the demon who might kill with gentleness, though she
had never heard of the double melody and its double
price, she listened. And she heard, taking in each note
and storing it in her heart, though she knew each would
someday wound as deeply as a knife.

A tear welled up in one eye, then the other, as she
began to cry. And still she listened, and heard the
sadness, and the loneliness, and the loves left long since
behind, but not forgotten.

His arms reached around her shoulders, warm
around her, and the song continued, along with her
tears. The tears became sobs, and the sobs subsided.

As the last note died away, his lips fell upon hers,
and her lips rose to his. She let her body respond to his
heat and his song, knowing that the child would be a
daughter, her daughter, for whom she would pay any
price. For whom she would have to pay any price.

And one tear, and one kiss—they were for the old
man who looked young and never had been.

One tear and one kiss, and a single great wish.

LXIV

THE MAN GLANCED OUT THE WINDOW, LETTING HIS EYES SLIDE
by the oval window that had once been the viewport of a
ship even more ancient than he was.

His peripheral vision caught a movement, a dash of
red, and his attention recentered on the scene outside.
Outside, where the warmth of late spring slowly re-

moved the last of the long winter snows. Outside, where only a scattered handful of snowdrifts remained, and where the golden oaks were putting forth the first leaves of the new season.

The figure in red was a woman, wearing a clinging pair of leather pants and a thinnish leather jacket. The jacket was doubtless imported, reflected the blond-haired man with a quirk to his lips. No local dyes or fabrics glittered that brightly, and the emerging local ethic opposed the use of synthetics except where no alternatives existed.

Looking around the central and golden wood-paneled room, he stepped back from the window. His smile was part amusement, part anticipation.

The winter, with the exception of a few pleasant interludes with those who needed what little he had to offer, had been long, as were all winters on Old Earth. While he could not refuse those in need, most were ignorant of life beyond the High Plains. As he had once been. Only one had been farther than Denv. Denv, while a model of the environmentally oriented and integrated community, remained laudably practical.

The woman whose shiny leather boots now clicked on the stone walkway he had built years ago seemed haughtier than his earlier visitors, as if she might attempt to control him.

Control him?

He chuckled at the thought. Some had, but not by attempting to do so.

"Will you stoop that low?" he asked the empty air.

He grinned a cold grin in response to his own question.

Clack, clack.

The heavy wooden knocker sounded smartly, twice.

He opened the door without a word, surveying the woman who stood on the stones before him, waiting for her to speak. Her face was pale, and her shoulder-length hair was black. So were her eyes.

"You don't look like the old devil of the hills." Her voice was hard, like the shiny finish of her black leather pants and glittering red jacket. The accent was Old Earth, unlike the clothing.

"If I were a devil, would you expect me to look like one?" He did not smile, for the imported fragrance with which she had doused herself was overpowering, far more effusive to him than it would have been to most men. The perfume and her attitude both repelled him, while freeing him to toy with her.

"Not very big, either," observed the black-haired woman.

"Am what I am." He paused. "Would you care to come in?"

"What's the price?"

"For what?"

He had almost stopped questioning those who came, stopped denying since denials did no good. Perhaps his acceptance was a sign of age, age that had not showed in his face or body, or perhaps he had repressed the anger because he feared its release.

But this woman, with her hard and demanding attitude, her expensive imported clothes, who used her body for her own ends, deserved questioning, deserved contempt.

"For what you are rumored to provide." Her painted lips tightened.

"Rumored to provide?"

"Off with the innocence, old devil. Those little girls, that boy. They all look like you. Never seen anyone else around here who looks so much like you."

He stepped back and half bowed, satirically gesturing toward the main room.

"Please enter, lady. What little I have is yours for the moment."

"Thanks." Her heels clicked as she walked past him into his home.

Her eyes widened as she took in the paneling, the

few carvings, the inlay work in the small table by the wall, and the antique books in the shelves.

"You must collect at double mastercraft."

He almost chuckled at her overtly mercenary nature.

"Not a credit. No need to."

"Not a credit," she mimicked. "Then how did you get all this?"

"Magic."

For the first time, the hard and self-assured expression on her face faded.

"Do you know who I am?"

"Should I?"

"I am Gramm Lostwin Horsten's daughter."

"And he is?" the former devilkid asked in a bored tone.

"Head Councilman of Denv."

"I am suitably impressed." So Lostwin had descendants around, descendants who had done well. Well indeed by their forebearer.

He smiled at the recollection of those times, and noticed that the brassy woman backed away.

She was not as young as her outfit proclaimed, well past first youth, and probably past thirty, perhaps even older if the devilkid genes ran strongly in the blood.

"Take it you have no offspring, and your husband may look to greener forests?"

"My reasons should not concern you."

"Your reasons are your reasons." He turned and closed the door, slipping the heavy bolt into place and shielding the action with his body.

For whatever obscure reason, she reminded him of another woman from the past, a copper-haired woman who had also used her body beyond her wisdom, and paid dearly. Even though there was little physical similarity, beyond a slender waist and full breasts, the woman before him, thrusting herself at him while demanding recognition, reminded him of the earlier lady.

Reminded him of her, without the subtlety, without the refinement.

"You never answered my question."

"About the price?" He smiled again as he moved back toward her. The smile was both hard and amused "No price, nor will I accept one. You pay the price from your own body and soul."

"Philosophy is cheap."

He did not contradict her, knowing this woman would not understand. How few there were who understood. How many women had there been, and how few like Caroljoy, or Faith, or Allison, or Lyr? Or even Constanza?

His eyes looked past the woman in red, who stood, a full pout on her lips, before the built-in shelves on which rested the ancient volumes he still collected and read.

He did not look at her, even as she shrugged her way out of the red jacket.

Swissshhh.

The jacket, tossed carelessly, landed on the desk, with one sleeve dangling halfway to the polished golden wood floor planks.

Under the imported red jacket, she wore a filmy form-fitting blouse, under which she wore nothing.

The devilkid could see her nipples, nonerect, and a creamy and pampered skin beneath the gauzelike blouse. His nostrils widened as he drank in the mixed odor of excessive fragrance, woman, fear, and imported powder.

"Sit down."

She turned her head toward him as he stepped into the center of the room, but did not move.

"Sit down!"

At his seldom-used tone of command, she sat, dropping into an old swivel in spite of herself.

"Now listen."

Explaining would do no good. Neither would a gentle approach, not that he was in the mood for gentleness. Not after her attitude. Not now.

He began the song with a near military stridency, a march-driving beat, keeping his eyes on the woman as he did. The power of the double-toned music caught her. She began to lean forward, her body moving toward him against her judgment.

Slowly, slowly, he began to weave in the theme of betrayal, adding the notes that sounded power. He could see her breathing deepen, as the music began to reach inside her.

She said nothing as he finished the first tune. Then, he walked over to the wall and extended the double-width pallet, spread the crimson and gray comforter.

He walked back to her and offered his hand.

She took it and followed his lead back to the pallet.

"Sit here."

When she sat, he knelt and pulled off, first, her right boot, then her left. He turned away from her, beginning the second song.

The second song screamed lust and power, power and lust.

As he reached the end, trailing off the last notes, he edged back toward her, noting the raggedness of her breathing, noting how she had opened the front of the thin blouse.

Her arms reached toward him.

"Not yet."

He could feel the cruelty of his smile, and nearly laughed, ignoring the desperation in her eyes.

He began a third tune, more demanding in its own way than the first two.

Before he finished, her hands were on his arms, tugging him toward the pallet.

"Please . . ."

"Not yet," he whispered between notes as he worked toward the finish of the third melody, dragging it from the depths where it had rested undisturbed for so long. His eyes glinted as he saw her remove the blouse and began to slide her nakedness from the tight trousers, her hips moving with his music.

He barely hesitated before beginning the fourth song, the hardest one, the one that mixed power, lust, teasing, and betrayal.

When the last note died, the woman who had worn red, who had thrust her hips and bared nipples at him, lay huddled on the corner of the raised pallet, curled into herself, even as her body shuddered to unaccustomed rhythms.

The devilkid ran his tongue over his lips, slowly removed his tunic and trousers.

The woman did not notice until his hand touched her shoulder.

"Bastard . . . devil . . ." Her voice held desire, hatred, fear, and desperation.

But she pulled him down and into her.

His right hand pinned both hers over her head, holding her helpless, for all that she did not struggle against him, but with him.

Finally, after long combat, her shudders lapsed. Then did he release her hands.

The one-time devilkid watched her breathing ease as the two lay in the indirect light of the late morning, watched as her nipples relaxed, and as the hardness crept back into her face. Watched as she shook herself and sat up.

Half sitting on the fold-down pallet, she reached for her trousers.

His hand disengaged hers from the clothing.

"Once is enough, devil man. You do well. Well as I've had."

She reached again for the trousers.

This time his hand was firmer, less gentle.

"Business is business," she said, with the hardness completely restored to her voice. "Now. What do I really owe you? None of this offage about no payment. Everything has its price."

He swung off the pallet, setting his feet lightly on the

smoothed plank flooring, then reached down and tossed her trousers across the room.

"True."

"Then what do I owe you?"

He laughed, a hard, barking, mocking laugh.

The woman shivered, although the air in the room was not at all cool.

"Humility . . . if anything."

"Humility?"

"Think everything is yours to take. Or buy."

Her eyes met his, then recoiled.

"It's been an interesting conversation, but I should be going."

She stood, but barely had her feet reached the floor before he stood next to her.

"Not yet."

She inched sideways, unable to back away from him because of the pallet behind her knees.

"This has gone far enough, little man."

Smiling, he did not move.

She inched toward her blouse, then leaned down to lift it.

His hand caught hers, so swiftly and with such power that her fingers opened and the gauzy garment floated back downward.

She moved her body toward him, sliding her skin against him, seemingly relaxing, letting her hands reach as if to go around his neck.

Her knee knifed toward his groin.

Thud.

She lay flat on the floor, momentarily, then began scrambling toward the desk and her jacket.

The devilkid did not move. Not until her fingers touched the dangling sleeve of the jacket. Then he seemed to flash across the space between them, his left hand slashing down and knocking the dart pistol from her fingers.

"Very interesting, lady," he said sardonically. "So

you were going to use the old devil, then assassinate him to retain the family honor?"

The whiteness in her face confirmed his statement.

"So what shall we do——"

Another quick kick toward his groin, but he blurred, and his hands shifted position. Abruptly he lifted her overhead, with his hands holding her tighter than iron bands. Then he carried her toward the pallet, releasing her suddenly.

Thump.

He watched as the impact left her breathless. Watched as she scrambled to get her feet under her. Watched as she dashed for the front door.

He pounced again, picking her away from the still-bolted exit and carting her back to the pallet. Her breathing was ragged.

Again, he stood there, naked, watching her, also naked, as her eyes darted around the room, as her eyes glanced from one door to the other, from front to rear. Waited as she looked at the wide and closed side windows.

"Sick! You're sick."

He said nothing, letting his eyes run over her skin, inhaling the mixed scents of previous arousal and current fear.

Once more, he did nothing immediate as she feinted toward the front door, then dived for the less obvious rear door.

He caught her, holding her overhead again, dropping her on the pallet a second time. Waiting, letting his eyes take in her fear and nakedness.

"What do you want? You want something different? Tell me. Tell me. I'll do it. Just let me go."

He shook his head.

She gathered her feet under her, but, shoulders slumping, settled into a sitting position on the edge of the pallet, looking at the floor.

He took one step toward her, deliberately, then stopped.

She looked up, eyes wide.

Then he took another. Stopped, letting his eyes rip across her nudity.

Her mouth opened, soundlessly.

He took another step. Now he was close enough to touch her.

She looked away, then back up, her mouth opening wider, tears forming in the corners of her eyes.

". . . no . . . no . . . no . . ."

He stepped back. Waited.

She seemed unable to close her mouth, panted raggedly.

Letting the heat build within him, he held back, knowing he was treading the thin edge of sanity. He raked her pale body again with his eyes.

As he stepped back toward her, she scuttled backward toward the top of the pallet.

Like a laser, he was on her. Pinned her hands over her head, forced her legs apart in a single rough body movement. Drove deep into her, ignoring the single scream that was sob, shriek, and cry.

Ignored the small voices in his mind, and let himself be devilkid, again, if only for a few fleeting moments. Let himself forget the iron discipline of the Commodore and the wisher of great wishes. Let himself pay her back for all those who had used him, for all those he had let use him.

His own payment would only last forever . . . and he drove into her to forget the long past and longer future.

LXV

THE JAYS BROKE OFF THEIR CHATTERING.

Gerswin stood in the target yard and balanced the heavy knife in his hand, listening for the sounds he half expected, half feared.

He paused, ears alert for the slightest indication of the hunters, trying to hold back the memories, to concentrate on the moment at hand, to let the old training and instincts take over.

Abruptly he slid the knife back into its hidden sheath. After checking the sling leathers and his pouch of smooth slingstones, he let his trained feet carry him from the shaded and walled target yard into the trees, off the few paths and toward the possible routes his attackers would take from the town.

He doubted if any knew the way, or that Lostwin's many times removed granddaughter would have been fool enough to give exact directions.

Click.

Faint . . . the sound came from his distant right.

Gerswin eased from tree to tree, taking advantage of the few winter bushes and patches of sparse undergrowth that were scattered beneath the old spruces.

Old spruces they seemed, yet none was as old as he.

As he moved cross-hill to position himself behind the group of towners, he counted as he went. Eight. Just eight, and none were crafters or woodsmen.

Gerswin smiled faintly. Some were still his tacit

allies, or feared the old devil of the hills more than they feared the growing strength of the towners.

Gerswin's expression turned bleaker as he began to stalk the rear guard of the party. His fingers brushed over the butt of the ancient, but quite serviceable, stunner he had brought.

The last man looked back, too late to utter a word. Gerswin's hands flashed—one choking off any outcry, the other leaving the man momentarily disabled.

Thrumm.

The rear guard had lagged far enough behind and to the right of his nearest companions that the single stunner bolt would not be heard.

Besides, reflected the hunter, not a one of his attackers had ever heard an Imperial weapon. Not in this time, not with the Empire gone from Old Earth.

Gerswin's second target was less than twenty meters from a heavier man Gerswin recognized as Verlint, the husband of the once-haughty lady.

The devilkid twirled the sling.

Swissshhhh.

The slingstone whispered through the spruce bough to the right of Verlint's companion.

Swissshhh.

Verlint crashed onward in spite of his efforts to step softly. The second man scratched his head and turned toward the soft sound. Gerswin moved.

Thrumm.

Within minutes, the second man was trussed and laid aside.

Verlint was next—a simple stalk and stun shot, since the five others were on the far side of the shallow ravine.

Thrumm!

Leaving Verlint trussed as well, Gerswin resumed his stalk, forcing himself to move carefully, despite the lack of caution on the part of those ostensibly tracking him.

The next man was a straggler, stunned quickly, and trussed almost as swiftly.

The remaining four moved together, whether from lack of response from their companions, or from nervousness. Less than four meters separated them. Two carried laser rifles, antiques that might work. Or might not, releasing all the energy in their power packs in a single unwanted detonation.

As if a laser were a good forest weapon to begin with.

Sighing silently, Gerswin decided to rely on herd instinct.

Craccckk!

The first slingstone slammed into the tree on the right side of the man farthest from Gerswin. He dived leftward, and began to scuttle toward the others.

"What's that?"

"Rouen? Where are you?"

"Where's Verlint?"

"Quiet!"

Gerswin grinned, melting back toward the other side of the group.

Cracckk!

"Devilkid!"

Cracck, cracckk!

"Down! Get down!"

"Where?"

Craacckk!

All four were huddled within meters of each other, crouching behind two boulders.

Craacckk!

The four edged even closer together, as if under siege.

The once and always devilkid checked the stunner. The power reserve would be more than adequate.

Slipping from spruce to spruce, like a shadow in the late afternoon, he moved to within meters of the quarry.

Thrumm!

"Dynlin!"

Thrumm!

"Get him!"

"How?"

Thrummm!

"Devil . . ."

Thrummm!

After wiping his forehead, Gerswin waited, listening to see if the forest sounds would resume, if he had missed someone, or if someone else were coming.

In time, a jay chattered once, then again. A squirrel scrabbled down a nearby tree. The hum of the scattered insects began to build.

At last, Gerswin began the tiresome process of lugging the unconscious men to a single clearing, trussing those he had not bound and disarming them all. The weapons he placed behind a stone-topped low hill, out of their line of sight.

Arranging the eight in a double line of four in the middle of the clearing, he sat down on the large stone to wait, letting his thoughts drift where they always seemed to drift. Into the past, into the darkness where he had met Caroljoy, into the Service where he had met Faith, and Allison, and where he had lost Martin and Corson. Into the shadows.

In time, he glanced up into the spruces overhead, noting the growing shadows, seeing the straight trunks, half hearing the jays, the buzzing of the flies, an occasional scurry of the still-rare chipmunk, and the chitterings of the ubiquitous squirrels.

If his memories were correct, when he had returned to Old Earth the first time as a junior lieutenant, the lands where he now sat had been nothing but wasted red-purple clay, where the cold winds blew summer and winter.

Nodding at the improvement, he glanced back at the figures on the needle-covered ground, then toward the hidden location uphill where his dwelling nestled into its own past.

Not that he could blame the eight men, who had

been out to protect what they thought was theirs to protect. All were too young, adults though they were, to understand that no one person could ever own another. Perhaps they were too wrapped in the fragility of their own masculinity to recognize that.

He laughed harshly, suddenly.

"You . . . of all people . . ."

He returned his thoughts to the squirrels, comparing the sleek animals that scampered along the branches to the scraggly refugees he recalled from centuries past. Shaking his head, he waited for his restless captives to wake.

"Who . . ."

Gerswin dropped his introspection, but said nothing. Just watched as the awareness, and the confusion, before him grew with each awakening man.

"Verlint! You here?"

". . . old man . . . you said . . ."

"How did we . . . what happened . . ."

". . . get here . . ."

". . . told you . . . not to get him angry . . . but you . . ."

Almost as quickly as the babble of voices had risen, the noise dropped away as each man strained at his bonds to see Gerswin sitting on the low boulder, waiting and saying nothing.

The silence drew out.

"Dirty ambusher!"

"Sneak! Used Imperial weapons!" The outburst came from Verlint.

"Like your laser rifle?" asked Gerswin. "Rather I used my knife?"

There was no answer.

"What should I do?" Gerswin's eyes raked the trussed figures. "If I let you go, just come back. Execute you, and the Council will have to order something. Means I'll have to disappear. Too old for that."

". . . doesn't look that old . . ." muttered the man lying next to Verlint.

"You don't fight fair," stated Verlint.

"Lost that ideal long ago. Fought to survive. Still do."

"That was then. This is now."

Gerswin smiled, and his expression chilled the afternoon like sudden night.

"You want a fair fight? Fine. One on one. Any one of you against me. You pick the weapons."

"No weapons," rumbled Verlint.

Gerswin shook his head sadly. "If that's the way you want it."

"You fight him, Verlint. Your problem," mumbled another trussed figure.

"I'll fight. Not just my problem."

Gerswin nodded in agreement with Verlint's assessment. A knife appeared in his hand, as if by magic. He was beside Verlint, and the knife flashed. Flashed again, and Gerswin stood back by the boulder as the dark-haired and bearded, heavy-shouldered Verlint freed himself from the just-severed leather thongs that had bound him.

"Wait."

Although Verlint had already started to move toward Gerswin, he stopped at the light, but penetrating, voice of command.

"You're too stiff. Might take a drink of your water. I'll wait."

Gerswin sat easily on the stone while the bigger man rubbed his arms, stretched, and shrugged his shoulders.

"Terms?" asked the man with the curly blond hair. "Falls, first blood, broken bones, or death?"

"Blood or bones, whichever comes first. Scratches are not blood."

"Death!" screeched the thin man at the end of the seven bound figures.

"You're not fighting. Besides, he could have killed us all. He didn't."

Gerswin stripped off his tunic, folded it, and laid his belt on top of the pile.

He moved toward the level end of the clearing, his back half to Verlint, listening in case the man might lunge for the weapons Gerswin had stacked behind the rock.

Verlint did not , but trailed Gerswin.

"Ready?" asked the heavyset man.

Gerswin nodded, his face impassive, concentrating on what he would have to do.

Verlint did not move, but centered his weight on the balls of his feet, ready to react to Gerswin.

Gerswin sighed, took a deep breath, and edged closer to the dark-haired big man, to whom he had easily spotted twenty centimeters and more than twenty kilos.

"Kill him!" screamed the thin man.

Verlint ignored the scream, as did Gerswin.

The devilkid blurred toward Verlint, who tried to dance aside. With a duck, a swirl, Gerswin slipped inside Verlint's too-slow arms, lifting the man overhead, then hurling him toward the needle-covered ground.

Crack.

Gerswin had held the bigger man's right arm until the last moment, when the strain snapped the bone.

Verlint did not move for long moments, then, ashen-faced, struggled into a sitting position, cradling the broken right arm with his left.

Gerswin trotted back to the rock, where he pulled his tunic back on and replaced his equipment belt and knives.

Verlint staggered to his feet, but did not leave the clearing where he had been thrown.

"What . . . are . . . you . . .?"

"Am what I am. Born here a long time ago. Die here, I hope, a long time from now."

The throwing knife appeared in Gerswin's hand, and he knelt by the first trussed figure.

Moving so quickly that there was little reaction, Gerswin severed the thongs holding all seven men before the first had finished stripping the leathers from his hands and feet.

"What do you really want, devil?" demanded the loud, thin man.

"To be left alone. To let anyone visit me who will. That is all I have asked since I returned."

Verlint nodded, then spoke. "And what if others do not listen?"

"Then I will do what I must."

All eight men shivered.

"Your weapons are here." Gerswin gestured toward the rock. "Suggest one man carry them all. Do not expect to see you again."

He stepped into the trees, sliding sidehill and out of sight before they could react.

He hoped that fear and reason would prevail—that and the hope of the women, the women who would come to be the leaders.

He smiled, wondering if the daughters could escape the sins of the father, fearing they might.

Fearing they might.

LXVI

[CV] "ARE THE LOSTLER HYPOTHESES CORRECT?"

[W] "That is a difficult question to answer directly. The children appear to have a life span around two hundred, roughly twice the Imperial/Commonality averages, but the aging factor is negligible. Muscular and neural development are better by a factor of two to three. Raw intelligence, as well as you can measure, averages thirty to fifty percent above the standard first quintile—"

[CV] "You mean thirty to fifty percent brighter than the twenty percent who are normally the brightest?"

[W] "That is correct."

[CB] "What about leadership?"

[W] "That is an intangible. How can one measure leadership? If you mean accomplishments, there is no doubt. His direct first generation offspring all manifest—"

[CB] "We know that, but can you predict or measure the difference?"

[W] "Only by the characteristics. For example, the traits marking the distinctions—eye coloration, reflex speed, musculature, curly hair—don't pass to the second generation except when both parents actually manifest them. But any child who is his has them all."

[CV] "What happens if a third- or a second-generation descendant without the traits has children with a direct child of his?"

[W] "It's recessive. No . . . that's not accurate. It is as though the traits wash out if they don't carry on as dominant."

[CZ] "Artificial insemination? Is that—"

[CV] "We couldn't do that! What about—"

[CB] "That wasn't the question. We have to investigate all the possibilities."

[W] "Assuming you could do so, by deception, I would assume—"

[CZ] "A willing woman, so to speak?"

[W] "—the probability is surprisingly low, according to the samples already obtained. While we could work on it, without understanding more of his body chemistry, I could not in good conscience advise that as a practical alternative. The high . . . viability . . . is offset by a low capacity for preservation."

[CV] "So we're back where we started from? One source of genius, one source of inspiration, and one source of leadership? After all your research . . . that's where we're left? Kerwin and Lostler were right?"

[W] "Substantially . . . yes."

Excerpt—*Council Records*
[Sealed Section]
Remembrance Debate
4035 N.E.C.

LXVII

THE BIDDING CONFERENCE WAS COMING TO A CLOSE.
The woman at the podium surveyed the group around the two long tables in the open courtyard. She wore a simple rust tunic and matching trousers, and her short blond hair showed tight natural curls. Green hawk eyes and a sharp nose dominated her lightly tanned face.

Her presentation of the Council's requirements was long done, and now she was presiding over the comments and questions that had ensued from the presentation.

"The power requirements are substantial, particularly for a planetbound system," observed the representative of Galactatech.

"For this project alone, we will accept the necessity of fusactors or any other appropriate self-contained system. We understand the technical limitations which preclude our normal methods." The Council representative's tone was matter-of-fact.

"All underground?" questioned the woman engineer from Altiris.

"An absolute necessity. You could create an artificial hill if it fits the overall plan."

No one else spoke for several seconds.

The Old Earth Council representative stood, her hawk-green eyes cataloguing the mixture of off-planet entities bidding on the project.

Her hand on the stack of datacubes, she asked, "Any other questions about the proposal?"

The Hunterian representative nodded, and the Councilwoman almost recognized him before belatedly realizing that the nod meant "no" from him.

"If not, all the technical specifications are in the cubes, as well as the bidding requirements themselves. I will stress again the absolute necessity for retaining the present locale and structure without disruption and without change. Any landscape changes must be out of the line of sight of the existing structure for the first phase of the project, until the distortion generators are fully operational."

She stood back as the interested parties came forward to authenticate their interest and to receive a datacube.

A half smile on her face, she listened as the comments drifted around her in the crisp fall-smoke air of the courtyard.

"Istvenn-expensive project."

"Barbaric . . . waste of resources . . . never stand for it at home . . ."

". . . sentimental gesture . . ."

". . . look for the technological challenge . . ."

". . . of course we'd take it . . . make us famous . . ."

". . . else could you expect? He did it, if you believe the myths, single-handedly. Have you seen the old his-tapes . . ."

For all the remarks and commentary, only three of the more than twenty invited to the conference declined to bid and to accept the datacubes.

The Councilwoman stayed in the courtyard long after it had emptied, looking at the screen on the portascreen, centered as it was on a hand-built dwelling nestled into the trees and against the hillside. The scene did not show the planned park, the hidden field generators that would be installed, the progressive sonic barriers to protect unwary intruders, or the years of debate that had made the conference possible.

She sighed, wondering if the project would solve the problems facing Old Earth, or at least the associated problems facing the Council. Those in the bidding group who had caught the expectation aspect had certainly been right.

What else could they do, needing what they needed? What else could they do, owing what they owed?

And what else could she do, daughter to father, owing what she owed?

LXVIII

"YOU ARE THE HIGH PRIESTESS?" ASKED THE ANGULAR MAN IN red. His accent was thick, with the rounded tones that signified that he came from beyond the Ydrisian Hub, from the far side of the Commonality.

"No. I am the Custodian." With calm and penetrating voice and hawk-piercing yellow-flecked eyes, she answered him.

"But you are . . . in charge . . . of the . . . shrine?" The angular man persisted.

"It is not a shrine. Merely a dwelling within a stasis field. I am responsible for its maintenance and security."

The man in rust-red glanced at his companions, a

man dressed in grayed green; a man not quite so angular, but darker of complexion and with a tight black mustache to match his short-cropped black hair; and a woman with silver hair, young despite the hair color, who wore also the grayed green tunic and trousers.

"Perhaps we do not understand. We understood this was a shrine to the One Immortal, the one who brought down the old ways . . . So it is told even in the far places . . ." His voice trailed off.

"You have come from quite a distance on slender hope," observed the Custodian, not relaxing her scrutiny of the three.

"We are scholars, of sorts, uh . . . Custodian . . . scholars of our world's past. Byzania, it was once called, but now Constanza, it is said, in recognition . . . but that is not important now, and too long to tell, for the ships come infrequently, and we have little time. You must understand . . ." He looked at the woman in grayed green, then back at the Custodian, dropping his eyes from the sharpness of her study. "You must understand that the climb back for us has been less than easy, harder than for most, and still we have no ships of our own."

"Yet you travel far."

"We have our culture, and in some things are considered advanced. We have mastered the house tree and its uses, as well as other secrets of the forests and the great rolling plains.

"The past, some say, is the key to the future, and some of those keys are missing. Others are only myth. Most puzzling is the mystery of the great Ser Corson, who shattered armies, it is said, with his words alone, and who brought us Constanza to set us free. But I digress. My words wander.

"A traveler mentioned to us your shrine, and we came to study but found nothing to observe, save a great park, and a shrine, a mysterious dwelling of the past, locked behind the great stasis fields. We were directed here."

"Why do you think our park, or anything we have here on Old Earth, would have any bearing on your past?" For the first time, the Custodian's words held more than her normal warm courtesy.

"That we cannot confirm, but it has been reported that Ser Corson was ageless, and in the entire Commonality and without, there is only one shrine to an immortal, only one legend." He paused, clearing his throat.

"Your pardon, but it is reported that he looked like you, with the eyes of the hawk, and the curled hair of the sun, and the strength of ten. That he stopped on Constanza for a brief time as a part of a greater mission that would take him to the end of time. And Constanza herself said that he would be found living yet when the suns died."

The Custodian's eyes softened. She sighed, then smiled. "Be seated, gentle folk. There may be some that I can add to your knowledge, but there may be more that you can add to ours."

LXIX

UNDER THE DUSKY VIOLET TENT OF THE EVENING, LIT BY THE flickering stellar candles called stars, stood a circle of smaller tents, each circular, walled but halfway, and comprised of alternating panels of black and white.

Those who gathered for the Festival of Remembrance, as they did on the last evening of summer every tenth year, set out the delicate foods, and wondered if the Captain would appear, not that he had ever failed them.

For this one evening, and only for that one evening in each decade is the Park of Remembrance closed to everyone but a select few.

And who are those few who might enter? Lay that question aside for a time and look upslope, to the cottage as it emerges from the mist of time.

View the man.

He wears a uniform of black and silver, freshly tailored, but no uniform like it now exists in the Commonality of Worlds, or in the outlaw systems. His hair is curled gold, and his eyes are clear, yellow-bright like a hawk's, and pierce with the force of a quarrel, equally antique.

As he strides down the curving walk from the small cottage under the tall oaks toward the tents of black and white, his step is quick, firm, as if he were headed for his first command.

The sky shades toward black velvet, and the first candles of night overhead are joined by their dimmer sisters. The breeze from the south brings the tinkling sound of a crystal goblet striking another object, perhaps a decanter of Springfire.

Glowlights are strewn in the close grass which appears close-clipped, but which is not, for it has been grown that way. Under the nearer tents are tables upon which rest crystal, silver, delicacies such as arlin nuts and sun cheese, and the spotless linen that is used so sparingly elsewhere in the Commonality.

The Captain steps from the fine gray gravel of the flower-lined walk. His heels click faintly on the four stone steps that will bring him down to the tents and those who await him.

Nineteen faces turn toward him, and even the breeze halts for a moment.

Slowly, aware of the unspoken rules, each of the

nineteen averts her gaze. One picks up a goblet of Springfire she does not want.

Another, red hair flowing, tosses her head to fling her cascade of fire back over her bare shoulders.

A third looks at the grass underfoot, points one toe like the dancer she is not before shivering once in the light night air.

The Captain slows, edges toward the second tent, the one where the two decanters of Springfire sit on the middle of the single white-linened table.

To his right is a blond woman, scarcely more than a girl, in a shift so thin it would seem poor were it not that the material catches every flicker of the candlelight and recasts it in green shimmers to match her eyes.

His eyes catch those green eyes, and pass them, and she looks downward.

From the table he picks a goblet, looks toward the decanter.

"May I, Captain?" a husky voice asks.

"If you wish." He inclines his head, the goblet held for her to fill, and his glance rakes her with the withering fire of the corvettes he has not flown in more than twenty centuries.

"Thank you."

His glass full, he bows to her. "Thank you."

She steps back, black-ringleted hair falling like tears as he turns and leaves the tent.

He takes a dozen steps across the grass between the black and white of the tents.

The slender, brown-haired woman who had been squinting to make out the silhouette of the cottage on the hill above catches her breath as his fingers touch her shoulder.

"No . . ." he says, as those fingers, gentle, unyielding, turn her to bring her face around. "Not . . . yet . . ."

His voice trails off, and his fingers slide down her arm from her shoulder to take her hand. He does not release his hold on her as he begins to speak again.

"You seem familiar. These days, everyone seems familiar. Once . . . wrote of the 'belle dame sans merci' . . . of enchanted hills. If you disappeared, you were gone for a century."

He chuckles, and the golden sound is that of the young man he appears. His face smoothes, and he leans down and places the goblet he has not touched upright upon the turf. He straightens.

"These days . . . you have the enchanted prince who cannot remember. What else can I claim?"

She takes another deeper breath, finally attempts an answer.

"No one . . . they . . ."

"Because my mind wanders, shattered with the weight of memory . . . assume I cannot reason . . . do not appreciate my position."

Momentarily his eyes glaze, as if he has looked down the long tunnel to the past and cannot see the object for which he has searched.

Her hand squeezes his fingertips, though she does not understand why, and she waits.

Again . . . he laughs, and the sound is harsh, barking.

"Sweet lady, not my princess, nor can I seal your eyes with kisses four. But walk with me."

From the corners of their eyes, the other sixteen, those not already dismissed, stand, wondering, waiting . . . unsure.

The Captain points, and his arm is an arrow that flies toward the stars.

"See—that faint one? Near the evening star. Beyond that, the tiny point, Helios, sun of New Augusta." He lowers his free hand, and his eyes, and resumes his walk.

"You are not . . . let me put it another way. Would you mind if I called you Caroljoy?"

"Tonight, as long as you want, I will be Caroljoy to you."

"Longer for me than you, sweet lady." He releases her hand and stands silently for a moment that is longer than a moment.

"Sweet lady, not my princess, nor can I seal your eyes with kisses four. But walk with me yet." As he speaks he bends toward her and offers his right arm. She takes it as they walk slowly down away from the circle of tents.

"That star I showed you, Caroljoy. Wasn't really Helios. Cannot see it from here. But it was where I pointed. Life. You point at something and . . . not what you thought."

"Martin never lived long enough to understand that. Caroljoy . . . my first Caroljoy . . . she understood . . . told me that. Didn't believe her."

The two stop at the top of the grassy slope that eases down to the lake where the black swans sleep on the water.

He stops, releases her hand and arm.

"Do you know? No. You would not, but you might. I can think. But I cannot try to remember. All I am is what I remember, and I must not."

His face creases into a smile that is not.

"Better this way. The longer sleeps through time give me some strength to be myself—'le beau capitaine sans merci'—for a time."

"Without mercy?"

"Without quarter."

He whistles a single note that is two-toned, then another. The melody builds until the stars twinkle their tears into the black lake, until the eighteen who have waited behind them slip away into the velvet night beyond the park, each one wondering what she has lost, and what her sister of this single night will gain.

At the precise moment the song has ended, without

a word, the Captain and his lady touch lips.

Without another word, they carefully seat themselves, side by side, holding hands, and facing the lake where the black swans sleep and where the dreams rise from the depths like the mist of the centuries past.

"My lady . . .?"

"Yes."

"Do you mind . . . knowing what you must know . . ."

Though she says not a word, her answer is clear as they turn to each other, as their arms reach around each other, and as the summer becomes fall, and they fall into and upon each other.

The swans sleep in the almost silence, in the music that must substitute for both love and worship, for the loves that he has lost and will always lose, and for the worship all who walk the grass of Old Earth have for their Captain.

Anachronistic? Barbaric?

Perhaps, but unlike other ancient rituals, there is no blood shed. There are no sacrifices, nor is anyone compelled against her will. Nor has any woman ever been required to spend a summer/fall evening in the Park of Remembrance. At least, not in all the centuries since it was first designed, not since the days before the temporal fields enclosed the hill and the cottage upon it. Not since the days of the Captain.